12/2023

D1525322

# AUNT BESSIE ASSUMES

## AN ISLE OF MAN COZY MYSTERY

## DIANA XARISSA

# AUTHOR'S NOTE

Aunt Bessie originally came to life (sort of) in my Isle of Man Romance, *Island Inheritance*. She was the source of the inheritance that prompted the heroine to visit the Isle of Man. So, yes, in that book she had recently passed away. Her life story was told through the recollections of other characters, as well as through letters and diaries.

After I finished writing the book, I couldn't seem to let go of Aunt Bessie. She fascinated me and I wanted to learn more about her. When I decided to start a cozy mystery series, also to be set in the Isle of Man (more about that later), I knew I needed an interesting and unique protagonist. Aunt Bessie seemed tailor-made for the job. Aside from the "being dead" part, that is.

Of necessity, therefore, this book is set circa 1998, about fifteen years before that romance novel, which was pretty much intended to be set in the year it was written (2013). Aunt Bessie is, thus, still very much alive. I'm hoping I haven't made any obvious errors in setting the story in the recent past. The biggest changes have, obviously, been in technology. So, for example, Aunt Bessie and her friends have mobile phones, but not "smart" phones.

For readers who enjoyed *Island Inheritance*, or other of my Isle of Man Romance series books, you will find the occasional character who crosses over between books and series. Obviously, in the Aunt Bessie books they will be younger versions of themselves. I hope you enjoy a little peek into their personal histories in that way. Similarly, if you start with the mysteries and go on to read the romances, you can find out what happens in later life to some of the characters from the Aunt Bessie books.

I've used British spellings and British and/or Manx words and terminology throughout the book (although one or two American words or spellings might have slipped past me). A couple of pages of translations and explanations for many of them, especially for readers outside of the United Kingdom, appear at the end of the book.

As to the setting, the story takes place in the incredibly beautiful Isle of Man. The island is located between England and Ireland in the Irish Sea. While it is a Crown Dependency, it is a country in its own right, with its own currency, stamps, language and government.

This is a work of fiction. All of the characters are a product of the author's imagination. Any resemblance to actual persons, living or dead, is entirely coincidental. Similarly, the names of the restaurants and shops and other businesses on the island are fictional. I've also taken considerable liberties with locations within the story, adding fiction shops and restaurants where they are convenient to the story rather than where they actually exist.

The historical sites and other landmarks on the island are all real; however, all of the events that take place within them in this story are fictional. (And I'm sure the food at the Ramsey and Cottage District Hospital is much better in reality than Bessie finds it here.)

Manx National Heritage is real and their efforts to preserve and promote the historical sites and the history of the island are extraordinary. All of the Manx National Heritage staff in this story, however, are fictional creations.

The Isle of Man Constabulary is also real, however their members in this story are very much fictional and they behave in ways that I'm sure their real counterparts never would.

The island was my home for over ten years and I hope that my writing conveys how much I loved it there. It is a truly unique and fascinating place, steeped in history and endowed with its own distinct culture and traditions. I hope to visit soon and I encourage all of my readers to do the same.

# CHAPTER 1

*E*lizabeth Cubbon, known as Bessie to her friends, rubbed her eyes and checked the clock by her bed. It was 6:06, which meant her internal alarm was a few minutes off today. She frowned as she sat up in bed and pushed back the warm duvet. Slippers in place, she padded over to the window and looked out. The glow from the nearest street lamp gave her just enough light to see the sheets of rain that were falling. She would definitely have the beach to herself this morning.

Half an hour later she was showered and dressed and waiting impatiently for the sky to lighten up a bit. Sunrise, this early in March, was still half an hour away. As rainy and overcast as it was, the sun wasn't going to make much difference, but she waited for it anyway. A hot cup of tea and toast with honey and homemade strawberry jam helped to pass the time as she watched out the window for the sun to come up.

At quarter past seven, when the sun had risen enough to lift just a bit of the gloom, she pulled on her thickest waterproof coat and a pair of Wellington boots. An umbrella would have been useless in the strong wind. Bessie loved walking on the beach and she wasn't about to let a little rain or wind stop her. It was, however, colder outside than she had realised and once she stepped out, she decided that today's morning walk was going to be a short one.

As usual, she headed straight towards the water. Some distance from the water's edge, she turned right and began her usual stroll towards the line of newer cottages in the distance. Most days she walked as far as the closest cottage before turning back towards home. In the summer she might walk to the cottages and well beyond. Today she planned to shorten her stroll considerably as the strong wind began to pick up and the rain streamed across her face.

In the dim light and pouring rain, she supposed it wasn't surprising that she didn't see the man until she had nearly tripped over him. One look had her turning around and heading for home. Even if she had brought her mobile phone with her on the walk, she couldn't have used it in the heavy rain. She walked as quickly as she could back to her cottage, hurrying faster than she had in many years.

She dialled a number she knew well.

"Laxey Neighbourhood Policing, this is Doona, how can I help you?"

The familiar voice was welcome. Doona only worked the early shift once or twice a week and Bessie felt fortunate that she was the one who answered the phone today. "Doona, it's Elizabeth Cubbon," she said, suddenly formal.

"Bessie? My goodness, aren't we formal on a Monday?"

"Sorry, Doona." Bessie felt flustered. "It's just that I've found a body, you see."

"A body?" Doona repeated. "What sort of body is that, then?"

"Well, a human one," Bessie answered. "A man, probably middle-aged I would think, although it's hard to tell since he's face down in the sand."

"And you found him where, exactly?"

"He's just lying on the beach." Bessie felt she was explaining herself badly. She took a deep breath and started over. "I went out for my morning walk, and I nearly tripped over this man who's lying on the beach. I'm sure he must be dead. It's too cold and wet for anyone to lie there otherwise."

"Aye, dead drunk, more like it," Doona replied. "How many complaints have we had about the folks in the new cottages getting drunk and behaving badly?"

"I don't think anyone's staying at the cottages yet, this season. Anyway, I really think he's dead," Bessie told her friend. "He's lying face down in the sand and he didn't move when I shouted at him. I think you'd better send Hugh and he'd better be quick. The tide's on its way in and the gulls are circling."

"I don't suppose you have any guests that could go and stand by the body until Hugh gets there?" Doona asked. "Someone should keep an eye on it, I suppose."

"No one stayed over last night," Bessie answered. "They usually don't on school nights."

Bessie had never married or had children of her own, so she acted as an honorary aunt to every child in the small village of Laxey, where she made her home. Her guest room was often occupied on weekends by some angry or unhappy teenager who felt misunderstood by his or her parents.

"That's a shame. I'm ringing Hugh on his mobile phone now, but it will take him a while to get dressed and get down there. He doesn't usually roll in here until half-eight or nine."

"I'll go and wait with the body," Bessie told her.

"Now don't you be silly," Doona replied. "You stay in where it's warm and dry. I'll tell Hugh to hurry."

"The poor man shouldn't be out there all alone," Bessie argued. "I'll go and stand with him and chase away the gulls and the tide."

"You'll struggle to chase away the tide, I think," Doona laughed. "I'll make sure Hugh knows you're waiting out in the cold for him. I'm sure he'll hurry faster if he knows that you're getting soaked and blown around."

"I wouldn't be too sure of anything with young Hugh," Bessie replied. "He's a nice boy, but I've never seen him hurry at anything."

"Just as well he's living here," Doona chuckled. "Traa-dy-liooar, and all that."

In spite of her offer, Bessie was in no hurry to get back outside

3

in the nasty weather to spend more time with the dead man. After she'd hung up the phone, she put the kettle back on and prepared herself another hot drink. She carefully poured it into an insulated mug and then, reluctantly, pulled her still wet coat back on. The man on the beach hadn't moved, which didn't surprise Bessie. There was no doubt in her mind that he was dead, whatever Doona thought.

The rain was easing off slightly and the sun was trying its best to warm the air as it rose before Bessie finally spotted Hugh's police car pulling into a parking space in front of her cottage. Bessie headed up the beach towards him, waving to him as he emerged from his car. He was frowning and struggling to pull on a light raincoat. He popped open an umbrella and Bessie held back a laugh as the wind immediately blew it inside out.

"This is beastly weather," he told Bessie as she approached him.

"We mustn't complain," Bessie told him. "Plenty of places are worse than here."

The man looked at her for a moment and then shook his head. "Can't think where," he muttered under his breath. Then he spoke loudly. "So what have we got then?"

"I nearly tripped over him," Bessie told the young policeman. "I was out for my morning walk and I didn't expect to find anyone lying on the beach, especially not in this weather."

Hugh nodded. "I expect he's from the new cottages," he told Bessie in an impatient voice. "Had too much to drink and now he's gone and passed out on the sand."

"I'm pretty sure the cottages aren't being used yet this year. Besides, I think he's dead," Bessie repeated what she'd already told Doona.

Hugh managed to get his umbrella the right way around again and he battled to keep it that way as the pair slowly approached the body. They watched silently as a seagull landed on the man's back and began pulling at the thinning hair that surrounded a bald circle on the back of the man's head.

"That has to hurt," Hugh remarked as he stopped walking. "Maybe

I'd better get some reinforcements down here. Dead people aren't really part of my job description."

Bessie sighed and turned towards him. "You should at least check that he's really dead," she encouraged the man. "Think how embarrassing it would be to get Inspector Kelly down here only for him to find that the man really is just drunk."

Bessie watched as different emotions flashed across the young man's face. She had known young Hugh Watterson since the day he was born and she could almost read his thoughts as he looked from Bessie to the body and back. His eyes and his hair were almost an identical shade of brown. He was in his mid-twenties now, and had grown to around six foot tall, but he still looked no more than fifteen. He was still sporting the same patchy attempt to grow a moustache that he had started when he'd actually been that age.

Hugh had joined the Isle of Man Constabulary as soon as he'd left school, but he was still as transparent to her as he had been at six when he used to stop in to see her after school, pretending he just wanted to say hi, really hoping for a biscuit or a slice of cake.

While he was reasonably smart, even his best friend would never call him enterprising. His worst enemy would simply say that he was lazy. Bessie could almost see him trying to work out what move would cause him the most work. She sighed and took a decisive step towards the body. The tide was still rising and it wouldn't be long before it would reach the man's feet.

Hugh crossed to her side and then held out a hand. "Aunt Bessie, you need to take a step back, please." Bessie stopped and then moved back a few feet under Hugh's suddenly serious gaze.

Hugh reached the man's side and pushed gently on his shoulder. Nothing happened. He pushed a second time, with more force.

"Sir?" Hugh shook the man's shoulder, shouting loudly over the lightly falling rain and the sound of the wind and waves. "Sir, you need to wake up. Sir?"

With a sigh, Hugh walked over to hand his umbrella to Bessie and then returned to the body. He began struggling to roll the man over onto his back. Suddenly he stopped what he was doing and looked over at Bessie. Bessie looked expectantly at him, but his expression told her nothing.

"I need to ring for backup," he said to Bessie. "I know that this is no job for a woman, especially an elderly woman, but could you stay with the body for a few more minutes while I do that?"

Bessie drew herself up to her full height of five feet, three inches and glared back at the man. "I'll thank you to keep your sexist and ageist remarks to yourself, young man," she told the policeman. "I am perfectly capable of standing here for a few minutes while you do what you need to do. The poor dead man deserves to have sympathetic company while he waits for whatever is going to happen next."

Hugh looked as if he wanted to argue, but only for a moment. "Keep the umbrella for now," he told Bessie as he headed back to his car. "And stay away from the body."

Bessie grinned as the wind howled and blew the umbrella inside out yet again. She wasn't going to stay any drier with it than without it, but she knew its presence made the young policeman feel a bit better about leaving her out in the storm. Once Hugh was back at his car, Bessie turned curiously towards the dead man. What she could see of him looked vaguely familiar, but she wasn't sure why.

Bessie had lived on the Isle of Man for almost her entire life. Most of her childhood had been spent in America, but that had been a very long time ago. She had purchased her little cottage on the Laxey beach when she was just eighteen and had lived there ever since. While Douglas, the island's capital, had been growing rapidly recently, thanks to changes in the tax laws, Laxey was still pretty much the same small village it had always been. Bessie fancied that she knew just about everyone in the area, and she felt sure that she could place the man if she could just see his face.

She took a cautious step towards him, wondering if she could somehow get a better look. She spun back around as she heard Hugh splashing back down the beach towards her. The rain had left puddles everywhere in the sand, and Hugh seemed incapable of missing any of them as he stomped along.

"Inspector Kelly is on his way and so is John Rockwell from Ramsey CID."

Bessie nodded. She knew Inspector Patrick Kelly; indeed, his mother had grown up in Laxey, although the family had moved to Douglas when the future Mrs. Kelly was in her late teens. She had eventually married a Kelly from somewhere in the south of the island and they had remained in Douglas.

Bessie remembered Mrs. Kelly bragging about her clever son who had joined the police department in London when she had seen her once in Douglas many years earlier. She'd heard through various sources that the woman had been even more pleased when Patrick took up a position with the force back on the island after some years in London. He was currently in charge of the tiny station at Laxey, with policing responsibility for both Laxey and Lonan, and Bessie occasionally ran into him when stopping to see Doona at the station.

"I know Patrick Kelly well enough," she told Hugh. "But I've never met John Rockwell."

"Inspector Rockwell is a good guy," Hugh shrugged. "He's from across."

Bessie nodded. "Where?"

"His last posting was in Manchester before he came here. I'm not sure where he's from originally." Hugh shrugged again and looked longingly at the umbrella Bessie was still holding.

Bessie shuffled closer to the man and tried holding the badly mangled umbrella at an angle that might offer some protection for both of them.

"Why did he leave his posting in Manchester?" Bessie asked, eager to learn all that she could about the man before his arrival.

"Apparently the wife wanted a nice safe place for the kids to grow up," Hugh repeated what he had heard. "They've a boy and girl and I hear they didn't live in a great area in Manchester and couldn't really afford to move."

Bessie nodded. The island was certainly a very safe place for a young family. "Where have they settled then?"

"They bought a four-bed semi in that new development in

7

Ramsey," Hugh answered. "They moved about six months ago and it's lucky they did, because the prices for those houses have shot up."

Bessie shook her head. "I don't know what's happening with house prices," she sighed. "All these bankers and the like moving in and driving up prices. Won't be long before no one will be able to afford anything. I know I should be grateful I got my little house so many years ago."

"Aye, you could be selling it for a lot of money now, you know," Hugh told her. "I heard that when Mrs. Clague sold the land that the new cottages are on she only got about a hundred thousand and now that land would be worth more than twice that."

"My advocate says that beachfront properties are at a premium right now," Bessie told him. "Mrs. Clague should have waited another year or two before she sold. Mr. Quayle reckons that prices are just going to keep going up."

"Aye, but Mrs. Clague was in a hurry, I gather."

"Oh aye, she wanted a spot in the new senior home in Douglas. I told her she should stay put, but she wanted the bright lights and the big city. Now she can walk to the shops and there's even a pub right next door. Last I heard she was having a wonderful time."

"You ever think about selling up and moving into a home?" Hugh asked, seemingly without thinking.

Bessie turned and took a step away from the man, taking the sheltering umbrella with her. She looked him up and down and then shook her head. "I am in a home, my home, and I intend to stay there until I die," she told him in an imperious tone. "I can't imagine why anyone would want to move into a home for the elderly and spend all their time surrounded by old people and nurses."

Hugh turned a burst of laughter into a cough and then quickly changed the subject. "I can't imagine what's keeping the bosses," he remarked.

"Your Inspector Rockwell probably got lost," Bessie suggested wryly.

"Ah, here they come now," Hugh waved an arm towards Bessie's cottage where the lights from several cars were now visible. Bessie shuddered as she realised that the new arrivals had driven in with their emergency lights blazing. By lunchtime, half the island would be thinking that she was dead.

Patrick Kelly was in his mid-forties, with brown hair that was thinning rapidly and hazel eyes that looked washed out and tired. He really needed to lose about twenty pounds. Stomping across the sand, he pulled his slightly too small raincoat as tightly as he could around his body as the still strong wind swirled around him.

A man Bessie assumed was John Rockwell followed him more slowly, taking time to study the scene as they approached. Of a similar age to the native Manxman, Rockwell looked as if he worked hard to keep in the best possible physical condition. His own raincoat looked not only warm, but was also a perfect fit. His hair was a lighter shade of brown than Inspector Kelly's and he didn't appear to have any trouble with it thinning.

Bessie could see a group of uniformed constables climbing from their cars and standing hesitantly in clusters by her cottage, waiting for their orders.

"What've we got?" Patrick barked at Hugh as he reached the younger policeman.

"It's a body, sir, a dead one," Hugh said brightly.

"I see that." Patrick shook his head. "I also see rain flooding the area and washing away all of the evidence, and an elderly civilian standing around getting soaked and getting in the way of the investigation."

Hugh flushed. "I brought an umbrella to shield the body," he offered, "but I thought that Bessie should have it. She's too old to stand in the rain without any protection."

Bessie opened her mouth to reply and then snapped it shut again. First Patrick called her elderly and then Hugh almost accused her of stealing an umbrella from a dead man. She was so mad she couldn't speak.

"Kelly, get a tent up." John Rockwell had reached the small group now and he quickly took charge. "There are plenty of men here to help."

Patrick nodded once and then, after shooting an angry look at Hugh, turned and walked back up the beach. Bessie could hear him shouting orders at the waiting men as he approached them.

"Now then, Hugh, isn't it? Tell me exactly what happened." Rockwell smiled encouragingly at the young policeman, who looked relieved.

"Doona, back at the station, she was rung at oh-seven-twenty-two this morning by a known member of the public, stating that she had discovered a body on Laxey Beach. Doona questioned the witness briefly, to establish exactly what she had seen, and then rang me and suggested that I check the beach. I arrived at oh-seven-fifty-five and found the body exactly as described by the witness. I, um, attempted to ascertain if the man in question was merely sleeping or was indeed dead by trying to roll him over. Upon doing so, I, er, well, at that point I returned to my car and rang for backup."

Hugh blew out a huge breath, as if exhausted by the recitation.

"I take it this is the witness in question?" The senior officer nodded towards Bessie.

"Oh yes, this is Aunt Bessie," Hugh confirmed. "Sorry, um, Miss Elizabeth Cubbon. She lives in the cottage just there."

Hugh pointed to Bessie's cottage and John turned his head and slowly looked it over before looking back at Bessie.

"I'm very sorry that you've had to stand out in the rain all morning, Mrs. Cubbon," he said to Bessie with a rueful grin. She was surprised to find that his eyes were an almost electric green that instantly fascinated her. Perhaps they were artificially enhanced, like Doona's, she surmised.

"I'm Inspector Rockwell from the Ramsey CID, by the way," the man continued. "Why don't we go inside and you can tell me exactly what happened."

"It's Miss Cubbon, actually," Bessie set the record straight. "And we've no need to go inside. It's a short story." She paused, expecting the man to argue but he simply nodded and waited for her to continue.

"I came out for my morning walk and nearly tripped over the

body." Bessie shrugged. "Then I rang the police. That's the whole story."

"Indeed?" Rockwell raised an eyebrow. "Do you always walk when it's pouring with rain and blowing a gale?"

Bessie snorted. "This isn't a gale. It's just a bit fresh. And I walk every day, whatever the weather. If I waited for sunshine, I wouldn't get very many walks in, would I?"

Again, the man raised his eyebrow and didn't speak. Behind them, the uniformed constables were struggling to erect a canvas tent over the body. Bessie turned to watch the action as the men fought the wind, the rain, and their own general incompetence. She had to bite back a laugh as a huge wind gust blew the half-erected tent over onto the beach.

"We aren't impressing you with our professionalism, are we?" Rockwell asked Bessie as they watched the men begin again.

"It really isn't that difficult," Bessie told him, shaking her head. "They just need to...."

The scream that echoed across the beach startled Bessie to silence.

# CHAPTER 2

The woman running down the beach towards them was wearing a flimsy white nightgown and, from the looks of it, nothing else. She screamed again, an almost inhuman sound, as she approached, and Bessie shuddered.

"Oh no, no, no," the woman sobbed as she was stopped by a pair of constables. "Danny needs me, you have to let me go to him."

Rockwell crossed the sand to the woman's side. "I'm Inspector Rockwell with the Manx CID. Can you identify this man?"

The woman looked at him with unfocussed eyes, seemingly unable to speak.

"Miss, can you tell me your name?" the inspector asked gently. He took an umbrella that was offered by one of the uniformed men on the beach and held it over the woman.

Bessie watched the interplay with interest. In spite of being soaked from her run across the beach, the woman's artificially blonde hair looked as if it had been styled recently. Her face was beautifully made-up and Bessie reckoned that the woman was wearing more cosmetics at that moment than Bessie had in her entire life. The rain seemed to be having little effect on the makeup, which to Bessie suggested expensive products. Bessie wasn't sure if it was the skilful application of eye makeup that made the woman's eyes appear to be such a stunning violet colour or if it were natural.

"Please, I have to help Danny," the woman sobbed after a moment. "He needs me."

"Miss, I'm sorry, but the best thing you can do for Danny now is answer my questions." Rockwell's words seemed harsh, but they clearly got through to the young woman.

"I'm sorry, I think I'm in shock." The woman used a shaking hand to brush a stray hair out of her eyes. "We're on our honeymoon."

Bessie shook her head sadly; she understood the woman's loss only too well.

"Can we start with the basics, please?" Rockwell took out his phone, safely covered in a waterproof case, and switched it on. "Normally I would take notes, but that's impossible in this rain. If it's okay with you, I'd like to record your answers. I don't want to do a full interview here, but a few basics will get us started."

The woman nodded reluctantly and once more brushed hair from her eyes. Bessie studied her carefully. At first glance Bessie had placed her in her mid-twenties, but now she decided that the woman was actually as much as a decade older than that. The soaking wet gown clung to every curve of the woman's perfect shape and Bessie found herself disliking the young widow even before she heard her story.

The woman clung now to Inspector Rockwell's arm as she began to speak. "I'm Vicky Robinson, well, Vicky Pierce now," she shuddered as she corrected herself. "That's Vicky, with two k's."

"V-I-C-K-K-Y?" he questioned.

The woman giggled as she gazed into the inspector's green eyes. "No, silly, V-I-K-K-Y."

Bessie turned away from the pair, certain that disapproval was written all over her face. The woman was almost flirting with the police inspector in front of her husband's dead body. That was no way for a lady to behave. Not that anything about Vikky Pierce gave Bessie reason to believe that she was a lady.

One of the uniformed officers handed Vikky a blanket and she

DIANA XARISSA

shot him a huge smile as she wrapped it around herself. Then she sighed dramatically.

"Sorry, where was I?" she simpered.

"You were going to tell me about the dead man." Inspector Rockwell's clipped tone seemed to startle the woman.

"Oh, oh, yes," she said. She looked over at the body that was now partially obstructed by the wobbly-looking tent that had finally been completed. Tears welled up in her eyes as she studied the scene.

"It's my husband," she said with a catch in her voice. "Daniel, Daniel Pierce. We got married on Saturday and came to the island to spend our honeymoon with his family at Theen-tray; that's his family's summer house here."

"I don't suppose you could spell that?" Rockwell asked. The woman looked at him blankly.

"T-H-I-E Y-N T-R-A-I-E," Hugh Watterson interjected. "It means 'Beach House' in Manx. The Pierce family bought the land and built the house about twenty-five years ago. It's just up that way, past the new cottages." Hugh gestured up the beach.

Rockwell nodded his thanks to Hugh and turned back to Vikky. "So you came to honeymoon in the family's summer home?"

"The whole family came. We came for the whole week to celebrate Daniel's father's sixtieth birthday."

Bessie nodded to herself. She knew the family, but only distantly. They were summer visitors, not full-time residents. That explained why the man seemed familiar. She must have seen him on the beach, during the summer months, many times over the last twenty-five years.

"Seems strange to honeymoon with your husband's family," Rockwell remarked in a mild tone.

"Oh, we all get along wonderfully," Vikky insisted. "I was just so excited about being Danny's wife that I would have agreed to anything anyway."

As the rain tapered off again and the skies brightened slightly, all around the quiet hum of the investigation began. Rockwell turned back towards Bessie and looked surprised to see her there.

"Oh, ah, I am sorry," he told her. "I should have sent you home ages ago."

"I thought you had more questions for me," Bessie answered, trying to cover for the fact that she had been listening intently to his conversation with the widow.

"And I'm sure I do," Rockwell agreed. "But right now I think I need to focus on my investigation and you need to get out of the rain."

"I'm sure you're right." Bessie grinned at him as she had an idea. "Why don't I take Mrs. Pierce back to my cottage so that we can both dry off? When you've finished down here, you can find us both there and we can answer your questions."

Rockwell only hesitated for a moment. It was clear to Bessie that she and the widow were both unnecessary distractions at the crime scene at the moment.

"That's a great idea," Rockwell told Bessie. "I'll be along as quickly as I can."

"Oh, no rush," Bessie answered. "Mrs. Pierce and I have a lot in common. I'm sure we'll find plenty to talk about."

Bessie put her arm around the younger woman and led her, unprotesting, up the beach.

As they reached the door to Bessie's cottage, the new widow drew a deep breath. "I should stay with Danny," she whimpered to Bessie.

"Leave everything to the experts," Bessie said in her most soothing voice. "You won't do anyone any good standing there getting soaked."

"I suppose not," the woman said softly. "Oh, your house has a funny name, too," Vikky said as she spotted the plaque next to the front door.

"Treoghe Bwaane," Bessie pronounced the Manx words for her guest. "It basically means 'Widow's Cottage,'" she explained.

"Oh, are you a widow too?" the younger woman asked as she plopped herself down in a chair at the kitchen table.

Bessie shook her head. "The cottage already had its name when I bought it," she explained. "But it seemed suitable because I bought it just after I lost my one true love."

"Really?" Vikky was intrigued. "Did he dump you or die or what?"

Bessie turned to look at her young guest. Could she really be that thoughtless and insensitive? She sighed to herself. It was her own fault for inviting the unpleasant woman into her home, she supposed. Sometimes she let her nosiness win out over her sense.

"He died," she answered shortly, hoping that the subject would end there.

"What happened?" the other woman continued to press Bessie.

This time Bessie sighed audibly. It wasn't as if she hadn't told the story hundreds of times before, it was just that she had already begun to dislike this flashy vulgar woman who wasn't behaving at all the way Bessie thought she should. Bessie simply didn't feel like sharing any personal information with Vikky Pierce.

"Any chance of a cuppa with the story?" Vikky seemed oblivious to Bessie's thoughts and she seemed to be recovering from her sudden bereavement strangely quickly.

"Tea? I'm surprised you have the stomach for it," Bessie said a bit snappishly as she turned on the kettle.

The woman looked startled for a moment and then began to shake. "You're right, of course; I can't imagine what I was thinking." Tears began to fall at an impressive rate as Bessie found mugs and filled her teapot with a couple of teabags.

"Now, now," she muttered towards the sobbing woman. "Everything's going to work out in the end, you'll see."

"How can it, with Danny dead?" the woman asked miserably.

"Oh, I'm sure you'll get over Danny eventually," Bessie replied. She wasn't usually so determinedly rude to guests in her home, but she really couldn't find anything to like in this woman.

"Oh, sure, eventually," the woman agreed as she wiped her eyes on a tissue from the box that Bessie handed her. "But that could take months. I'm ever so devastated now."

Bessie forced herself to count to ten before she replied. "I'm sure everything will work out in the end," she repeated herself. "The police here are excellent and I'm sure they'll find out what happened to your husband in no time."

"He must have drowned, or had a heart attack or something,"

Vikky said, her eyes filling with tears again. "I should have been with him."

Bessie poured out two cups of tea and found a box of biscuits that she quickly emptied onto a plate. Then she joined the young woman at the table, choosing a seat opposite her guest. She handed the woman her tea and a small plate to use for her biscuits.

"There probably wasn't anything you could have done," Bessie muttered a polite response that was at odds with her actual thoughts. "Anyway, the police are very good at their jobs; I'm sure they'll work it out quickly enough."

"I hope you're right," the woman said intently. "I have to know what happened to Danny. I feel as if this is all my fault."

Bessie nodded. "I'm sure that Inspector Rockwell will be able to answer all of your questions in due course."

"He spent his summers here just about his whole life," Vikky told her. "They used to stay in a bed and breakfast in Ramsey before they bought the land and built the cottage here. Danny and his whole family love the island so much. We even talked about moving here." The widow's voice broke as she spoke and tears began to fall again.

Bessie stared at her, puzzled and unsettled by her behaviour. "Drink your tea," Bessie counselled. "And then we can find you something to put on."

Bessie watched the woman blush under her heavy makeup. "I wanted to look nice for Danny when he got back," she explained. "I did my hair and makeup and put on my sexiest nightie. We had, well, we had a bit of a disagreement last night and we needed to patch things up."

"Yes, well, I'm sure I can find something for you to put on that will be more suitable for being out and about in this weather," Bessie replied.

They finished their tea in silence, Vikky nibbling her way through half a dozen biscuits, and then Bessie and her guest headed upstairs. Bessie had always been slender, and she wasn't about to let age become an excuse for letting her figure go. She should have plenty of things that would fit the young widow. Unfortunately, Vikky was several inches taller than she was, so any trousers that she lent the woman were going to be rather short on her.

Vikky sat on the edge of Bessie's bed, marvelling at the pink walls and the plethora of cuddly toys that filled every spare space in the room.

"Why do you have so many cuddly toys?" Vikky asked after a moment.

"I never experienced the joy of having children of my own," Bessie told her as she dug through her wardrobe. "I've been fortunate, however, in that many of the children in the area have adopted me as an honorary auntie. For some reason that seems to include buying me cuddly toys at every opportunity. I suppose I don't have to keep them all, but I could never find a reason to part with any of them."

Bessie grabbed a long tweed skirt and a large woollen sweater from the wardrobe. She also found a pair of thick tights that were size "extra-tall" which she had purchased by mistake. After a moment's hesitation, she added a pair of plain white cotton underpants to the pile. No doubt the other woman had never worn anything so ordinary, but at least they would be comfortable.

"Here you are. It's the best I can do." Bessie handed the clothes to Vikky who stood up and dropped the police blanket she had still been clutching around herself. "Cool, I can look like somebody's old auntie," Vikky muttered as she flipped through the clothes.

"Feel free to stay in your nightie," Bessie replied coolly.

"Oh, no," the woman backtracked quickly. "I didn't mean to sound ungrateful," she insisted. "Everything is just too much today. I'm sure I must be behaving very badly."

Bessie resisted the temptation to agree with her. "I should let you get changed then," Bessie suggested, heading towards the door.

As she turned back towards Vikky, she was shocked to see the other woman had already pulled off her nightie and was climbing into the borrowed underwear. Apparently modesty belonged to a different generation, Bessie thought as she made her way into the hall to wait for Vikky to finish.

Vikky followed her out of the room only seconds later, and the pair made their way back downstairs. Now Bessie led her guest into the small sitting room that was next door to the kitchen.

"Please have a seat; we might as well be comfortable while we wait for the police to arrive."

"Yes, I suppose so," Vikky said hesitantly. "Maybe I should go down and talk to them there," she suggested.

"I'm sure you'd just be in the way," Bessie told her.

"You were going to tell me what happened to your lover," Vikky suddenly remembered.

"We weren't lovers," Bessie said primly. "We were in love."

"Oh, sorry, I didn't mean anything," Vikky waved a hand. "Anyway, what happened?"

Bessie smiled grimly at Vikky. She was prepared to tell the story, but she was determined, in exchange, to find out some things about her guest as well.

"My family moved to America when I was just a baby, really," she began. "Then, after fifteen years there, they decided to move back to the island. I had fallen madly in love with a man I met through a friend, but my parents wouldn't let me stay behind with him. They made me leave him when they returned to the island."

"That's awful. You shouldn't have gone with them," Vikky told her.

"I was under eighteen; I couldn't have stayed on my own. Anyway, this was a great many years ago. Children obeyed their parents in those days."

Vikky snorted. "You wouldn't catch me leaving a man I loved just because my parents said I had to," she insisted.

"Yes, well, as I said, the times were very different then," Bessie said patiently.

"So they dragged you back here and you bought this cottage?" Vikky checked that she understood the story.

"There was a bit more to it than that," Bessie told her. "Matthew, that was the man I loved, decided to come and get me."

"Good on him!" Vikky shouted.

"Yes, well, unfortunately for him he fell ill on the journey here and died just before his ship docked in Liverpool."

"He was sailing? Why didn't he just fly over?"

"There weren't any commercial transatlantic flights in those days." Bessie shook her head. "And even if there had been, tickets probably would have been far too expensive for someone like Matthew to afford."

"So then you bought the cottage?" Vikky asked.

"Yes," Bessie nodded. "Matthew wrote a new will just before he left America, leaving everything he owned to me. It wasn't a lot of money, but it was enough to buy this cottage, which was much smaller in those days. I've extended it twice, you see."

"It must have been pretty small," Vikky said, looking around the space.

"It was really only two rooms when I bought it," Bessie told her.

"Danny's family's cottage is huge," Vikky replied. "It has separate wings for staff and stuff like that."

"From what I've heard, Danny's family has a great deal of money."

"Yeah, they own a bunch of stuff like grocery stores and shopping malls," Vikky shrugged. "I loved Danny because he was a good person, not because he was loaded."

"That's good to know," Bessie said, forcing herself to keep the doubt out of her tone. "So now that he's gone, who inherits his share of the fortune?" she asked boldly.

"Me," Vikky giggled. Bessie couldn't keep the shocked expression off her face.

"Oh dear, that didn't sound good, did it?" Vikky shook her head. "I'm just so confused. I can't even begin to believe that Danny's gone. He was always so much more serious than I was. He insisted that we rewrite our wills just before the wedding. I imagine that means I'm going to be a very rich widow."

With those words Vikky burst into tears again. Bessie sighed as she got up to find another box of tissues. Perhaps it had something to do with the generation gap, but she was finding it very difficult to muster up any sympathy for this woman.

The day wore on and, as Bessie made frequent trips to the kitchen for more tissues and endless cups of tea, she could just see the tented area where the police were busily going about their work. The rain finally stopped altogether and even the wind slackened as morning turned to afternoon.

Bessie offered the use of her phone to Vikky, if she wanted to ring anyone, but she demurred.

"I don't want to break the news to Danny's parents myself and I can't begin to explain anything. I just want to sit here and feel numb."

Bessie made soup with tea and toast for lunch, which they ate at the kitchen table. "You need to try to eat something," she told Vikky when she shook her head at the soup.

"I'm just not hungry," Vikky moaned. "How can I eat when I know that Danny is...."

"You have to keep your strength up," Bessie counselled her. "The next few days are going to be difficult; you need to stay strong."

She knew she was a fine one to talk. When she found out that Matthew had died, she had refused to eat for nearly a week, sobbing almost continually and only sleeping when her body gave in to exhaustion. But she didn't need to tell Vikky any of that. With one more final urging, the younger woman fell on the soup and toast as if she hadn't eaten in days. Within minutes, half a loaf of bread was gone and Vikky was halfway through a third bowl of soup.

"You were right," she told the older woman as she emptied the bowl the third time. "I really needed that."

Bessie bit her tongue and looked out the window at the activity further down the beach. The police vehicles that were parked in her driveway and along the road next to her house had been coming and going throughout the morning. When Bessie spotted the ambulance that arrived shortly after lunch, she quickly moved her guest upstairs and away from any chance to watch her husband's body being removed.

"I have an office up here," she told Vikky as she ushered her upstairs. "And I have a lot of books. Maybe you'd like to read while you wait."

Vikky wrinkled her nose. "I'm not really much of a reader," she replied. "Where's your telly?"

Bessie fought back a frown. "I don't have a telly."

"Too cheap to pay the licence fee?" Vikky snorted.

Bessie bit back a dozen angry replies. After several deep breaths, she finally spoke. "Television has simply never interested me," she told the woman, keeping her tone as even as she could manage. "Money is not an issue."

"What did you do before you retired?" Vikky asked.

Bessie bristled. This woman was unbelievably rude. "I don't believe that's any of your business," she couldn't stop herself from saying.

Vikky looked stung. "Oh, am I prying now? I thought, since we talked about my marriage and your dead boyfriend and whatever that we could talk about stuff. Never mind."

Bessie was saved from having to reply by a loud knock on her door. The two women hurried down the stairs, both welcoming the interruption.

Hugh Watterson stood at Bessie's door. The rain had stopped some time earlier but Hugh, who had been out in it for hours, was still almost dripping wet. He forced himself to smile at the two women.

"Inspector Rockwell has asked me to collect Mrs. Pierce and bring her over to the station. He needs to talk to her and he felt that the station was the best place." Bessie grinned at the look on Hugh's face as he looked into her cosy kitchen. No doubt it would be hours before he could get changed out of his wet clothes and relax.

"I don't want to go to the police station," Vikky protested. "It isn't like I've done anything wrong."

"No, of course not," Hugh was quick to agree. "But the Inspector wants to get right to interviewing susp..., er, witnesses. He's gone back to the station and asked me to bring you. Other constables have been sent to gather up the rest of the victim's family."

"You're going to bring Danny's parents to the police station? It's worth going just to see that." Vikky laughed now and looked around. "I didn't even have my bag or my phone, did I?" she said to Bessie.

"You didn't bring anything with you," Bessie assured her. "As for what you were wearing when you arrived, well, I'll drop that off to you another day. You don't want to be worrying about it all afternoon."

"Thank you." Vikky didn't seem to be paying much attention to Bessie. She was staring down the beach, where teams of uniformed constables were slowly walking along the sand, studying every inch of it. Bessie could see that the tent was still standing, but it was obvious that the body had been removed.

Hugh noticed where she was looking and exchanged a quick glance with Bessie. "Let's get going then," he blustered. "Off we go."

Vikky was shaking as Hugh took her arm and guided her out towards his car.

"Thank you, Aunt Bessie," he called over his shoulder.

"It was no problem," she replied to the man, waiting for a similar word of thanks from Vikky.

Vikky climbed into the passenger seat of the police car without looking back.

Bessie frowned. Manners should always trump tragedy, she thought to herself as she went back inside. She tried hard to understand the other woman's feelings, but there were no two ways about it. Bessie couldn't make herself like Vikky Pierce, no matter how sorry she felt for her.

# CHAPTER 3

*B*essie bustled around her cottage, quickly washing the lunch dishes and tidying them away. She went back upstairs and rescued the left-behind nightie. The label identified it as pure silk and dry clean only, so Bessie simply threw it into a shopping bag to take back to Vikky later. If it had been sensible cotton, Bessie would have washed it for the other woman out of simple courtesy.

She folded the police blanket carefully and put it into a second bag. She would return it to Doona, who would take care of laundering it. Even if she did wash it, Doona would have to do it again anyway. Doona had explained it to her once, something about having everything the police used washed in the same detergent for reasons having to do with evidence. Bessie wasn't sure she understood, but she knew there was no point in washing the blanket herself.

Chores finished, she sank down on a couch in the sitting room and then realised that her morning routine had been completely disrupted by events. She hadn't even turned the ringer on her phone back on. She sighed as she got to her feet again. Her mobile phone was used for emergencies only and was in her handbag, probably switched off. She had a single line into the house, and that phone sat in the kitchen next to the overpriced answering machine that her advocate had nagged her into getting.

When she went to bed at night, Bessie always turned the phone's ringer off. It was a minor concession to her age. She felt she was too old now to be running up and down the stairs in the middle of the night if the phone rang. Any call between nine at night and six or seven the next morning was going to be a wrong number anyway. Bessie's friends would never bother her at those hours, and she couldn't imagine any emergency that couldn't wait until morning.

With all of the comings and goings with the police cars and the ambulance, Bessie was unsurprised to find that she had twenty-two messages on the machine. She made herself a cup of tea and pulled out a pad and pen to write down the important ones.

Bessie split the list into two columns, those who had rung because they were genuinely concerned and those who had rung out of sheer nosiness. It didn't take long to return the handful of calls from the sincerely worried. The others could wait a bit longer to get their skeet, she decided.

She was just reassuring her advocate that the excitement hadn't been too much for her when she heard a knock on her door. Hugh Watterson was back.

"I'm sorry, Aunt Bessie, but I'm meant to ask you to come into the station to make a statement," he said apologetically. "I told Inspector Rockwell that I could take your statement here, but he wants to talk to you himself."

"I suppose inspectors can make whatever rules they like," Bessie shrugged. She had no real objection to going to the station; she often spent time there visiting with Doona anyway, but it would have been nice to have been given options.

Hugh opened his mouth and then snapped it shut. Bessie wondered what he wanted to say, but didn't pry.

"Just let me get my bag," she told Hugh. "You pop in and make yourself a cuppa. The kettle has just boiled."

Hugh grinned at that and Bessie could hear him grabbing a cup and making himself tea as she headed towards the stairs. She always welcomed houseguests and the neighbourhood children always knew they could "run away" to Aunt Bessie's whenever they felt the need, but Bessie wasn't the sort to wait on her guests hand and foot.

As soon as they were old enough to not get hurt, she taught them to make their own tea and where the biscuits were kept. Everyone knew that, at Bessie's, biscuits had to be put on a plate and then eaten neatly so that the plate caught the crumbs. Visitors also quickly learned that they should wash their cups and plates for themselves when they were finished. Bessie was terrific at providing tea and sympathy, but she wasn't going to clean up after everyone on top of that.

A few minutes later she was bundled up into Hugh's police car and whisked away into the centre of Laxey. Hugh pulled into the police station car park and smiled at Bessie.

"At least the rain has stopped," he remarked.

Bessie looked up at the grey skies and nodded. "Could start again any time," she replied.

"Hardly surprising in March," Hugh shrugged.

They climbed out of the car and headed into the station through the back door. Bessie had never entered from the back; when she visited Doona she always came in the front way. Doona's desk was in the building's lobby, and Bessie had never had any reason to go past it into the station itself. Now she looked around with interest at the small offices that they passed as they made their way into the building.

She was disappointed in what she saw. Many of the doors were closed, but the ones that were open just looked like ordinary offices. Their occupants could have been advocates or insurance agents as much as policemen. She saw no sign of Vikky Pierce, or indeed anyone else. The station felt almost deserted.

Doona had told her that there were a few small temporary holding cells in the basement of the building, but Hugh didn't take her anywhere near those, either. Instead, he escorted her into the lobby and left her with Doona while he went to let Inspector Rockwell know that she had arrived.

"Oooo, there you are," Doona squealed when she spotted Bessie. "How are you? Was it frightfully awful?"

Bessie hugged her friend and was surprised to find tears welling up in her eyes as she was squeezed tightly. Doona was in her mid-forties, twice-married and twice-divorced. She was a few inches taller and about thirty-five pounds heavier than Bessie. She wore her heavily highlighted brown hair in a short bob and alternated between thick glasses and contact lenses that artificially gave her sparkling green eyes.

"Oh now, don't you be crying," Doona told her. "That widow woman has used up every blessed tissue in the whole station and I haven't had time to pop out to buy more."

Bessie smiled. "Vikky Pierce? She used more than a few tissues at my house as well. In between gossiping and eating like a horse."

Doona shook her head. "Come and sit down. Inspector Rockwell won't be ready for you for a bit. You can tell me all about it."

Bessie handed the bag with the police blanket to her friend and then slid into the chair next to the reception desk that Doona manned. She smiled at Doona, feeling lucky that they had met and become good friends before today's events.

"Fastyr mie," she told Doona.

"Oh aye, fastyr mie," Doona replied with a laugh.

"We really have to stay in practice," Bessie insisted. The friends had met a few years earlier in a beginning Manx language class for adults. While neither had developed any proficiency in the native language of their homeland, they had quickly become close friends.

Doona had grown up in the south of the island. She and Bessie only crossed paths when Doona moved to Laxey to take the job at the Laxey station as a civilian officer, following her second divorce. At their first language class Bessie had confessed to feeling bad that she had never learned the language that her parents and especially her grandparents had spoken. Everyone laughed when Doona announced that she had just signed up in the hopes of meeting single men. It was especially funny since the class consisted of six women, all falling somewhere between Bessie and Doona in age.

"I've signed up to start again in April," Bessie told Doona. "I'm taking Beginning Manx again, since I haven't exactly mastered it."

Doona laughed. "I'll sign up, too. Maybe this time there will be some men in the class. Or maybe the teacher will be a single middle-aged man looking for the perfect woman."

"You'll be lucky if there's a stray man in the class," Bessie laughed. "Marjorie's teaching it again, so you're definitely out of luck there."

Doona shrugged. "It's fun anyway, even though I'm terrible at it."

"It's a tough language," Bessie told her. "I heard my parents speak it occasionally and I still can't manage it."

"They should have taught it to you," Doona sighed.

"Once we moved to America, they didn't see any advantage to doing so. And once we'd moved back, I moved out."

Doona nodded. She knew Bessie's story well. "I should be glad they didn't teach it to you as a child," she remarked. "If they had, we wouldn't have met."

"I suppose we would have met today," Bessie said wryly.

"Yes, I suppose so," Doona laughed. "Anyway, what happened?"

Bessie fought back a sigh. "I went for my regular morning walk and nearly tripped over a dead man. Luckily, that's an unusual morning for me."

Doona nodded. "It's pretty unusual for us as well," she confided. "And from what I hear, he didn't get dead accidentally."

Bessie stared at her friend. "What do you mean?" she demanded.

"I can only tell you what I'm hearing through the grapevine," Doona told her. "None of this is official. But I've heard he had a knife stuck in his chest."

Bessie sat back in her chair, stunned by the news. "But no one gets murdered on the Isle of Man," she argued. "Okay, there was that man in Douglas in 1982, but he was from across and brought his troubles with him."

"There's more that goes on than makes the papers," Doona

confided. "But even so, Laxey has always been one of the safest places on the island."

"What else don't I know?" Bessie demanded. "I know the widow was brought in for questioning; how did she seem to you?"

Doona shook her head. "I could get fired for talking about an active investigation," she told Bessie with a frown.

Bessie frowned herself. "What good is having a friend on the inside if I can't get any good skeet out of her?" she demanded.

Doona grinned. "I told you the most exciting thing I know," she reminded her friend. "And I can tell you that Inspector Rockwell is stepping on just about every set of toes he can find," she whispered.

"Why am I not surprised?" Bessie asked. "He seemed like the type when I met him on the beach."

"Oh, he is," Doona agreed. "Inspector Kelly isn't very happy with the way the CID is taking charge. He thinks that, since Laxey is his jurisdiction, he should be in charge. Inspector Rockwell insists that the CID trumps local jurisdiction. At this rate, the Chief Constable might have to separate them."

"Men!" Bessie rolled her eyes. "They should all be focussed on finding the killer, not worrying about who gets to be in charge."

"I think they're both more interested in who gets the credit when the killer gets locked up," Doona said. "The family is important across. This case is going to get lots of publicity, here and there. I think Mr. Pierce already has the Chief Constable on speed dial so he can keep up-to-date with developments. There will be lots of plaudits for the person who catches whoever did it."

Bessie groaned. She liked to think of Laxey as an undiscovered gem; the last thing she wanted was any publicity.

"I just hope young Hugh gets some of the credit when it comes," Doona told her friend. "He has his faults, but he's really a good kid and he works hard when he has to."

Bessie wasn't sure she totally agreed with her friend's assessment of the young policeman, but she didn't argue. "Surely you can tell me your impression of Vikky Pierce?" Bessie asked.

"I didn't get much chance to form an impression," Doona told her.

"Hugh brought her in and turned her over to Inspector Rockwell pretty sharpish."

"She wasn't left sitting around in the waiting room like I am, then."

"I hope you aren't complaining!" Doona giggled.

"Not really," Bessie replied. "So you didn't even meet the devastated bride, widowed just days after the happiest day of her life?"

Doona snorted. "It's not my place to say," she said, "but she didn't seem too devastated when she sailed in here. I recognized your clothes, by the way. You shouldn't have."

"I didn't want to leave her sitting around in a soaking wet silk nightie," Bessie answered. "Especially in my house."

Doona laughed. "What a mental image that creates," she giggled. "Still, I bet Inspector Rockwell will want the nightie."

"Why on earth would he want that?" Bessie was shocked.

"To test for blood stains and stuff," Doona told her. "Surely you've realised that the widow is the chief suspect."

Bessie nodded slowly, her brain struggling to keep up with everything that was happening. "I suppose I didn't really think about it," she said after a moment. "I mean, I didn't really think about it being murder. I just assumed he had a heart attack or something."

Doona patted her hand gently. "Murder is hard to imagine."

Bessie shook her head. "I might have made lunch for a murderer?"

"You made her lunch?" Doona choked back a laugh when she saw the look on Bessie's face. "I mean, that was really nice of you, but why?"

"It was lunch time," Bessie said weakly. "I wasn't thinking."

"I get the impression that you didn't like her very much," Doona remarked.

"I didn't like her one little bit," Bessie said tartly. "But I didn't think of her as a suspect. I really didn't think about the dead man. I've had a lot of different experiences in my life, but this is the first time I've found a body. I suppose I should have thought about it more before I invited the woman into my home."

"You should indeed," Doona said. "There's no telling what the woman is capable of."

Bessie just stopped herself from shaking her head again. "It all just seems slightly unreal. People don't just stab other people, not in my world, only in my favourite fiction."

Doona shrugged. "I've seen a lot since I took this job with the police. But this is the first murder we've had to deal with in Laxey. Luckily, it is pretty unusual."

She got up and took a couple of short steps to the kettle that was on a table behind her. As Bessie sat lost in her thoughts, Doona made tea for them both.

"Here," she handed a mug to Bessie. "I've made it extra milky and sweet. It will help for sure."

Bessie made a face. She'd drunk considerably more than her normal amount of tea already that day, but she forced herself to drink the warm liquid. She could almost feel its warmth spreading through her body and restarting her stunned brain. "There must be other suspects," she said now.

"I suppose the whole family has to be looked at," Doona agreed. "And the staff and anyone else who comes along. I don't know that much about it, yet, but I imagine I'll be typing all of the reports as they come in. Of course, I can't tell you anything until it's all over."

Bessie thought about that for a moment. "I understand," she assured her friend. "I just hope they sort it out quickly."

"I'm sure we will."

The voice from the hallway startled both women. Bessie turned her head and met Inspector Rockwell's eyes. He looked amused by the idea that he had interrupted the conversation. Behind him, Bessie could see Patrick Kelly and Hugh having a chat.

"I just need a few minutes of your time," Inspector Rockwell told Bessie. "Just to get a formal statement of exactly what you saw today."

Bessie nodded and got to her feet. Doona had busied herself with paperwork as soon as Rockwell had appeared. Bessie managed to catch her eye as she rose.

"Thank you for the tea," she said formally.

Doona winked at her. "No problem. Good luck."

"I hope I don't need it," Bessie muttered as she walked slowly across the room. One advantage of her age was that she could take her time crossing to the man. She didn't mind him thinking that she was slow; it gave her time to compose herself. She reached his side and smiled up at him.

"I'm not quite as fast as I used to be," she smiled, determined to be friendly.

"We all have to get old, I suppose," the man answered absently.

Bessie bristled at the remark, but kept her smile firmly in place. Old was not a word she liked to associate with herself, even if it might be accurate.

Rockwell led her back down the short hallway to one of the offices that had been behind a closed door when she and Hugh had arrived. He ushered her inside and waved her towards a chair.

Bessie took a quick look around at plain wood furniture planted haphazardly in the unadorned white room. She supposed it must be an office, because of the furniture, rather than a room intended for questioning suspects, but the space could hardly have been any more cold and unwelcoming.

"The Laxey Constabulary has kindly arranged for me to use this office during my investigation," Inspector Rockwell told Bessie as she shifted around in the hard wooden seat, struggling to find a comfortable position.

"It needs a bit of decorating," Bessie told the man, as he took his own seat behind the desk. She was surprised when he laughed at her words.

"Decorating is the last thing I'm concerned with," he told her. "I'm trying to find a murderer. This room is perfectly serviceable as it is."

"I suppose," Bessie shrugged.

"Right, I don't want to take up too much of your time," the inspector told her. "So I'd like to get right to my questions, if that's okay."

"Certainly," Bessie agreed.

"I'm going to record this and take notes as well, if that's okay?"

"It's fine."

"Terrific." The man smiled briefly and then consulted the notes he had on the desk in front of him.

"You're Ms. Elizabeth Cubbon, correct?"

"Actually, it's Miss Elizabeth Cubbon," Bessie told him. "While I applaud modern women for finding a title that allows them to hide their marital status from all and sundry in the same way that men can use 'Mister' to do so, I've never been fond of 'Ms.' as a title for myself. I've never married, but not due to lack of opportunity. I'm quite content with my status as 'Miss' Cubbon, thank you."

Inspector Rockwell blew out a long breath and then made a short note on his paper. "Right, so then, Miss Cubbon," he said carefully, "how old are you?"

"I hardly see why that is any of your concern," Bessie told him sharply. "What does my age have to do with your investigation?"

Another long breath was coupled with a long pause before the man spoke again. "We gather a certain amount of information from all of our witnesses, regardless of its immediate obvious relevance," he said eventually. "A witness's age can be important for understanding how he or she sees the world, for example. A twenty-year-old will see certain things very differently to a sixty-year-old."

Bessie sighed. "Age isn't something that I worry about," she told the man. "The last interesting thing that happens when you age is getting your free bus pass at sixty. I've had mine for a good many years now. I suppose I should be looking forward to a telegram from the Queen, but that's still a good many years into my future."

Rockwell looked as if he might press her further for a moment and then he frowned and made a few more notes on his papers instead. "Perhaps we can come back to that topic later," he muttered as he shuffled through the sheets on his desk.

Not bloody likely, Bessie thought to herself, biting her tongue hard to keep herself from saying it out loud.

"Okay then, Miss Cubbon," Inspector Rockwell smiled. "Can you please just take me through the last twenty-four hours or so. Start with yesterday afternoon and run me up to now."

"Yesterday?" Bessie frowned. She wanted to argue that yesterday didn't much matter, but she felt like she had been arguing with the inspector enough already.

"If you don't mind."

"Of course not," Bessie finally said grudgingly. "Let's see, yesterday I had lunch at home. I had soup and a small chicken salad sandwich. Then I spent some hours working on the research for a paper that I'm due to give at a conference at the Manx Museum later this year. I had dinner with my advocate and his family. His wife was kind enough to collect me and then he drove me home after dinner." Bessie took a breath.

"Sorry to interrupt," Inspector Rockwell held up a hand. "Can I just get the name of your advocate, please?"

"Doncan Quayle, Senior," Bessie answered without further comment.

Inspector Rockwell glanced at her and then made another note. "Sorry, please continue."

"After dinner I read for a short time and then I went to bed. I slept until six, got up and dressed and had some breakfast and then headed out for my morning walk. Not far from home, I nearly stumbled over the body of a man. I rang the police from my home and waited with the body until Hugh Watterson arrived. When yourself and Inspector Kelly arrived, I was told to wait at home and I returned there, along with the dead man's widow, who had turned up in the middle of everything. We kept each other company for a few hours. I made some tea and then soup and toast while we waited. Eventually, Hugh arrived and took Mrs. Pierce away. Some time later, he returned and collected me and brought me here."

"Thank you," Inspector Rockwell said. "Now I have just a few questions."

Of course you do, Bessie thought sourly.

"Do you know what time you went to bed?"

"It would have been somewhere between ten and eleven," Bessie told him. "I usually try to get eight hours of sleep, but I was in the middle of a good book last night and I read a bit later than I usually do."

"Do you remember waking up in the night at all? Did you get up for a drink of water or anything like that?"

Bessie shook her head. "I've always been a good sound sleeper," she told the man. "I didn't wake up once."

Rockwell nodded, but looked unhappy. "Right, do you always go for a walk in the morning?"

Bessie nodded. "Every morning, if I'm able, regardless of the weather," she told him. "I believe our bodies are 'use it or lose it.' I like to keep my mind sharp and my body as fit as I possibly can."

"I'd have to say that I agree with that." The man unconsciously patted his stomach. It was obvious, looking at him, that he worked hard to stay fit.

"You said something about working on a paper for a conference? What's that about?"

"I'm an amateur historian," Bessie explained. "I've been working with Marjorie Stevens at the Manx Museum Library on a number of projects. I've been indexing nineteenth-century wills and writing about my findings for the last few years. Lately, Marjorie's been teaching me how to read seventeenth-century handwriting so that I can help her index some of the documents available from that time period as well. In May, I'm going to be talking at a conference at the museum about some of what I've found so far and what I hope to do in the future."

Inspector Rockwell nodded, a slightly surprised look on his face. "Okay, so you worked on your research and then you had dinner with your advocate. After dinner you finished an interesting book and then went to bed. You slept well and then got up at six for a walk. The weather didn't bother you?"

"No sense waiting around for a nice day," Bessie told him. "By the time one gets here, I might not be able to walk any more."

"What time did you set out on your walk?"

"It was around quarter past seven. I waited for the sun to start coming up, since it was so dark and gloomy out."

"You didn't take an umbrella?"

"It was too windy."

The man nodded slowly. "So you were walking in the wind and the rain and it was nearly dark. I'm surprised you didn't fall over the body."

"I very nearly did," Bessie told him. "I walk nearly the same path every day. I have done for many years. Of course the tide and wind bring driftwood and all sorts up onto the beach, so I'm always careful. But I wasn't expecting to find a body lying there."

"Did you touch the body?"

"Not intentionally," Bessie shuddered. She closed her eyes and tried to think back. "I don't think I did," she said eventually. "It was dark and wet, but a full-grown man is pretty hard to miss. I saw him before I got close enough to actually fall over him."

"Didn't you try shaking him to wake him up?"

"No," Bessie said. "I'm not sure why, but there was no doubt in my mind that he was dead. Possibly because the weather was so nasty. No one, no matter how drunk, could possibly have been sleeping in that."

"I suppose I can't argue with that," Rockwell told her. "So you rang the police and then went back to stay with the body until the police arrived?"

"Yes, although I made myself a quick cup of tea first. I put it in a travel mug and took it with me to try to keep myself warm while I waited."

"Why didn't you take the travel mug with you on your walk in the first place?"

"I like to walk as briskly as I can," Bessie explained. "I would have had a cuppa as soon as I got in, but the whole point of the walk is to get exercise. Waiting for Hugh, however, was just standing around. I didn't want to catch a chill."

Rockwell nodded. "And when Hugh arrived, what happened?"

"We had a quick chat and then he decided to ring for backup."

"Can you remember exactly what you said in that 'chat'?"

"Yes, but I'm sure Hugh can as well. You'd do better getting it from him. I'm sure he's had to do a full report on this morning."

"It's always good to have two reports of the same conversation," Rockwell told her. "You'd be surprised how often they vary."

"Probably every time," she said. "People's memories are unreliable, but Hugh and I didn't talk about much of anything. I told him about finding the body and then we exchanged a bit of local gossip and waited for his backup to arrive."

"Did you discuss the identity of the murdered man?"

"No," Bessie told him. "I didn't have any idea who he was, and if Hugh knew him, he didn't mention it."

"Did you discuss how the man died?"

"Again, no. I thought he must have drowned or something. Hugh didn't offer any opinions about what might have happened."

"And when the widow arrived and identified the body, did you recognize her?"

"I'd never seen her before today."

"And yet you invited her into your home. You lent her clothes and you fed her lunch. Are you always so welcoming to strangers?"

"Probably not," Bessie told him honestly. "But I felt badly for her. She was meant to be on her honeymoon, and instead she found her husband's body. The weather was awful and I hated the thought of her standing there watching the police poke and prod her husband."

"So what did you two talk about?"

Bessie shrugged. "A little bit of everything, really," she said vaguely. "Nothing specific."

"Did she tell you anything about her relationship with her husband or with his family?"

"She said that she and the family get along well and she was happy to spend her honeymoon with them. She said something about having a small disagreement with her husband last night. That was why she had her hair and makeup all done this morning. She wanted to look her best when he got back."

"Got back from where?"

Bessie frowned. "She didn't really say where he'd gone," she told the inspector.

"And did she speculate on how he might have died?" Rockwell asked.

"She said he must have drowned or had a heart attack," Bessie recalled.

"And yet when I mentioned murder, you didn't seem surprised."

Bessie shrugged. "How long have you lived here? You must know how fast the gossip chain is. I heard a rumour that it was murder almost as soon as Hugh left my cottage with the widow and I started ringing back concerned friends." She held her breath as she waited to see if he would believe her. She didn't want Doona to be in any trouble.

Rockwell shook his head. "The rumour mill on this island is more efficient than its newspapers," was his only comment on the matter.

"So it was murder?" Bessie pushed her luck.

"We won't know anything for sure until we get the coroner's report," the inspector told her. "But for now, we are definitely treating it as murder."

Bessie nodded. "I suppose that makes sense."

"I'm glad you think so," Inspector Rockwell said dryly. He had a few more follow-up questions for Bessie, but only a few.

"Thank you for coming in," he said after they had quickly gone through her day one last time. "I'll have Hugh take you home. He can collect the widow's nightie from you for our lab tests."

Bessie nodded, grateful that Doona had already mentioned the idea. She didn't want Inspector Rockwell to know how shocked she had been when Doona had suggested it.

"You haven't done anything like run it through the wash, have you?" the inspector asked.

"Of course not," Bessie said, grateful that the inspector would never know how close she had come to doing just that.

Hugh was waiting in the lobby when Inspector Rockwell escorted her out.

"I'll take you home, then, shall I?" he asked as Doona handed Bessie her coat.

"I'd be ever so grateful," Bessie told the man.

She had never learned to drive, relying instead upon buses, taxis and the kindness of her friends. It was only in the last ten years or so that the matter had begun to become more of an inconvenience. Public transportation was losing its popularity with generations of people who seemed to believe that having their own private automobile was vital. Bessie was still managing, but she was beginning to think that she might just have to take some driving lessons and get her own car if things kept going the way they were.

# CHAPTER 4

*B*ack at home and rid of the suspect nightie, Bessie felt unsettled. She walked around her cosy cottage, tidying and straightening things that didn't need to be straightened. After a while, she decided to try again to take a short walk on the beach. Police tape and a shivering uniformed constable kept her from walking along her normal route. Instead, she turned in the other direction and made her way slowly across the sand.

She rarely walked this way because the road and a boat launch crossed the beach not far from her home. Busy in spring and summer, the area was all but deserted today. Bessie passed a single fisherman, sitting on the edge of the wall that ran along the road into the sea. A few lazy seagulls circled above her.

Temperatures were still chilly, and Bessie made it a short walk. Back at home she made herself her evening meal and sat down with her favourite Agatha Christie novel. Miss Marple would have already solved the case, she mused to herself as she turned the pages. The phone startled her when it rang just before nine. Bessie had ignored it for most of the afternoon, as more friends and acquaintances rang to find out about the murder, but now she answered.

"I wanted to catch you before you turned in," Doona told her friend. "I just wanted to check that you're okay after today's, um, excitement."

"I'm fine," Bessie insisted. "I had a short walk and a nice supper and now I'm reading Miss Marple and relaxing."

"Don't you be getting any ideas from Miss Marple," Doona cautioned her. "Leave this one for the police."

"I don't have any intention of getting involved in the investigation," Bessie assured her. "I just hope your police can work it out quickly. I love living alone, but I will definitely sleep better when the murderer is behind bars."

Doona offered to stay the night with her friend, but Bessie wouldn't hear of it. A few minutes after she'd hung up, just as Miss Marple was about to announce who the killer was, Bessie heard a loud knock on her front door.

She dropped the book in surprise and then laughed at her jumpiness. It was probably just one of the neighbourhood kids wanting to stay the night because of a fight with his or her parents. She walked slowly into the kitchen and flipped on the lamp outside her front door.

"Hugh Watterson? What on earth are you doing here at this hour?" she demanded as she swung the door open.

"I, er, well." Hugh blushed under the steely gaze and then cleared his throat. "The thing is," he told her, "I was worried about you, being here all alone. I thought that since I used to stay with you when I was having a hard time at home, maybe you'd let me stay for a night or two now, just until the killer is locked up."

Bessie smiled at the young constable. "Oh, Hugh, that's very kind of you," she told the man. "But really, I'm fine on my own."

"I know you are," Hugh assured her. He looked back and forth twice and then leaned forward to whisper to her. "The thing is," he confided, "I'm hoping to help solve this case. And I think that being here, on the beach, might give me an edge. I'm closer to the suspects and everything, you see? If you let me stay, I can keep an eye on you in case the murderer comes back, and I'm closer to the action. We both win. What do you think?"

Bessie bit back her first thought and waited a second to consider his words. She had thought about the murderer coming back, and it seemed extremely unlikely that he or she would do so, but perhaps it would be helpful to have someone in the cottage with her. She was used to having guests; Hugh wouldn't be any more trouble than anyone else. And it would be nice to feel as if she was helping him out in his police work, too.

Hugh was watching her with an expectant look on his face. "All right," she said eventually. "You can stay, at least for tonight."

Hugh looked so excited that Bessie almost laughed out loud. She watched as he raced back to his car and grabbed a small suitcase out of the back. She had never seen the young man so energised. A moment later he bounded up the single step to her door and she had to step back quickly before he bounced right over her in his eagerness to get inside.

"The guest room is still in the same place," she told Hugh.

"I was thinking it might be better if I slept on the couch in the sitting room," Hugh replied. "Just in case."

"Just in case what?" Bessie demanded. "What do you think is going to happen?"

Hugh shrugged. "I don't know, but if it does happen, I want to be ready."

Bessie bit back a laugh. One thing she knew about men, in spite of never marrying, was that there was little point in arguing with them if their minds were made up. "Suit yourself," she said. "Blankets and pillows are in the linen cupboard at the top of the stairs. Get whatever you need and get settled in. I was just heading to bed when you arrived, so, if you don't mind, I'll go now."

Hugh followed Bessie upstairs where she quickly provided him with a pile of blankets and pillows. She continued on to her own room, where she got ready for bed and then listened for a time as Hugh stomped around the cottage, presumably getting himself settled in for the night. Eventually the noises stopped and Bessie slid down under the covers. It had been a very eventful day, one she wasn't eager to repeat.

It was three minutes past six when Bessie's internal alarm woke her the next morning. She sighed as she looked out at another rainy day. At least it appeared that the wind was calmer. Not that she could get much of a walk in anyway, at least not in the direction she wanted to go. She dressed quickly and headed down the stairs. She could hear Hugh's snoring before she even reached the top step and by the time she was at the bottom she couldn't help but laugh at the sound.

She bustled around the kitchen, making tea and toast for herself and her guest. He was staying to help keep her safe; making breakfast seemed the least she could do. With the table set and the toaster full, she headed down the short hallway to the sitting room.

"Hugh?" she called gently. "Hugh, are you ready for some breakfast?"

Hugh didn't move from his spot, sprawled across her largest sofa.

"Hugh? It's Bessie; it's time for breakfast." Bessie took a few steps into the room and spoke loudly, but she seemed to make no impression on the sleeping man. It was just as well that no one had tried to murder me in my sleep last night, she thought. Hugh would have slept right through it and his snores would have drowned out any cries for help.

She studied the sleeping man for a moment longer and then shook her head. If he was that tired, she would just let him sleep. Back in the kitchen, she ate her own breakfast and sipped her tea. After some thought, she decided to postpone her morning walk until later in the day. And she worked out the perfect place to walk to as well.

A cacophony of noise at seven suggested that Hugh had set an alarm before he went to sleep the night before. After several minutes of odd noises, Hugh finally stumbled into the kitchen about quarter past the hour.

"Oh, ah, good morning, Aunt Bessie," he yawned. "You're already up and dressed, I see."

"Yes," Bessie answered. "I get up at six every morning. I'd go for my morning walk now if the police didn't have half the beach blocked off for their investigations."

"Oh, rather, well, yes." Hugh rubbed his eyes. Bessie doubted that he was used to human interaction this early in the morning. "That is, I'm sorry about that, but we have to keep the beach closed until we know for sure that we've found all of the evidence. We'd never hear the end of it if we missed something important."

Bessie nodded. It made sense; it just wasn't what she wanted to hear.

"Anyway," Hugh continued, "I've got to get back to my flat and have a shower before work. What are you going to get up to today?"

"You know you're welcome to use the shower upstairs," Bessie told him.

"Oh, that's very kind of you," Hugh shrugged. "I'd rather stop home, though. Make sure everything's okay there, check my answering machine for messages, that sort of thing."

Bessie nodded, wondering idly if Hugh was hoping for a message from anyone in particular. There had been rumours about him and some girl from the neighbouring village of Lonan a while back, but the talk had died down pretty quickly. That was something to chat with him about tonight if he came back again, she decided.

"So I'll be back around nine tonight, if that's okay?" Hugh said as he slurped up the last of the tea that Bessie had left out for him. "What did you say you were going to do today?"

Bessie smiled. She hadn't said, but she supposed there was no harm in telling the man. "I thought I would go and pay my respects to the family."

"Whose family?"

"Why, Daniel Pierce's family, of course. I found his body, and I've known the family for years. They've been summering here for over two decades. Whatever the circumstances of the man's passing, it's only polite to pay my respects to his family."

Hugh narrowed his eyes at Bessie. "You're not thinking of doing any amateur detective work, are you?" he demanded. "I know you read all those mystery books where little old ladies solve the crimes and leave the police looking dumb. You don't have any ideas like that, do you?"

"Of course not," Bessie soothed. "I'm just doing what is right and

44

proper under the circumstances. Considering everything that's happened, they probably won't even let me in the door at the Pierce cottage, but at least I can feel better that I tried. As I said, it's only right."

Hugh nodded. "Mind you, if you see or hear anything that you think is suspicious around there, you will let me know, right?"

"You or Inspector Rockwell," Bessie said with a smile.

"Oh, yeah, of course," Hugh replied. "Of course, it would be a shame to bother Inspector Rockwell with most things. I mean, he's a busy inspector and he doesn't even know you. He might not under-stand how well you know the people on the island."

Hugh shook his head. "Never mind," he sighed. "I know I'm wasting my time thinking I might solve this thing before the inspector does. I'm doomed to spend my entire career in uniform walking the streets of Laxey."

"There are worse jobs," Bessie said mildly.

Hugh smiled, although it looked forced. "I know, and I do love what I do," he told her. "But I would love to move up as well. I want to make people proud."

Bessie nodded, and then remembered the rest of the rumour she had heard. Apparently the young lady in Lonan had moved on from Hugh to another policeman, one who worked in Ramsey at the larger and presumably more prestigious station.

Hugh was gone before Bessie had time to worry any more about his love life. Not for the first time, she thanked heaven that she was beyond having to worry about such things herself. She had had two serious affairs of the heart and a few smaller flirtations in her day. Now she felt that she could look back on them with some true perspective, and she was happy that she had ended up where she was: on her own, but never lonely.

She took care of a load of laundry and a few other small chores around her cottage. Then she ate a small lunch before heading out towards the Pierce cottage. While she would have preferred walking along the beach, that was impossible, so instead she walked carefully along the narrow road that connected all of the beachfront properties.

45

She wore her boots and raincoat and carried a small umbrella that did its best to protect her from the steadily falling rain.

As she made her way along the stretch of tiny terraced cottages that everyone in Laxey called the "new cottages," she was surprised to see a truck parked just off the road. Thomas Shimmin, a middle-aged, heavy-set man, was just coming out of the very last cottage as she crossed behind it.

"Hey, Aunt Bessie," he called as he waved. "Walking on the road since the beach is closed?"

"Exactly," Bessie agreed. "But what brings you down here today? I wouldn't have thought the cottages would be booked for this time of year."

"Aye, no, they aren't," the man nodded. "But with all the trouble yesterday, I wanted to make sure for myself that everything was ship-shape in all of them, you know?"

Bessie nodded. "And did you find anything out of place?" she asked.

"No, thankfully everything seems to be exactly as we left things in November when we shut the cottages down."

"Well, that's good news. When do your spring and summer bookings start, then?" Bessie asked.

"We have bookings in April, for Easter week," the man told her. "I suppose I'll be spending a lot more time down here starting soon. We've lots to get ready before then."

"There can't be that much to do, can there?" Bessie asked. "I mean, the cottages were just built a few years ago."

"With the wind and the weather, they need a surprising amount of upkeep," Thomas told her. "And with the constant round of rentals all summer long, the interiors need regular maintenance as well."

Bessie nodded. "Hard work is good for you," she reminded the man as she continued along the road.

"Oh, aye," he replied. "But a lottery win would be better."

They both laughed at that, and then Bessie pushed onwards. A short distance past the new cottages, she could immediately tell when she had reached the edge of the Pierces' property. A huge fence had been erected only recently and Bessie winced at its ugly intrusion into the landscape. How they'd ever received planning permission for that thing she'd never understand.

As she approached the driveway where a gate appeared in the long fence, she noticed several cars parked along the road. Before she had much time to wonder what they were doing there, car doors were opening and she found herself surrounded by several men and women, all shouting at once.

"Who are you and what are you doing here?"

"Do you know the Pierce family?"

"What are you doing on this road?"

Reporters, Bessie realised, and aggressive and nasty ones at that. She stopped walking and stood as straight and tall as she could. Clearing her throat seemed to silence the mob momentarily.

"If you'll excuse me," she said in the politest tone she could muster. "I'm just taking a walk."

"Oh hey," one of the reporters called. "You aren't the old biddy who found the body, are you? The police said some old woman who was walking on the beach tripped over the body. That wasn't you, was it?"

Bessie glared at him. "You couldn't possibly be calling me an 'old biddy,'" she told him through gritted teeth. "Now, if you don't let me through, I'm going to ring the police. It can't be legal, you blocking someone from walking on a public road."

The reporters grudgingly stepped back a bit and Bessie pushed her way through them. After a moment, they settled for following behind her, throwing odd questions at her that she chose to ignore.

"So do you know the Pierce family?"

"Have you lived on the island long?"

"What can you tell us about the police on the island? Do they have any chance of solving this murder?"

Bessie pushed the call button on the gate, still ignoring the reporters who buzzed around her. After a moment, Bessie heard a buzz from the telephone that was mounted into the side of the gate. She picked up the receiver.

"Oh, my goodness, Bessie Cubbon, is that you?" the voice on the other end of the line said.

"Yes," Bessie said cautiously. "Who is this?"

"Oh, it's Bahey Corlett, me mum was Jane Corkish and me dad was Patrick Corlett. They used to have the pub on the Laxey corner."

"Oh, Bahey," Bessie spoke as quietly as she could. "What are you doing at Thie yn Traie?"

"Oh, you must remember, I worked for the Pierce family for years," Bahey told her. "First on the island and then across. I retired about three years ago, back here, but when the tragedy happened, I came to help as quick as I could."

"That was good of you," Bessie told her old acquaintance.

"But what brings you to the cottage?"

"I came to pay my respects," Bessie replied.

"Oh, aye, and that's only proper, with you being neighbours and all. And besides which, you found poor Danny, didn't you? And you were so very kind to Miss Vikky as well. We'll just have to get you in, but keep those reporters out, won't we?"

The phone went dead in Bessie's hand and she slowly returned it to its stand.

"Told to bugger off, were you?" one of the reporters sneered at her.

Bessie didn't even favour him with a glance. A moment later Bessie could see two enormous men walking towards her from the other side of the gate. The men were clearly hired muscle and the reporters all turned their backs as the men approached.

"You guys should just go, you know," the taller of the guards said conversationally as he reached the gate.

"We've checked with the police. We're perfectly within our rights to stand here on this side of the gate," one of the reporters answered.

"Whatever," the guard muttered. "You want to stand out in the rain all day, that's your business."

It wasn't just raining, it was cold and overcast, and Bessie felt a momentary pang of sympathy for the men and women who were stuck watching a gate and hoping that something might happen. That pang vanished a second later as it became obvious to the reporters that the guards were there to open the gate to admit Bessie. Then the questions began to fly once more.

"Who is she?"

"Why does she get in?"

"Give us a name, love, just something we can work with?"

Photography equipment was pulled from bags, and suddenly Bessie found herself being photographed from every possible angle as the guards unlocked the gates and opened them just far enough for Bessie to squeeze through. She quickly folded up her umbrella and slipped through. A moment later, both men opened huge umbrellas over Bessie's head and they used them to block her from the cameras and the prying eyes of the press.

"Let's get you safely inside, then," one of the men said to Bessie as the trio began to walk back down the long driveway.

Bessie had never been to Thie yn Traie, although she had heard a lot about it, especially when it was being constructed. Of course, she could see it from a distance every time she walked along Laxey Beach, but it was set quite far back from the water's edge, perched halfway up a small cliff, and Bessie had never felt the need to explore more closely. As she and her escorts rounded a curve in the drive, she suddenly saw the house in all of its splendour.

It was enormous. From the beach side of the property, Bessie had only ever been able to see a large two-storey home set into the fairly steep cliff, but from here she could see the sheer scale of the mansion. Again, she wondered about planning permission as she studied the multi-storey structure. Vikky Pierce had told her that the "cottage" had several separate wings, and now Bessie could see how they seemed to spread, tentacle-like, all across the ground.

She shook her head. The whole thing was a monstrous tribute to money over style and good taste. She could hardly wait to see what the inside was like.

The two men escorted her towards a side door near the row of garages. As they approached, Bessie counted garage space for seven cars. The door swung open as they reached it and Bessie found herself engulfed in a huge hug.

"Ah, Aunt Bessie, it's been too long," Bahey said when she finally ended the embrace. "You look wonderful, at least for our age."

Bessie smiled ruefully. Bahey was only about ten years younger than Bessie. When they first met, that gap had seemed insurmountable to them both. Bessie, in her early twenties, had little time for girls just into their teens. Now the gap seemed tiny as the two women inspected each other's lined and careworn faces.

"I think it was Tynwald Day, about three years ago, when I saw you last," Bessie recalled. "You mentioned then that you had just retired."

"You still have a great memory," Bahey sighed. "I seem to forget everything these days."

Bessie ignored the compliment. "Didn't you say you'd purchased a flat in Douglas?" she asked instead.

"I did, indeed," Bahey nodded. "Mr. Pierce was kind enough to help me save up for my retirement over the years. Thanks to him, I had enough to buy a little place outright. It's just off the promenade. You should come and visit me one day."

"I'd like that," Bessie told her. There were so few of her own generation left; she would quite enjoy an afternoon of reminiscing with the slightly younger woman.

"But you haven't come to waste time talking with me," Bahey shook her head. "It's kind of you to come and pay your respects; so few people do these days."

Bahey looked around as if checking that they were alone. "Lots of people ringing and coming around to try to get the latest skeet, but no one who really cares," she said, nodding seriously at Bessie.

Bessie wasn't sure that she qualified as someone who really cared, but she did feel that her visit was motivated by the right reasons. She murmured what she hoped Bahey would take as an appropriate response.

"I have to ask," Bahey said with tears in her eyes. "You saw the body; do you think Mr. Daniel suffered at all?"

Bessie shook her head. "I'm sure it was quick," she told the younger woman, patting her arm as she spoke.

"I'm sorry," Bahey said, wiping her tears with the back of her hand.

"I never married, never had children. Mr. Danny and Mr. Donny always felt a little like my own boys. I'm sure Mrs. Pierce would forgive me for feeling that way."

"Of course," Bessie soothed. "You must have been pleased when Daniel found a wife, then?" she asked suggestively.

Bahey scoffed. "She has them all fooled, the Pierces, but I can see through her. She didn't really love Mr. Daniel; she was just after his money."

"And now she's got it," Bessie said.

"Not if Mr. Pierce and Mr. Donny have anything to do with it," Bahey whispered. "Oh, they still seem to think she's wonderful, but they're businessmen first. They don't think Miss Vikky should inherit everything after just a couple of days of marriage. They're hinting that they might contest the will unless Miss Vikky takes a small payoff and goes away quietly once all the fuss has died down."

"Really?" Bessie shook her head. "I suppose I should be glad that there was never enough money in my family to cause these sorts of fights."

"Aye, mine either," Bahey shrugged. "I got a little bit of money when me mum and dad passed on, but I let my sister have everything else. I was across and being looked after by the Pierces well enough. Now that I'm back on the island, she's given me some of me mum's old furniture to make my flat feel more like home. It'll all go to her son anyway, when I go, but at least we never had to fight over it."

"I remember your sister as well," Bessie said. "She was a school teacher in Foxdale for many years, right?"

"Aye, she's still there. Foxdale don't suit everyone, but she seems to like it. Her husband passed about nine years ago, but she reckons she's happy enough on her own now that her boy is grown and gone. But enough of this reminiscing. You'll have to come and visit me soon so we can catch up properly. You came to see the Pierces. Come through to the great room and I'll let Mr. and Mrs. Pierce know that you're here."

Bessie followed Bahey down a long corridor from the garage wing into the main house. There was so much to see that it was hard for her to take it all in. The house appeared spotless and perfectly maintained. Walls looked freshly painted and carpets didn't look as if anyone had ever walked on them. Bessie tried to peek into as many rooms as she could as they walked along, but Bahey walked too fast for her to get more than a vague impression of expensively furnished but soulless spaces.

At the end of the corridor, Bahey flung open a door and switched on some lights. "Here we are," she told Bessie. "The great room," she said in a hushed tone. She ushered Bessie inside, turning on more lights as they walked into the space.

Bessie turned around slowly as she studied the room. It was huge, certainly larger than the whole ground floor of her cottage, with massively high ceilings as well. It was informally divided into several areas, each containing groups of chairs and tables. The back wall of the room was almost entirely made up of windows that stretched at least two-stories high. There was a long bar covered in black granite just in front of the windows, with bar stools dotted along in front of it. While Bahey had turned on several lights, with the overcast skies outside, the room felt cold and unwelcoming.

Bessie turned to Bahey. "It's sort of a grim room, isn't it?"

Bahey laughed. "I've always thought so," she agreed. "But the family loves it in here. Anyway, I'll just tell Mr. and Mrs. Pierce you're here."

Bahey disappeared back through the door and Bessie took another slow look around the room. She didn't like it any better the second time. Unwilling to choose which area to sit in, she made her way over to the wall of windows. She could just about make out her own cottage, a tiny dot on the horizon. The police tape still blocked off the beach and Bessie could see a single uniformed officer walking slowly along the perimeter of the tape. Whether he was looking for evidence or just guarding the area, she couldn't tell.

Bessie swung around when she heard the door open behind her. She immediately recognised Mr. and Mrs. Pierce from their annual summer visits. Mr. Pierce was tall and grey-haired, with broad shoulders and an almost military bearing. His wife was petite and looked exhausted and much older than the late fifties that Bessie knew was her age. The couple took a few steps into the room and stared at Bessie.

"Mr. and Mrs. Pierce, please accept my deepest sympathies for your loss," she said as she crossed to them across the large room.

Mrs. Pierce looked at her with unfocussed eyes. "Do you have children?" she asked in a shaking voice.

"No, I was never blessed with children of my own," Bessie replied, taking the woman's hand as she reached her side. "I can't begin to imagine the pain you're suffering."

"It's unbearable," the woman told her, squeezing Bessie's hand painfully. "I can't bear it. The doctor has had to give me piles of pills just so that I can breathe."

Bessie nodded. "I am so very sorry," she repeated. "I'm not sure if you even remember me, but I live in the cottage just down the beach from you." Bessie waved her hand vaguely in the direction of her home.

"Of course we remember you. Everyone who spends any time in Laxey at all knows Aunt Bessie," Daniel Pierce, Sr., answered brusquely. "It's kind of you to pay your respects."

Bessie nodded and pulled her hand away from Mrs. Pierce just long enough to shake hands with the dead man's father. Although Mr. Pierce seemed steady enough, when she was close enough to shake his hand Bessie realised that a lot of his strength was currently coming from whisky.

"And of course you found the body," a voice from the doorway startled them all. Bessie turned to find a heavy-set man of about thirty-five staring at her.

"Ah, Donny, there you are," Mr. Pierce waved the man into the room. "Aunt Bessie, this is our younger son, Donny. Donny, Aunt Bessie is a neighbour who came to pay her respects."

"And she's the one who found the body," Donny repeated himself.

"Are you?" Daniel said, looking at Bessie with confusion on his face.

"Well, yes, technically," Bessie admitted, not knowing why she should feel guilty about that.

"I didn't realise," Daniel told her. "I don't know that it really matters." He shook his head and then headed towards the bar. "Anyone else need a drink?"

"You shouldn't be drinking this early in the day," Donny told his father.

"I'll have a nice glass of white wine." Mrs. Pierce had followed her husband to the bar.

"And you shouldn't be drinking at all," Donny said in an exasperated tone. "You've been given a load of medication that doesn't mix with alcohol."

"I'll only have one," Mrs. Pierce promised her son as she reached for the glass her husband held out to her.

"But...."

"Oh, leave them alone," a bored voice sounded from the doorway. "Let them get drunk if they want, they're in mourning."

Bessie studied the woman who now entered the room. She was young, maybe twenty-five, blonde and very pretty, but she had a spoiled and petulant look about her that rather ruined her natural attractiveness.

"You aren't helping, Sam," Donny sighed.

"I wasn't trying to help." The woman shrugged her shoulders and then turned to Bessie. "So who are you then?"

"I'm Elizabeth Cubbon," Bessie answered. "I live just down the beach from here and I came to pay my respects to Mr. and Mrs. Pierce."

The girl raised an eyebrow. "Being neighbourly, not nosy?"

Bessie found herself almost liking the young woman. "Just neighbourly," she assured her. "You haven't told me your name," she added.

"Oh, I'm Samantha Blake, but everyone calls me Sam," the woman shrugged. "I'm Donny's girlfriend, for lack of a better word."

Donny made a sound that Bessie couldn't even begin to interpret.

"The children all came for my husband's birthday," Mrs. Pierce told Bessie. "He turned sixty on Sunday and we had a small family party here. There was supposed to be a bigger affair back in London next month, although I don't think we'll go ahead with that now."

"We never should have come," Daniel Pierce muttered darkly into his drink. "Danny would be okay if we had just stayed home."

"Really?" Bessie couldn't keep the doubt from her voice. There was no polite way to press the issue, though. Luckily, Daniel continued.

"He must have stumbled across some homeless person or maybe a drug deal or something on that beach," the man told Bessie. "And he got stabbed because of it."

Bessie counted to ten before she replied, carefully working to keep her voice even. "I've lived on that beach since before you were born," she told the man just a little sharply. "We don't have homeless people or drug dealers spending time there."

Daniel shrugged and then swallowed the rest of his drink. "We should have insisted that they honeymoon somewhere warm," he muttered. "And we should have insisted on a proper wedding, too."

"Was the wedding a small event, then?" Bessie asked, letting the subject change.

Samantha laughed and then answered for Daniel. "The wedding wasn't much of anything," she said. "Vikky dragged poor Danny off to the registry office and got him locked down before he knew what hit him."

"Sam, that's enough," Donny said tersely. "Danny loved Vikky very much. They dated for six months or so before they got married and they were going to have a proper bash in a few months, once the weather was nicer. The thing was, neither one of them wanted to wait to actually get married and start their lives together."

"Didn't turn out to be much of a life together, though, did it?" Samantha drawled.

"Sam!" Donny looked at her furiously.

"I don't know why you have to be so horrible about me." This time Bessie recognised the voice from the doorway.

"Vikky, please don't pay any attention to Sam." Donny rushed over to Vikky's side and took her arm. "How are you feeling?" he asked in a concerned tone.

"I'm okay," Vikky answered softly. "I think I'm still in shock."

"That isn't surprising under the circumstances," Donny said soothingly. "Come and sit down and rest."

"I didn't know we had a guest," Vikky said as she suddenly noticed Bessie.

"I just came to pay my respects." Bessie was tired of repeating herself. "I do hope you're feeling better today," she added.

"Oh, you're the woman from yesterday, aren't you?" Vikky asked. "You were there when I found Danny."

"Yes," Bessie said gently. "I was there and then you came back to my house for tea, remember?"

Vikky wrinkled her nose and Bessie could see her trying to concentrate. "I suppose so," she said eventually. "The doctor was here earlier and he gave me something to make me feel better. I'm sort of out of it a bit."

"Never mind," Bessie told her. "You've had a huge shock."

Donny led the young widow to a seat near the window and then sat down next to her, still holding her hand tightly. Bessie glanced over at Samantha, who rolled her eyes and sighed deeply.

Mr. and Mrs. Pierce seemed oblivious as they sipped their drinks. They were both staring into space in different directions. Bessie shook her head.

"I suppose I should be going, then," she said generally.

"Oh, thank you for coming," Mrs. Pierce answered vaguely.

Vikky glanced up and waved before turning back to her conversation with Donny, who simply ignored Bessie.

"I'll walk you out," Samantha offered. "I would hate for you to get lost in this monstrosity."

Bessie smiled at the younger woman. "I'd appreciate that," she told her.

"Mr. Pierce seems pretty certain that the murder was random," Bessie remarked as the pair made their way through the house.

Samantha laughed. "And yet he can't explain how the weapon came from this very house."

"The knife came from Thie yn Traie?" Bessie asked in surprise.

"Yep," Samantha grinned. "Not only that, but it was part of a set that Mr. and Mrs. Pierce just gave the happy couple as a wedding present on Saturday night."

"My goodness," Bessie exclaimed. "How on earth can Mr. Pierce explain that?"

"Oh, he has some theory about Danny taking the knife on the walk with him, you know, for protection." Samantha waved a hand. "It's all nonsense, of course, but it's what he wants to believe."

"How on earth did you find out about the knife, anyway?" Bessie asked curiously.

"When you're as important as Mr. Pierce, the police share information with you," Samantha said with a shrug. "I think the Chief Constable himself rang and talked to him."

Bessie frowned. Doona was worried about saying anything she shouldn't, and yet the Chief Constable was having cosy chats with the victim's father.

They had nearly reached the front door now, and Bessie deliberately slowed her pace. "So do you have your own theory about what happened?" she asked the young blonde.

"Sure," Samantha shrugged. "But no one wants to hear it."

"I'd love to hear it," Bessie told her eagerly.

A wary look came over Samantha's face. "Yes, well…." she prevaricated.

"Sam, where are you?"

Samantha jumped as Donny's voice echoed down the corridor.

"I'm just showing our guest out," she called back down the hall.

"Well, hurry up, will you? Vikky wants to go for a walk and I need you to sit with my parents."

"And it's all about what Vikky wants," Samantha said grimly, turning back towards Bessie.

"You were going to tell me your theory on the murder," Bessie reminded her.

Samantha sighed. "But now I have to go baby-sit the grieving parents while Vikky takes my boyfriend for a ride."

"I thought Donny said she wanted to go for a walk," Bessie said sweetly.

Samantha laughed. "For an old lady, you're kind of cool," she told Bessie. "Meet me tomorrow around one at the Laxey Wheel and we can chat about my theory."

"Oh, but...." Bessie didn't get to finish. Instead Donny suddenly came storming down the hall towards them.

"Come on, Samantha, I need you," he demanded.

The beautiful blonde rolled her eyes at Bessie and then said a quick goodbye.

"Don't forget, the Laxey Wheel at one," Samantha whispered in Bessie's ear just before she followed Donny back towards the great room.

Bessie frowned as the pair disappeared from view. She wanted to hear Samantha's theory and she didn't want to wait until tomorrow. After a moment, she sighed and then turned to the door. She pulled on the coat and boots she had left at the door and grabbed her umbrella, then she pulled the door open and looked out at the cluster of reporters who were still hanging around at the top of the drive. Sighing even more deeply, she stepped outside.

"Aunt Bessie?" The voice came from her left. She turned to see one of the security guards from earlier standing there.

"You probably don't remember me," the man said, looking at her shyly. He grinned and Bessie suddenly placed him.

"Robert, Robert Clague," she smiled. "Your parents ran the Laxey post office for a few years in the eighties. Of course I remember you. You still have the same shy smile that you had when you were seven. You tried to eat your own body weight in shortbread every time you stopped to visit me."

The man laughed. "That's about right," he told Bessie. "I still remember your shortbread biscuits. They were something special."

"I didn't realise you were working for the Pierce family now," Bessie said.

"Oh, I'm not," Robert corrected her. "I work for Manxman Security

Services. The family has hired us to help out because of what happened yesterday."

Bessie nodded. "That makes sense."

"Anyway," Robert continued, "I'm done for the day; how about I give you a ride home?"

"That would be wonderful," Bessie couldn't help but gush a bit. She had found the visit emotionally draining and the thought of fighting her way through the reporters and then walking home the long way around seemed almost too much.

"I haven't made shortbread lately," she said in an apologetic tone. "But I'm sure I can find you something to go with a nice cup of tea when we get there."

"That sounds great," the man answered. He escorted Bessie to a newer model car with the security company's name painted on the side. They climbed in and Bessie was surprised when Robert drove off in the opposite direction from the gates.

"There's a service entrance around the back," Robert told her as the house disappeared from view. "There may be a few reporters out there as well, but most of them are at the main gate. There's more to see there."

As it happened, only a single reporter was sitting inside a stationary car just outside the service entrance gate as they approached. Robert tapped a code into a panel near the gate and it slid open soundlessly. The reporter barely looked up.

"I imagine we aren't interesting in this car," Robert shrugged.

On the drive he brought Bessie up-to-date on his parents, who were now retired and living in Blackpool. Over tea and biscuits he politely, but consistently, refused to answer any questions about the Pierce family. Bessie couldn't even get him to admit to having formed any impressions of any of the family members in the limited time he had spent in their company.

After a short time, he was on his way. As soon as he was gone, Bessie listened to her answering machine messages and rang back the few people whom she was actually interested in speaking with, ignoring the rest.

# CHAPTER 5

"*I*'m coming over after work," Doona told her when Bessie rang her back at the police station. "And I'm bringing Chinese, so you don't have to cook."

Bessie didn't argue. She loved Chinese food and she was always happy to have a night off cooking. "You'd better bring extra," she told Doona. "Hugh might be here."

"Why would Hugh be there?" Doona wondered.

"He's sleeping on my couch at the moment. He has some crazy idea that I need protecting."

"Good for him," Doona cheered. "I told you he's really a good guy."

"I'm reserving judgment for now," Bessie told her friend.

Doona just laughed and then said her goodbyes.

Bessie spent what was left of the afternoon cleaning the bathrooms, her least favourite job, and then working on her research. She was due to give the paper in early May, and at the moment she had little more than a vague notion of what she was going to say.

Two solid hours of hard work left her feeling far more confident about the conference. She pushed back from her desk and checked the clock. Doona would be arriving in around an hour. Bessie smiled to herself. She'd worked hard all afternoon and she didn't need to worry about cooking anything. It was definitely time to curl up with a good book.

She had an agreement with the bookstore in Ramsey; they sent her the newest releases in a number of different series that she enjoyed and billed her monthly. She'd received a package from them yesterday afternoon, but with all the excitement, she hadn't even opened it yet.

Now she carefully cut through the tape and pulled open the box, inhaling the wonderful papery aroma of new books. She smiled at her new acquisitions, excited to find four new titles from some of her absolute favourite authors. After a moment's indecision, she grabbed the latest in an American private detective series and, cup of tea to hand, settled in to read.

Loud and persistent banging dragged her back home from the California seaside. Bessie looked around, slightly disoriented at the sudden return to reality.

The banging didn't let up, so Bessie closed a bookmark into the book and headed towards the door.

"I was starting to worry about you," Doona told her when Bessie let her in.

"I was lost in the latest Sue Grafton," Bessie explained.

"Ooo, I just got that one myself," Doona answered. "I'm saving it for the weekend so I can read it straight through."

While they talked, Doona was busy unpacking several large bags of food. The kitchen filled with sweet and spicy smells that made Bessie's mouth water.

She'd only just pulled plates from the cupboard when there was another knock on the door.

"I thought I smelled Chinese food," Hugh grinned as Doona let him in.

"You have perfect timing," Doona smiled back at him. "You're just in time for dinner."

The threesome filled plates and then settled in comfortably around Bessie's table.

"So, how was your visit to Thie yn Traie?" Doona asked, after most of the food was gone.

"Interesting," Bessie answered. "They're a strange lot."

"How so?" Hugh asked.

"Well, the dead man's father thinks the killing was random, for a start."

"Anything is possible," Hugh said.

"I heard a rumour that the knife came from the house," Bessie replied.

"I couldn't possibly confirm or deny any rumours," Hugh said stiffly. He then caught Bessie's eye and winked at her.

"Right," Bessie said. "So Daniel Pierce, Sr., is convinced that there are deadly homeless men wandering around Laxey Beach, either that or murderous drug dealers. Meanwhile, his wife, I'm afraid I didn't catch her first name, has been medicated by some well-meaning doctor who probably doesn't realise how much the woman drinks."

"Her name is Margaret," Doona told Bessie. "I saw it on her statement."

Hugh shot Doona a look.

"What?" Doona demanded. "I'm not telling her anything that isn't public knowledge."

"Just be careful," Hugh said quietly. "We both have to be careful talking to civilians. Inspector Rockwell doesn't like gossip and rumours."

"I'd suggest he's moved to the wrong little island, then," Bessie laughed. "Gossip is what keeps this island running."

"So the victim's parents were odd," Hugh said. "Did you meet anyone else?"

"Apparently Danny had a brother," Bessie said. The other two nodded.

"He seemed odd as well. Not exactly sad at the loss of his brother, and it seemed to me that he's getting awfully cosy with the widow as well."

Hugh shook his head. "I bet Samantha isn't too happy about that," he commented.

"Samantha didn't seem happy about much of anything," Bessie said.

"Samantha is the gorgeous blonde, right?" Doona checked. "She came in to the station with the family, but no one was talking to her while they waited."

"She's supposed to be Donny's girlfriend, but they didn't seem to be getting along very well this afternoon," Bessie told the others. "I'm going to meet her tomorrow afternoon at the Laxey Wheel so we can talk properly."

Hugh shook his head. "I don't think you should be getting so involved in this," he told Bessie. "Paying your respects is one thing, but arranging to meet up with one of the suspects is another. Amateurs have no part to play in a police investigation."

"Nonsense," Bessie told him. "I'm not getting involved in anything. The poor girl needs someone to talk to, that's all. Things are very tense at Thie yn Traie at the moment and she needs a break and a sympathetic ear. We probably won't talk about Danny at all, just Donny and the wicked widow woman."

Doona laughed. "That's a good way to describe her," she told Bessie. "I don't know why I don't like her. I only spent two minutes with her. But there is definitely something unpleasant about her."

"She just lost her husband. I don't think she was too worried about being pleasant," Hugh suggested.

"She isn't just unpleasant," Bessie said. "She's impolite."

Hugh shook his head. "I didn't get that at all. She seemed like a lovely young woman dealing with an unexpected tragedy in the best way she could."

Bessie shrugged. "I don't think Samantha is very fond of her. I expect I'll get an earful about her tomorrow."

Hugh frowned. "If Inspector Rockwell finds out that you're running around meeting up with suspects, he isn't going to be happy."

"I can't see that what I do is any of his business," Bessie replied stoutly. "He has a murderer to find. He doesn't need to worry about me having a friendly chat with someone. Why would Samantha be a suspect anyway? What possible motive could she have for killing Danny?"

Hugh shrugged. "I have no idea what her motive might have been," he told the others. "But she knew the dead man, which isn't the case for most of the population of the island. And she had access to the knife, again unlike most of the island's residents. Unless Danny took the knife out with him on his walk, the murderer has to be someone in that house."

"I can't believe his own parents would kill him," Doona said.

"It has been known to happen," Hugh replied. "Although in this case, I'm inclined to agree with you, barring any evidence to the contrary. Mrs. Pierce seems especially devastated by the loss. I didn't get much chance to form an impression of Mr. Pierce. He wasn't so much questioned as tiptoed around. He's a very important man across and that means we have to tread carefully around him."

"So if the parents are out of it, that leaves the widow, the brother and his girlfriend as your only suspects?" Bessie asked.

"There's some household staff as well," Hugh told her. "A driver, a housekeeper and a few young girls who worked as maids and whatever. We can't rule anyone out at this point, and I shouldn't be talking about it."

Of course the widow had the best motive, didn't she?" Doona asked. "All that lovely money. What sort of motive might Donny have had?"

"Has to be money, doesn't it?" Hugh answered. "Although apparently he isn't in line to inherit anything from his brother anyway. Mr. Pierce told the inspectors all about the complicated trust arrangements they have in place. He said that his own father and his father's brother had a huge falling out over the business when they were running it and they nearly bankrupted the company before they finally came to an agreement. After that, they set up all sorts of complicated legal bits and bobs to prevent it from happening again with the next generation."

"Legal bits and bobs?" Bessie remarked. "I should ask Doncan about that."

Hugh smiled at her. "That might not be the technical term, but whatever he said, the gist of it was that that Donny won't gain anything, at least financially, from his brother's death."

"I suppose he could have a whole host of other reasons for wanting his brother dead, though," Doona suggested.

Hugh shrugged. "He seemed really broken up about it," he told her. "But then, maybe he's just a good actor."

Bessie nodded slowly. "I really should talk to Bahey again," she remarked. "If anyone knows that family, it's her."

Hugh scratched his head. "Bahey who?"

"Bahey Corlett; she worked for the family for years, both on the island and across. She was there when I visited, even though she retired a few years ago," Bessie explained.

Hugh shook his head. "I don't think I've met her. I haven't been out to the house, except for a drive along the road to have stern words with the reporters who are plaguing the family."

"They are really dreadful. Can't the police do anything about them?" Bessie asked.

"Not really," Hugh shrugged. "It's a public road. As long as they stay on the road and don't try to get onto the actual property, they can stay. I understand that the Pierce family has hired their own security, anyway. The men from Manxman should be able to handle a few reporters."

"I actually know one of them," Bessie told him. "Robert Clague grew up in Laxey."

"I think you know just about everyone on this island," Doona joked.

"And not one of the people I know would murder anyone," Bessie answered.

"Don't be so sure," Hugh cautioned. "You never know what it might take to drive someone over the edge. We don't have a lot of murders on the island, but I've been studying up on different crimes. Sometimes the guilty party is the least likely suspect."

"In this case, then, you need to take a good look at Mrs. Pierce," Bessie told him. "She must be the least likely suspect."

Hugh shrugged. "I'm not taking a good look at anyone," he said glumly. "I'm holding down the fort at the station, looking for lost kittens and truant schoolboys, same as always."

Doona gave Hugh's arm a sympathetic pat. "Someone has to keep the station running and look after the rest of Laxey," she said soothingly. "Let Rockwell and Kelly run around asking questions and looking for clues. You just keep your ear to the ground. I'll bet you hear more interesting information than they will ever get from their interrogations."

Hugh shrugged again and then changed the subject. "What time are you meeting Samantha at the Laxey Wheel?" he asked Bessie.

"One o'clock," Bessie answered. "I'm not sure why she picked there, but I suppose there are worst places to meet."

"All those stairs," Doona said with a frown. "I'm not sure I like the idea of you climbing all those stairs and being so far off the ground with a murder suspect."

Bessie laughed. "I'll be perfectly fine. After all my years on this earth, I think I'm a pretty good judge of character. If that girl was going to kill anyone, it would be Vikky, not her boyfriend's brother, and certainly not me."

"I have to say I have some sympathy for her there," Doona answered. "Vikky was already at the station when the rest of the family showed up and she literally fell into Donny's arms. I'll bet Miss Samantha's nose has been out of joint ever since."

A knock on the door surprised them all. Bessie got up to answer it, followed closely by Hugh. When she reached the door, she turned to look at him, hovering only inches behind her.

"For goodness' sake," she whispered, "go and sit down. I don't want you scaring some poor ten-year-old who just got told off for not doing his homework."

"If I were sure it was a ten-year-old, I would be happy to sit down," Hugh hissed back as the person on the other side of the door tapped again.

Bessie glared at Hugh, and he took half a step backwards. She shook her head and sighed deeply, but he refused to retreat further. Neither of them was expecting Inspector Rockwell on the other side of the door.

"Inspector?" Bessie knew the greeting sounded more like a question than a welcome and quickly corrected herself. "This is a surprise, but please, do come in," she offered.

The man stepped into the cottage and looked around the kitchen. If he was surprised to see Doona and Hugh there, it didn't show on his face.

"We were just going to have some tea and fortune cookies," Bessie told him as she pushed the cottage door shut. "Please join us."

"That's very kind of you," the man replied, taking the few steps to the table and sitting at an empty place.

Hugh had returned to the table while Bessie and his boss were talking; now he settled back into the seat he had left earlier. Doona quickly cleared away the rest of the debris from their meal, passing Bessie the unopened box full of fortune cookies.

Bessie started the kettle and then put the cookies onto a plate. She added a few different varieties from her own stocks and then put the plate in the middle of the table. Everyone sat silently as they waited for the kettle to boil and for Bessie to make the tea.

Once everyone had their drink and their choice of treat, Bessie sank down into her chair and smiled tentatively at her new arrival.

"So what brings you here tonight, Inspector?" she asked, trying to make the request sound conversational rather than nervous.

Inspector Rockwell smiled at her. "Everywhere I go in Laxey, everyone tells me the same thing. If you want to know the skeet up here, talk to Aunt Bessie."

Bessie nodded; she couldn't possibly argue with that.

"So I want the skeet," the man continued. "Who's the most likely suspect in Daniel Pierce's murder? Who do most people think did it?"

Bessie took a long sip of her tea as she gathered her thoughts. She was probably foolish to feel flattered that he was asking, but the feeling was still there. She exchanged looks with Doona and Hugh, both of whom looked uneasy.

"I haven't had much chance to talk to people since I found the body," Bessie prevaricated. "And the ones I have talked to have been more interested in hearing about my experience than in speculating who might have killed the poor man."

"But you must have heard some conjecture," Inspector Rockwell pressed her gently. "This is all off the record, by the way," he added. "I'm not looking for an official statement, just your thoughts and ideas."

Bessie shrugged. "Don't they always say that it's the person closest to us whom we have to fear most? Most of the people I've talked to think the widow had the best motive."

Inspector Rockwell nodded. "But they'd only been married a few days," he reminded Bessie. "Surely she could have put up with him for a little bit longer before getting rid of him."

"Maybe he had already worked out that she was only interested in his money, so she had to act fast," Doona suggested.

A slightly awkward silence greeted that idea before Inspector Rockwell changed the subject.

"What do you think of the idea that it was drug related?" he asked Bessie.

"A few years ago I would have said 'no way,'" she replied. "But the world is changing and even Laxey is changing. The world of drugs and dealers and that sort of thing is something that I only know about through fiction. All I can tell you is that I've never seen anyone on Laxey Beach doing anything that I thought was related to illegal drugs."

Rockwell nodded slowly. "We have a lot of avenues to explore," he told her and the others. "Sometimes we get the most important clue through unconventional means. Obviously, a murder investigation is no place for a random civilian, but you're something of an institution in Laxey. If anyone is going to hear that little bit of information that we need, it's you. I would be extremely grateful if you would pass along anything and everything that you hear to me."

Bessie shrugged. "Hugh is staying with me at the moment," she told the man. "He seems to think I need protecting. I'm happy to share the things I hear with him every night."

Rockwell frowned and opened and closed his mouth several times before finally speaking. "That would be great," he said in a choked tone.

He stood up quickly, draining the last of his tea once on his feet. "Thank you kindly for the tea and biscuits," he told Bessie with a smile. "I can see why you love your little cottage. It really is something special."

Bessie rose to see him out, but Rockwell waved her back into her chair. "Hugh can see me out," he told them all. "Thank you again."

Hugh jumped up and quickly walked to the door behind his boss. The two disappeared outside. It was several minutes later when Hugh returned, just as Bessie was trying to work out how she might eavesdrop on the conversation taking place on her doorstep.

"Oh, I do hope you aren't in any trouble," Doona told the man once he had sunk back into his seat, a slightly dazed look on his face.

"I don't reckon I am," Hugh said after a moment.

"So what happened?" Bessie demanded impatiently.

Hugh ran a hand over his face and then shook his head. "He actually congratulated me on being here. Said it was a smart move. Said that protecting you was probably a good idea and that you were the perfect person to hear anything if people started talking. Oh, he wasn't really happy that you said you'd tell me what you heard rather than him, but he got me to promise that I'd pass everything along as soon as I got it, which I would have done anyway."

"So he wasn't upset to find us here?" Doona checked.

"He did remind me that I'm supposed to be getting information from Bessie, not giving information to her," Hugh grinned. "But he didn't seem too worried."

"Did he say anything about not talking to Inspector Kelly about all of this?" Bessie asked, suddenly suspicious.

"Not exactly," Hugh answered. "He said something about not bothering Inspector Kelly with the bits of gossip and innuendo that I might pick up from Bessie," Hugh told her. "I think he's hoping that Bessie's contacts will help him solve the murder before Inspector Kelly does."

Bessie frowned. "I don't want to get between those two," she complained. "Anyway, I think my loyalties should be to Patrick Kelly. He's a native, after all."

"Just focus your loyalties on Hugh here, and don't you worry about the dueling inspectors," Doona suggested. "If you ask me, Inspector Rockwell is more likely to share the credit if he solves the case than Inspector Kelly, but that's just my opinion."

"Hurmph," Bessie sighed. "I don't expect I'll have anything to contribute anyway," she told the others. "Whatever happened out on the beach, I'm pretty sure it didn't involve anyone local, so it's highly unlikely that any gossip I hear will matter."

"Of course, you are meeting with one of the suspects tomorrow," Hugh reminded her. "She might have something interesting to say."

Bessie only nodded. The whole topic was beginning to upset her. It was one thing reading about murder and mayhem in her favourite books, but in real life such things were physically and emotionally exhausting.

"I need to get out of your hair and let you get some sleep," Doona announced. "Tomorrow is going to be another busy day for all of us."

Hugh was smart enough to start washing up the dishes while Bessie saw her friend to the door.

"Ring me the minute you get done with that woman," Doona instructed her friend. "I want to know what she said and I want to know that you're safe."

"She'll be plenty safe enough," Hugh answered from the sink. "I'll be having my lunch right around one o'clock tomorrow and I think the picnic tables at the Laxey Wheel are the perfect spot to sit and eat."

"That's a great idea," Doona enthused. "Maybe I'll join you."

Bessie sighed. "For goodness' sake," she exclaimed. "I'm meeting a young woman who needs someone to talk to. Just because she is very tangentially attached to a murder doesn't mean I need a full complement of body guards."

"I suppose I can eat lunch wherever I want," Hugh said, giving Bessie a stubborn grin.

"I'll stay at the station, then," Doona told her friend. "But you still have to ring me the second you finish with her."

Bessie assured her friend that she would do so and then locked up the cottage's front door for the night. While Hugh finished washing, she grabbed a towel and dried the dishes. When they were all tucked back up in their proper places, Bessie headed upstairs to bed.

With her face washed and her teeth brushed, she climbed into her most comfortable nightgown and crawled into bed. For several minutes she lay snuggled under the covers, wondering how one man could make so much noise trying to be quiet. When the banging and crashing from the lower level finally stopped, she fell into her normal sound sleep.

# CHAPTER 6

$\mathcal{B}$essie didn't bother trying to wake the loudly snoring constable the next morning. She made herself tea and toast and then waited for his alarm at seven to do the job for her. Once Hugh was moving around, albeit slowly, Bessie headed out for a walk on the cool but mercifully dry day. She didn't go far, but she felt like she needed to stretch her legs and get away from everyone for a short time. She had lived on her own her entire adult life and having Hugh in residence, even after just two nights, was already starting to wear on her.

She was slightly disappointed to see that Hugh was still at the cottage when she returned.

"Not gone to work yet, then," she said as soon as she was in the door.

"Ah, I was just going to head out now," Hugh stammered. "I had a shower here this morning so that I didn't have to stop at home."

"You know you are more than welcome to do that," Bessie lied easily, wondering if he hadn't bothered to stop home because he knew the message he wanted wouldn't be there, or if she was reading too much into his changed behaviour.

"I just wanted a quick word with you before I went," Hugh added. "I'm sort of worried about you and the Laxey Wheel thing."

Bessie frowned at her young guest. "Don't be silly," she nearly snapped. "I'm meeting an unhappy young woman for a short chat. Everything will be fine."

"Nevertheless, I'll be having lunch at the wheel," Hugh reminded her. "And I want you to program my mobile number into your mobile phone in case you need me in a hurry."

Bessie considered arguing with him, but she couldn't muster up the enthusiasm. Besides, it did no harm having his number in her phone.

Once Hugh was satisfied with the arrangements for later in the day, he headed out to work and Bessie breathed a sigh of relief. She spent several minutes tidying up around the house. Hugh had been very careful to keep his things in a very neat pile in one corner of Bessie's sitting room and she worked around that pile, dusting and vacuuming. When she found herself frowning at the pile for the third time, she decided that she needed to get out of the cottage.

She had used the same taxi service for more years than she chose to remember. A few years ago they had relocated their dispatch centre to Ramsey, which often meant longer wait times for Bessie if she didn't pre-book. That usually wasn't an issue; Bessie rarely did things on impulse. Today was an exception.

She was lucky, therefore, that the company had a driver in the Laxey area when she rang. The man who pulled up in front of Bessie's cottage just minutes later was one of her favourites.

"Dave, I'm glad to see you," she greeted him.

"Always a pleasure to see you, Aunt Bessie," he answered with a wide smile. "And I know you've had more than your share of excitement lately, so I won't be bothering you with questions."

Instead, the pair chatted about Dave's family as he drove Bessie along the coast into Ramsey.

"It isn't like you to go into Ramsey on a Wednesday," he remarked as he pulled into a small car park lot to let Bessie out.

"No, I just needed a change of scenery," Bessie answered. "After everything that's been going on, I thought a spot of retail therapy might help."

Dave laughed. "The wife claims that's the only sort of therapy that actually does anyone any good," he told Bessie.

"I reckon it's at least as useful as any other sort," Bessie said with a smile.

"I'll see you back here at eleven, then," Dave confirmed their arrangement.

"Perfect."

Bessie started her visit to the shops at her favourite bookstore. She settled her account and then spent several minutes browsing.

"Oh, Aunt Bessie, we just got a great-looking new cookbook in stock," one of the shop assistants told her. "It's got tons of pictures."

Bessie smiled. She loved cookbooks, especially ones with pages of glossy photos of gorgeous looking food that she knew she could never recreate. At her age, she no longer harboured any illusions that she might one day become a better cook. She prepared what she liked, which meant simple food that was quick to fix and required few ingredients. However, that didn't dull the pleasure she received from drooling over recipes for dishes she would never dream of attempting.

Half an hour later, the cookbook and a new mystery novel by an author she'd never heard of before tucked into her shopping bag, Bessie headed out of the store. She had an hour left before Dave would return, so she wandered slowly up and down the street of shops. She spent a few minutes in each of the charity shops digging through their piles of second-hand books and was rewarded with an only slightly dog-eared copy of an Agatha Christie mystery that was missing from her collection.

She was annoyed to find that she was starting to get tired as she headed back to meet Dave. I must do more walking for longer stretches, she told herself sternly. A few days off and I'm already out of shape.

Dave ferried her back to Laxey, dropping her off on "Ham and Egg Terrace," where she had a quick lunch. Originally built as terraced cottages for the mine workers, the row of homes got their nickname from the meals that were once served to island visitors in the cottage's front rooms. Now a single pub stood at one end of the terrace. It served fresh food incorporating as many Manx ingredients as they could source.

After lunch, Bessie briefly considered ringing Dave and asking him for a ride over to the Lady Isabella, as Laxey Wheel was named, and then scolded herself. The wheel was only a short walk from the terrace of cottages. She shouldn't have even considered it, even if she was carrying a shopping bag full of books.

While she kept a steady pace, she walked somewhat more slowly than she wanted to and she ended up arriving at her destination about ten minutes after one.

The wheel was practically deserted on this overcast and slightly chilly March day and, as Bessie watched it turning lazily as she approached, she felt a shiver run down her spine. A few benches and picnic tables were scattered around the base of the wheel and Bessie had to resist the urge to wave to Hugh when she spotted him sitting all alone at one of them. He looked miserable, nibbling on a limp-looking sandwich. If they ever did this again, she would have to pack him something more appealing for his lunch.

She paused at the large sign that gave a brief history of the wheel. Although she must have been there hundreds of times before, she still stopped to reread the key facts.

"The 'Lady Isabella,' was named after the wife of Charles Hope. He was the serving Lieutenant Governor of the island in 1854, when the wheel was built. It is the largest working waterwheel in the world, once essential for pumping water out of the mines in Laxey."

Bessie loved her history, but the technical details of the wheel held less interest for her. The only one that always caught her eye was the diameter. The Lady Isabella was seventy-two feet and six inches in diameter. She always wondered if the extra six inches were part of the design or a small miscalculation by the builders.

A single Manx National Heritage worker was standing at the bottom of the steps that led to the wheel's viewing platform. He knew

Bessie on sight and waved her on as she fumbled in her purse for her membership card.

"I think I know a member when I see one," he chuckled as Bessie headed past him and began the long climb up the winding staircase.

"Am I going to have the view all to myself?" Bessie asked, worried that she might have missed Samantha by being late.

"There's one or two folks up top," the man grinned at her. "But if you stay for long I bet they'll give up and head for the pub."

Bessie smiled back and then focussed on her climb. Halfway up she stopped to catch her breath and look out at the already amazing view. She was reminded once again of how much she loved her island home. The views were simply spectacular. Bessie wondered what the miners who had toiled away in the mine that the wheel had once serviced would think of it now being a tourist attraction.

She shut her eyes and tried to imagine how Laxey in the second half of the nineteenth century must have looked. It was impossible to think that the tiny town had once been home to over six hundred miners and their families. With a sigh, Bessie continued her climb.

When she reached the top, she was disappointed to see that only three other people were there and Samantha wasn't one of them. She nodded a quick "hello" to Mark Blake, a young man who had recently come to work at the Manx Museum in the "special projects" department. He was somewhere in his twenties and incredibly enthusiastic about the island and its history.

"Hello, Bessie," Mark shouted a greeting as he and his companion made their way towards her. "My brother Michael is just here visiting for a few days." Mark made quick introductions before the pair headed off down the steps, their conversation drifting back towards Bessie as they went.

"We'll skip the mine for now, if you really want to. We can head over to the old cottages instead," Mark was telling his brother. "They were built for the mine workers around 1860 and are still occupied today."

Michael shot Bessie a slightly dazed look as he followed Mark down the steps. Bessie shook her head. Mark would never understand why everyone didn't share his enthusiasm for the island's past.

With the pair gone, Bessie turned her attention to the only other person on the viewing platform. As she approached the man, she studied him.

Donny Pierce looked as if he hadn't slept since the last time she saw him. He was staring out at the breathtaking landscape in front of him, but he didn't seem to be seeing it. Bessie was only a step away from him when he finally seemed to notice her.

"Oh, uhm, good afternoon," he said formally.

"Good afternoon," Bessie replied politely. "I don't know if you remember me?" she asked tentatively.

The man sighed and ran a hand over his face. "You came by the house yesterday, didn't you?" he said slowly. "Betsy or something like that. You know Bahey and my parents."

Bessie nodded. "It's Bessie, actually," she corrected him gently. "But what brings you out here in this miserable weather?" As if to prove her point, a light rain began to fall.

Donny shook his head. "It seemed brighter earlier," he shrugged. "And the girls wanted to get out of the house."

"The girls?" Bessie asked.

"Sam, er, Samantha and Vikky. Things are pretty tense at Thie yn Traie right now and they both wanted a break."

Bessie nodded. "Your mother must be, understandably, very upset."

The man nodded. "Yeah, she's taken Danny's death really hard. He was her firstborn and, really, if I'm honest, her favourite."

Bessie tutted at him. "Mothers don't have favourites," she said sternly.

The remark raised a small smile from the man. "I don't know," he shrugged. "Anyway, her doctor's given her a bunch of tablets and she seems to be washing them down with bottles and bottles of wine. My father has chosen whisky as his coping mechanism. The cottage isn't really a fun place to be and the girls needed a break."

"Nice of you to accommodate them," Bessie remarked.

Donny gave her another small smile. "I suppose I needed a break,

77

too," he admitted. "The police won't let any of us leave the island at the moment, so a bit of sight-seeing sounded quite appealing. Anyway, it seemed like a good idea an hour ago."

"The trip to the wheel hasn't gone the way you expected?" Bessie suggested.

"No, I suppose you could say that."

Bessie stayed silent, waiting to see what he might add. After a long minute while they both took in the view, Donny sighed deeply.

"Coming to the Laxey Wheel was Samantha's idea," he told Bessie. "Apparently some distant ancestor of hers once worked in the mine here. I can't imagine what it must have been like in those days."

"Me either," Bessie told him. "I was just thinking about that as I was climbing up here."

"You never saw the mine when it was working?" Donny asked.

"The mine stopped operating in 1929, when I was still living in America," Bessie told him.

Donny looked like he had a dozen more questions for Bessie, but then he sighed again and fell silent. After a few minutes, Bessie restarted the conversation.

"So Samantha wanted to have a look at the wheel?" she asked, trying to pick up where he had left off.

"What? Oh yes. Samantha wanted to see the wheel and the mines and whatever else we could find. We made all of the arrangements last night, before bed. Then, this morning, Vikky overheard our plans and asked if she could come as well. Samantha wanted to say 'no,' but I couldn't see any harm in including her. She needed the change of scenery as much as anyone."

Bessie nodded slowly. "So you brought them both here."

"Yeah, and they started fighting in the car before we even left the cottage and argued all the way to the car park," Donny looked bewilderedly at Bessie. "They really seem to hate each other, and I've no idea why."

Bessie studied the man, wondering if he was really that stupid about women. "Perhaps Samantha thinks you are falling for Vikky," she suggested.

"Vikky is my brother's widow. She's my sister now," Donny sighed again. "I won't deny that she's a very attractive woman, but she just lost her husband. Even if I weren't involved with Samantha, I wouldn't be trying to move in on Vikky, at least not yet."

Bessie stared out towards Laxey and tried to work out how to reply to the man's words. The "at least not yet" seemed telling to her. Donny was interested in the attractive widow; he was just waiting for the right time to make his move. She sighed. People so often made their own problems.

"So where are Samantha and Vikky now?" she asked. She and Donny were still alone on the platform.

"They both went stomping off in different directions," he shrugged. "I suppose I'll ring them both when I'm ready to go. I'm dreading the drive home, though."

Bessie gave his arm a sympathetic pat and began to turn away. She stopped when Donny grabbed the hand that she had used to pat him.

"Bessie, please, I hate to keep you standing out in the rain, but, well, can you spare me just a minute more of your time?"

She turned back towards him curiously. "Of course," she said gently.

"I just wondered," he began hesitantly. "Oh, never mind."

"What is it you wondered?" Bessie coaxed.

"You know the island and what goes on here," Donny said. "What do you think happened to my brother?"

Bessie shook her head slowly to give herself time to think. "That's a question for the police," she said finally. "I know the island, but I don't know anything about murder. From what I've seen, I can't begin to guess who might have wanted to harm your brother." She was surprised when Donny choked back a laugh.

"He really had everyone fooled," he said harshly. "My mother won't believe a bad word about him. The police seem to think someone in the family is responsible and I don't want to speak ill of the dead, so I haven't told the police absolutely everything. Maybe I should fix that? What do you think?"

"I think you should tell the police anything and everything that you know," Bessie said, a touch primly.

Donny shook his head. "He was my big brother," he answered with a catch in his voice. "I always looked up to him, you know?"

Bessie nodded. "I had an older sister. I know exactly what you mean. But the best thing you can do for him now is help the police find out what happened."

The man nodded slowly. "He was taking drugs," he blurted out.

Bessie struggled to keep her face from registering shock. "Drugs?" she repeated.

"Yeah," Donny sighed. "I just found out a few weeks ago. He started missing work or turning up late. My father is getting ready to retire early, or he was anyway, and more and more of the responsibility for running the company has been falling on me and Danny. Except in the last month or so, it's been all me. Danny hadn't been coming in, or he'd come in late and then leave early. And he'd been, uh, all over the place with his decision-making. I finally confronted him a few days ago, before the trip, and he told me everything."

"Everything?"

Donny shrugged. "Probably not everything, but he told me plenty. He was hooked on some prescription painkillers that he got to help with headaches. He said it started out with just one a day, but he found out that he liked the way they made him feel. They just wiped out all his worries. Fast forward a few weeks and he was hooked big time. He was using multiple doctors to get more and more prescriptions and then he found another source, a black market one." Donny turned away from Bessie and leaned against the platform railing, his eyes filling with tears.

"I begged him to get help," he told Bessie. "I offered to pay for it, offered to cover it all up from our parents, offered to do whatever it took. He said he wasn't ready yet. I think he married Vikky because he was out of it on drugs. I can't believe he would have ever done that any other way. He loved being single. And I suppose he was out of it when he redid his will. That's one of the reasons why I'm supporting my father's efforts to get Vikky disinherited."

"Really?" Bessie tried to keep the shock from her voice.

"Hey," Donny answered, "I like Vikky a lot, but she had to know that my brother was doing drugs. I think she knew and she took advantage of it. My father and I will make sure she gets some sort of payout, but she certainly doesn't deserve Danny's share of the company."

Bessie bit back a dozen replies. "So he wasn't interested in giving up the drugs?" she asked, changing the subject away from the widow.

"No, at least not yet. He said something about being straight-laced and responsible his whole life and needing a few months to just have some fun." Donny shrugged. "I suppose some people would call it a midlife crisis."

Bessie nodded. So many more men than women seemed to suffer from such things. She had always been aware of the passage of time and the fragile nature of existence, but it appeared that some people, on realising that they had hit middle age, felt the need to do something radically unlike themselves in order to prove something to someone.

Doona, for example, got a tattoo on her fortieth birthday. Unfortunately, she had chosen to have it done at a location that was more about affordability than artistic ability. Luckily, the tattoo was small and, as it was on the back of her shoulder, she didn't have to look at it herself. Bessie often wondered if she was tired of saying "No, it's a butterfly, yes, really," all summer long when she wore sleeveless dresses, but it wasn't something that Bessie felt she should ask her friend.

"And Vikky knew about the drugs?" Bessie asked.

"She must have," Donny insisted. "If Danny wasn't hiding it from me, he wouldn't have been hiding it from his girlfriend, either. I don't think he cared who knew, aside from our parents."

"I take it they wouldn't have approved," Bessie remarked.

Donny laughed. "They would have fired him, cut him off without a cent and written him out of their wills. My mother and father have very strong opinions about drug taking, in spite of their own behavior at the moment. The family firm is tied up in all sorts of complicated legal entities, and every single one of them has clauses about substance abuse."

"So what do you think happened to your brother?" Bessie asked.

Donny looked around the empty platform and then lowered his voice for no reason whatsoever. "I think he arranged a middle of the night meeting with a drug dealer and the dealer killed him," he whispered.

"Where did the dealer get the knife from?" she asked, annoyed with herself when she realised she was whispering as well.

"Danny must have taken it with him for protection," Donny said, a touch smugly. "He couldn't possibly have been comfortable dealing with drug dealers and the like. He was probably terrified. And he was probably carrying a great deal of cash as well. Taking the knife with him for protection makes perfect sense."

"You really need to tell the police everything you've told me," Bessie said, her mind spinning from all the information that had just fallen into her lap. "They need to know about your suspicions."

"I suppose so," the man said in a reluctant tone. "It's all really just my own personal theory, though. I can't prove any of it. I suppose there must be drug dealers on the island who would supply prescription medication?"

Bessie frowned at him. "I have absolutely no knowledge of such things," she told him tartly. "I'm sure the police will be able to work out if your theory is plausible or not. But they can't investigate it at all if you don't tell them."

"I know you're right," Donny sighed. "I think my big fear is that my parents will find out about Danny's drug problem. My mother is so distraught already, I hate to add to her unhappiness."

"I understand that," Bessie said, now patting his arm again. "But surely she would prefer to see his murder solved, whatever unpleasantness that might reveal."

"I suppose so," he agreed after a moment. "And I imagine she would rather it was a drug dealer than the alternative."

"What alternative is that?" Bessie asked.

The man shook his head. "The only alternative I can think of is that Vikky killed him," he said softly. "And that would be much worse."

"You really think she's capable of murder?"

"No," Donny said too loudly. He took a deep breath. "I don't know what to think," he said eventually. "I mean I introduced them, you know? I met Vikky through mutual friends and I thought she would be perfect for my brother. I was even happy when they got married, even though I thought Danny only agreed because of the drugs. I thought she would be good for him, once he got his habit sorted."

"Why would she kill him? They had only just married," Bessie played devil's advocate.

Donny laughed unpleasantly. "They were fighting almost all the time," he told Bessie. "The night of the, um, er, the night Danny died they started fighting at dinner and kept at it until Vikky finally stormed away to go to bed. Danny said he was going to just sleep in one of the spare bedrooms rather than try sleeping with Vikky."

"What were they fighting about?" Bessie had to ask.

"I don't know. Vikky thought Danny was flirting with Samantha and Danny thought Vikky was flirting with me." The man ran a hand over his face. "Then Vikky got a text from an ex-boyfriend who apparently didn't know she was now married. Unfortunately, Danny had her phone at the time and he read the text. Apparently it was sort of, um, rude and suggestive." He shook his head. "I think they both realised that they had sort of rushed into marrying and they were both regretting it."

"Surely divorce is a better option than murder," Bessie said sensibly.

Donny shrugged. "Vikky wouldn't have been given much money in a divorce settlement after only a few days," he said.

Bessie frowned at him. "I thought you said you liked Vikky," she said. "It sounds like you're ready to put her on trial for murder."

"I do like Vikky," Donny insisted. "But if it wasn't something related to drugs, I can't imagine who else could have done it. Obviously, neither my parents or myself had anything to do with it;

Samantha didn't have any motive, and anyway, she spent the night with me. There simply isn't anyone else."

Bessie gave him a measured look. "I'm sure the police are considering every possible option," she said eventually. "You should tell them everything you've told me and then let them worry about it."

The man nodded. "I'm really angry at Danny for doing this to us," he confessed.

"That's perfectly normal," Bessie informed him. "But you still must want to see his killer behind bars."

Donny shrugged and then turned away from Bessie. "Thanks for the chat," he said dismissively. "I suppose I should round up the girls and head back home. My parents might have noticed by now that we're gone."

"Which way did you say Samantha went?" Bessie asked. "I'd love to have a quick chat with her about her Manx ancestry."

He shrugged again. "I think she was heading towards the mine. She said something about wanting to see where the men worked. I think she was just too lazy to bother climbing the steps up the wheel."

"Thanks." Bessie thought of a million things to say, but chose to say nothing further. She turned and slowly headed back down the ninety-six steps. The rain was falling gently but steadily as she reached the bottom.

# CHAPTER 7

*A*s she stepped away from the stairs, Hugh came up alongside of her and took her arm.

"I was starting to get worried about you," he told Bessie as they walked slowly away from the Lady Isabella. "Henry, the Manx National Heritage guy, wasn't sure how many people were up there, but he was pretty sure none of them were women. What were you doing up there all that time?"

Bessie patted his arm, touched by the obvious concern in his voice. "Samantha wasn't up there," she told him, "but Donny Pierce was, and he had a lot on his mind."

"Anything you need to tell me right away?" Hugh asked. "Because I really need to get back to the office. With both Inspector Rockwell and Inspector Kelly popping in and out all the time, I can't afford to take an extra-long lunch."

"I've told the man that he should go to the police with his information," Bessie said. "If he hasn't come in and talked to anyone by the end of the day, I'll fill you in tonight."

Hugh nodded. "If you're sure it isn't anything urgent, I've really got to dash."

Bessie patted his arm again. "You go and get back to work. I'll see you tonight."

Hugh hesitated. "What are you going to do now?"

"I'm going to try to find Samantha. I suspect she got tired of the cold and the damp and found her way to a pub somewhere."

"Be careful and ring me if you need me," Hugh instructed her. "And don't go climbing the Lady Isabella again."

Bessie smiled. "No worries, I don't have any desire to climb all those steps again in a hurry."

Hugh nodded and then gave her one last worried glance before he rushed off back to his car. Bessie shook her head. Even with a murderer running around, she felt safe on her little island. It was sweet of Hugh to worry about her, but totally unnecessary.

Donny had suggested that Samantha had been heading towards the mine when they split up. Even though he'd said that at least an hour had passed since then, the mine seemed as good a starting point as any.

Bessie walked carefully along the uneven ground, heading for the entrance to the old mine shaft. On arriving, she stopped at the opening and read the sign that was partially blocking it.

"Manx National Heritage welcomes you to the old Laxey Mine. Only a small portion of the tunnel leading to the old mine is visible, but you are welcome to walk inside and see for yourself where the miners would have begun their day in the short tunnel that remains accessible. Because there is always a risk of rock fall, all visitors must wear hard hats. Please be careful and enjoy your visit."

Bessie glanced at the rack of ugly white hard hats that sat next to the sign. She kept her gray hair short and neatly trimmed; the hat would make little difference to her style. That didn't mean that she wanted to wear it, however. The hats were ugly and uncomfortable. For a moment she debated simply ignoring them and heading into the tunnel. Then she sighed deeply and grabbed the nearest one. Plopping it on her head, she made her way to the mouth of the tunnel.

It would have been just her luck, if she'd left it off, to find Mark Blake or some other Manx National Heritage bigwig inside the tunnel when she got there. She'd never hear the end of the teasing if he'd spotted her. The last thing she wanted a reputation for was rule breaking. She sighed as she stepped into the dimly lit tunnel. It was empty. She took a couple of steps forward and then shrugged. She would have to look for Samantha elsewhere.

The sound of a mobile phone ringing stopped her as she was turning around. She glanced around the narrow tunnel, trying to work out where the annoying notes were coming from. Someone must have dropped their phone in the tunnel when they were sight-seeing, she decided. She might as well play Good Samaritan and find it for them.

The sound was coming from deeper into the space and she walked forward quickly, hoping to find the phone before it stopped ringing. At the end of the tunnel, just in front of the locked doors that led into the actual mine shaft, sat an old-fashioned mine cart, part of the display. As Bessie walked towards it, she decided that it must be where the sound was coming from.

She stopped in front of the cart and glanced down into it, hoping that the phone would be lit up enough to help her find it in the near-darkness. She took a sharp step backwards as the phone's light revealed far more than just the ringing mobile. As her mind tried to process what she had seen, her feet were carrying her backwards, towards the mouth of the tunnel.

As Bessie stepped outside, she took several deep breaths and then pulled her phone from her pocket. She frowned as she punched the third number on her speed-dial list.

"This is Hugh." The voice on the other end helped steady Bessie's nerves, at least a little bit.

"Hugh, it's Aunt Bessie," she began. She heard the quaver in her voice and took another deep breath.

"What can I do for you, Bessie?" Hugh asked politely.

"It's Samantha; I've found her," Bessie replied.

"Great, did she have anything interesting to say?"

"No," Bessie shuddered. "She's dead."

Bessie pulled the phone from her ear as she heard a huge crashing noise. A moment later, she cautiously put it back.

"Aunt Bessie?" Hugh sounded terribly flustered. "Sorry, I, uh, I dropped the phone. I'm sure I didn't understand you. What did you just say?"

"I said Samantha is dead," Bessie answered sharply. "You really should be paying more attention."

She heard Hugh take a deep breath. "Where did you find her?" he asked after a moment.

"In the Laxey Mine," Bessie said. "She's in the mine cart, all curled up. Her phone was ringing." Bessie was annoyed to hear tears in her voice as she spoke. She cleared her throat in an effort to stem them.

"Okay, I'm on my way," Hugh told her. "I was just pulling out of the car park by the wheel when my phone rang, so I won't be long. Just wait there for me and don't let anyone in or out of the mine until I get there."

He hung up before Bessie could protest. "How exactly am I supposed to do that?" she muttered at the phone. In the end, it didn't matter, as no one approached the mine in the five or so minutes that it took for Hugh to turn up.

She watched his car's arrival, his lights blazing and siren blasting, with a frown. Surely there was no need for so much rush; the woman was dead, after all. She sighed. Boys and their toys, she decided. Hugh probably loved having an excuse to flash his lights and blare his siren. She was impressed to see him hurrying from the car towards her, though. It was the fastest she'd ever seen the man move.

"Is there anyone else in there?" he asked as he reached her side.

"No, the place was empty when I got here. I only went in a few steps and I was going to leave when I saw it was empty. Then a mobile phone started to ring and I thought I might as well find it and rescue it." Bessie shook her head. Sometimes it didn't pay to try to be helpful.

Hugh nodded and then disappeared into the mine tunnel. Only a few seconds later he was back, pulling out his phone and making calls. Bessie watched for a few minutes and then, when he'd just finished one call and was about to begin another, interrupted him.

"I'll be in the pub if you want me," she told him, pointing to the end of "Ham and Egg Terrace."

"You probably should stay until the inspectors get here," Hugh told her.

"Sorry, I need to get out of the rain and have a cup of tea," Bessie said stoutly. "The inspectors can find me there whenever they want to chat."

Bessie turned her back on the still protesting Hugh and stomped away through puddles that were growing larger by the minute. A cup of tea and a piece of cake, she decided. Or maybe a hot pudding, like jam roly-poly with lots of custard; that would be good. She completely blocked everything from her mind except her immediate plans. Behind her, a new crime scene investigation began.

Bessie was happy to put her heavy shopping bag on an empty chair and settle into another. She drank her tea and ate her sticky toffee pudding with extra custard while, around her, the entire room buzzed with excited chatter. By the time she finished, six police cars were dotted throughout the small car park near the mine and two ambulances were vying for space near its entrance.

"I wonder what's going on at the mine," the girl clearing the dishes from Bessie's table remarked idly.

"I couldn't possibly guess," Bessie answered, unwilling to discuss what she had seen with anyone if she didn't have to. The girl walked away and Bessie shut her eyes and drew a breath. The tea and sugary treat hadn't been enough to erase the image that seemed burned into her brain.

Finding Daniel Pierce's body had been a somewhat upsetting experience for her, but this was in a different league. For one thing, she had immediately assumed that Danny had died of natural causes. Perhaps more importantly, he had been lying in such a way that she couldn't see his face. That had given Bessie the chance to feel somewhat detached from his death. Besides, the man had been a relative stranger to her. She was vaguely aware that he had been present on Laxey Beach in years gone by, but she didn't think she'd ever spoken to the man.

Samantha's death was completely different. Bessie shut her eyes tightly and then opened them quickly as, once again, the ghastly image haunted her. Samantha had been curled up in the mine cart with the phone resting near her head. In the eerie blue light that the phone emitted, Bessie had just been able to make out the surprised look on Samantha's lifeless face. The only other thing that really registered in Bessie's split-second look was the knife that was sticking out of Samantha's chest. She found it impossible to reconcile the body she had seen with the vivacious and beautiful woman she had spoken with only twenty-four hours earlier.

Bessie ordered herself another cup of tea. She was thinking seriously about getting herself a second pudding as well when Inspector Kelly walked into the room. He quickly spotted her and made his way to her table.

"You should have stayed at the crime scene," he barked as he sat down next to her uninvited.

"It was so cold and rainy," Bessie said in a weak voice. "I just felt like I needed to sit down. I think I was in shock."

The inspector looked at her like he didn't believe a word she had said, but he didn't argue. "I need you to run me through finding the body," he told Bessie.

A crashing noise behind him had him jumping to his feet. The startled waitress was staring down at Bessie's second cup of tea, which she had dropped.

"Oh, I am sorry," she stammered. "I just, that is, you said, oh my...."

Inspector Kelly frowned. "Is there an office or another room that I can use for a few minutes?" he asked the waitress.

"Um, sure, yeah." The girl was trying to mop up the spilled drink and collect the broken pieces of cup. "You can use the back room," she finally offered as she stood up with hands full of soaked paper napkins and cup fragments. "Just through the arch. We use it for parties and stuff."

The Inspector nodded once. "I think some privacy is in order," he told Bessie, gesturing for her to follow him into the back.

Bessie rose slowly, picking up her shopping bag and using the time to gather her thoughts. She wasn't feeling terribly impressed with Inspector Kelly at the moment, but that didn't mean she wasn't prepared to tell him everything.

In the end, though, she wasn't given a chance. The Inspector sat down at a table right inside the door and motioned for Bessie to join him.

"Hugh reported that you went into the mine, saw that it was empty and then heard a mobile phone ringing, is that correct?" he began.

"Yes," Bessie answered, surprised at the detailed question.

"You then tried to find the phone and found the body instead, correct?"

"Well, technically, I found both the body and the phone," Bessie answered.

The man rolled his eyes. "Yes, all right, whatever," he muttered. "Do you have anything to add to your statement?"

Bessie sat back and studied him for a long minute. "I don't recall making a statement," she said finally.

The man sighed. "I'm a very busy man," he told Bessie. "I have Hugh's statement and you've just confirmed what he reported. If you stop by the station tomorrow, Mrs. Moore will have what we discussed typed up and ready for you to sign."

He was gone before Bessie could frame an appropriate reply. "Well, he's never going to solve the crime that way," she muttered to herself as she got to her feet. "Fancy not even asking me why I was at the mine," she shook her head and made her way back through the pub, heading for the door. It swung open before she reached it and Bessie took a step backwards to allow the man coming in some space.

"Ah, Aunt Bessie," the man said brightly. "Just the person I wanted to see."

Bessie grinned up at Inspector Rockwell. "I'm awfully popular right now," she remarked. "Inspector Kelly just left."

"Did you give him a statement?" Rockwell frowned.

"Not exactly," Bessie answered. "He already had Hugh's statement, so he just wanted to verify a few things."

"I'd like to do a bit more than 'verify a few things,'" the inspector told Bessie. "Maybe we should grab a table and some tea."

"You're welcome to use the back room," the same waitress said brightly. "I'll bring some tea through in a minute."

Rockwell nodded and offered Bessie his arm. Feeling somewhat more appreciated, Bessie took it with a small smile.

The inspector waited until the tea had been delivered before he spoke. "I'd like you to run me through your day," he told Bessie, after he'd added milk and sugar to his cup and taken a long drink. "Actually, start with when I left your cottage last night, if you don't mind."

Bessie smiled and settled back in her chair; Inspector Rockwell now rising even further in her estimation.

"After you left, Doona went home and Hugh and I went to bed. Well," she corrected herself, "I went to bed. Hugh is insisting on sleeping on the couch."

The man nodded and made a small note on a pad of paper that he had pulled from his pocket. "Go on," he said encouragingly.

"Right, so I got up at six, as usual, had a walk and then did some cleaning. After that I took a taxi into Ramsey and did some shopping. The taxi brought me back to Laxey and dropped me here for some lunch. After lunch I walked over to the wheel and climbed up. Mark Blake from the Manx Museum was at the top, along with his brother, and we exchanged a few words. The only other person there was Donny Pierce. I chatted to him for a short while and then headed back down the stairs."

"I want a complete account of your conversation with Mr. Pierce," the inspector told her. "But that can wait until after you finish your general statement."

Bessie nodded. "I headed for the mine, but when I got inside it was empty, so I turned around to go. Then I heard a mobile ringing. I tracked the phone down to the mine cart and when I looked inside I found Samantha's body as well. I immediately left the mine and rang Hugh. Once he arrived I came over here and had tea and sticky toffee pudding while I waited for whoever wanted to talk to me."

Inspector Rockwell nodded and made a few notes before he spoke.

"Sticky toffee pudding sounds wonderful. I still haven't had any lunch and now it looks as if it might be some time before I get any." He ran a tired hand over his face before he continued. "Anyway, your statement matches what Hugh has reported, but I'm much more interested in what you haven't said than in what you have."

"Meaning what exactly?" Bessie asked.

"Well, firstly, meaning what on earth were you doing climbing the Laxey Wheel on a wet and cold day in March? I can almost understand why Donny Pierce and the others were here, but why you?"

Bessie sighed. She hoped she wasn't about to make the inspector angry or get Hugh into trouble. "I was supposed to be meeting Samantha here," she said reluctantly. "When I was at Thie yn Traie yesterday we arranged to meet here at one o'clock today."

Inspector Rockwell nodded slowly, his face flushing with what Bessie assumed was repressed anger. He took a long slow breath before he spoke again. "I see," he said tightly.

Bessie smiled innocently at him, sipping her tea so that she wouldn't start apologising. In her mind she had done nothing wrong, but the look on John Rockwell's face suggested that he didn't agree.

"If you had thought to mention that to me last night," he said eventually, "we might have been able to have some people in place here. We might even have been able to prevent Samantha's murder."

Bessie shook her head. "I was meeting an upset young woman who was having a hard time with her boyfriend and his family. She just needed someone to talk to, not a police bodyguard."

"And yet she's dead."

Bessie frowned and then felt unwelcome tears welling up in her eyes. Was it possible that Samantha had been murdered because of their plans to meet today? "I can't believe that our planned meeting had anything to do with her murder," she said eventually, as much to herself as to the Inspector.

"Why not?"

"Well, why would it?" Bessie demanded.

"Why don't you take me back through your conversation with her yesterday?" Inspector Rockwell suggested.

Bessie closed her eyes and tried to remember exactly what had been said. "She walked me to the door," Bessie began. "We were talking about Daniel Pierce's theory, about the killing being random. I suggested that she must have her own theory and she admitted that she did, but she didn't want to discuss it then. She suggested the meeting time and place."

"Who could have overheard your conversation?"

"I don't think anyone could have," Bessie tried hard to remember. "We'd left the family in the great room. Donny came out while we were talking, but he was too far away to overhear anything except our goodbyes." Bessie paused and shook her head again.

"What is it?" Inspector Rockwell asked.

"Robert Clague," Bessie said slowly. "He suddenly appeared next to me in the hallway as I was leaving. I suppose he might have been able to overhear the conversation. But he didn't have any reason to kill anyone. He's only just been hired by the family for security. I doubt he even knew the younger Daniel Pierce and he must have just met Samantha yesterday when he came to work for the family."

Rockwell nodded absently, making notes in his notebook. "Interesting," was his only comment.

The Inspector took Bessie through her day several times over, checking and rechecking her story. Then they spent a very long time discussing her conversation with Donny Pierce at the top of the wheel.

"Donny gave his statement to Inspector Kelly," Rockwell said after Bessie had completed the third retelling of the conversation. "I think Kelly is quite fond of the idea that all of this trouble is drug-related."

"Why? I hate thinking that there might be drug problems on this island."

Rockwell shrugged. "I think he's hoping to catch a murderer and break up a drug cartel in one fell swoop. He's angling for a promotion into Douglas."

"I hope you aren't planning to move to the capital as well," Bessie said with a sigh.

"Oh, no," Rockwell smiled at her. "I really like it up north. Ramsey already feels like home, for me anyway." Something flashed across his face that Bessie caught and would wonder about later.

"I'm glad you like it here," Bessie replied.

"I really do," the man assured her. "I also enjoy being head of my own small investigative division. The Douglas CID is bigger but, dare I say it, more convoluted. Up here I get to run things the way I see fit. Of course, if I don't get this murder solved, I might find myself out of any job."

Bessie frowned. She was starting to like the man, in spite of his origins. Well, not everyone could be born Manx. "I hope that doesn't happen," she told the man.

Before Rockwell could answer, his phone buzzed insistently. He pulled it from a pocket and frowned at it.

"I have to take this," he told Bessie apologetically. "It's the Chief Constable."

Bessie nodded as he rose and walked towards the far corner of the room. Within seconds, however, he was back.

"And now I have to run," he said, his tone somewhere between apology and exasperation. "I'd like to stop by and visit you tonight," he told Bessie. "Hopefully, around the same time as last night, if that's okay?"

"Certainly," Bessie agreed.

"I'm sure Hugh and Doona will be there as well," he told her with a smile. "We can bash around a few ideas and see what we come up with."

Bessie grinned back at him. Yes, she was definitely starting to like him.

She finished her tea and then sat back in her chair. Neither inspector had actually told her that she was free to go, but she was sure she had outstayed her welcome at the small pub. She rose to her feet and headed slowly towards the front room, hoping there might be a taxi waiting at the rarely used taxi rank outside.

She was only halfway to the door, carrying the shopping bag that now seemed to weigh a ton, when it burst open and Hugh bounced in, seemingly full of an unusual amount of energy.

"Ah, there you are, Aunt Bessie," he said brightly. "I've been instructed by Inspector Rockwell to see you home safely."

Bessie nodded. "It was kind of the inspector to think of me," she remarked as they made their way out of the pub after Bessie had settled her bill and exchanged a few words of thanks with the proprietor.

"He's convinced you're the key to solving this thing," Hugh whispered to her once they were safely buckled up in Hugh's car. "He told me to make sure I take especially good care of you."

Bessie smiled. "Well, that is all very nice, but I really don't know anything, you know."

"But you have the best connections of anyone in the area," Hugh reminded her. "Inspector Rockwell wants to tap into your network."

Bessie shook her head. "I doubt that anyone I know actually knows anything useful," she told Hugh. "But I'm happy to help as much as I can. I quite like Inspector Rockwell."

"He's a good guy," Hugh said, a touch of surprise evident in his voice. "He seems to know what he's doing as well."

Bessie wondered if Hugh was contrasting Rockwell to Kelly, but didn't voice the question. Whatever Hugh thought of his competing bosses, he would be wise to keep it to himself.

Back at home, Bessie worked hard to find things to do to keep herself busy. She returned every phone message on her answering machine and rang a few other friends as well. If Inspector Rockwell wanted to hear all of the latest skeet, the least she could do was try to find out as much of it as she could. Luckily none of her friends had heard about the incident at the Laxey Mine yet, and she wasn't about to mention it. An hour later her head was full of marriage, divorce and baby news, but she had learned nothing of interest about the murder on her doorstep.

Keeping herself busy, she pulled two containers of her homemade spaghetti sauce from her freezer. Spaghetti Bolognese would be perfect for dinner for them all tonight. Although she was already tired from all of the walking she had done that day, she headed up the hill to the small shop at the top.

Catering to a small community that was increasingly ignoring it, the shop carried a little bit of just about everything. Bessie bought a few pounds of minced beef and an extra box of dried spaghetti noodles. She also added a freshly baked baguette, some butter and a bulb of garlic; a large bag of "mixed salad greens" finished off her selections.

Back at home, she cooked the mince and then added it to the sauce in a large pot. She left it simmering on the stove while she curled up with the book she had never managed to get back to the previous evening. Aside from an occasional break to stir the simmering sauce, she managed to put the very real victims that she had discovered out of her mind as she immersed herself in the fictional murder mystery.

She sighed as she turned over the last page. Everything was wrapped up neatly and the murderer was on his way to prison. She could only hope for a quick and easy resolution to the real life case as well. She stretched and then checked the time. It was past six and she was surprised that Doona hadn't appeared yet.

Her telephone message light was blinking frantically at her when she headed back into the kitchen. She'd forgotten to turn the ringer back on yet again. "You did that deliberately, so you could read without interruption," a little voice in her head said accusingly. Bessie ignored the voice and played through her latest messages.

It appeared that word had now leaked out about her discovery of the second body. Bessie didn't even bother to write down the caller's names this time; they were mostly the same people she had spoken to earlier in the day. She wasn't in the mood to ring anyone back right now and she had no doubt that they would ring again if they didn't hear from her.

There were only two messages that interested her. Doona had rung to say that she, Hugh and Inspector Rockwell would all be arriving around half-seven. She was to ring Doona back at the station before seven to let her know what sort of food they should bring. A quick call to the station to reassure Doona that she had their evening meal well in hand left Bessie with only one other call to return. Thoughtfully, she replayed the message that had been left.

"Oh, Bessie, oh darn, I hate these machines. Oh, it's, um, it's Bahey, Bahey Corlett. I'm still staying at Thie yn Traie, but I'm having lunch with my sister Joney tomorrow and I thought maybe you would like to join us? We could talk about old times and things. Ring me back?"

Bessie wrote down the number that Bahey had left, wondering exactly what "things" the other woman had in mind. There was no doubt that Bahey would have a lot of inside information about the Pierce family. How much of that she would be willing to share was another matter. There was only one way to find out.

She nearly changed her mind about lunch when she discovered that the sisters were meeting in Foxdale at Joney Kelly's house. It wasn't that she had anything against Foxdale; it was just a long journey and taxis were expensive. Bahey solved the problem by offering to pick Bessie up along the way.

"Mr. Pierce is going to have one of his staff take me in one of their cars," she explained. "I never learned to drive, either. We can easily pick you up. Mr. Pierce won't mind."

It was past seven when Bessie finally got off the phone with Bahey. She quickly filled her largest pot with water and put it on to boil. Then she mixed up garlic butter and spread it thickly over the baguette she had sliced open. By the time her guests arrived, she had lightly tossed the salad with some homemade dressing and had set the table for four.

Doona arrived first, and she gave Bessie a huge hug.

"Kys t'ou?" she asked.

"Ta mee braew," Bessie answered with a grin. "Actually, I'm not really fine, I'm quite upset, but I don't know how to say that in Manx."

The two friends laughed as Doona hugged her again.

"Was it awful?" Doona asked.

"It was pretty bad," Bessie shrugged. "I've been keeping myself really busy. I finished that book I had started and I did some shopping so I could cook for us all. As long as I'm busy, I don't have to think about it."

"Well, I brought a bottle of wine," Doona told her. "Make sure you have a few glasses to help you sleep."

Bessie shook her head. "You know I'm not much of a drinker. I'll have a glass with dinner, but I don't think it will help me sleep." She shuddered when she thought about trying to sleep tonight. Closing her eyes still brought back that same unwanted image. She looked at Doona and forced herself to smile. Doona looked far too worried about her, that wouldn't do.

"I'm fine," Bessie insisted. "It was just a shock, that's all. Some spaghetti and a good long talk with everyone will set me to rights."

Doona nodded slowly, doubt still evident in her eyes. She didn't get a chance to reply, however, as just then Hugh arrived. The women heard the car approaching and Bessie pulled the door open as he parked.

He was holding something awkwardly as he climbed out of his car. Bessie frowned, puzzled, as he juggled the oddly shaped parcel and his car keys as he walked to her door. It was too dark to work out exactly what he was holding.

At the door he stopped and then blushed and pulled the package from behind his back. It was a large bouquet of flowers. Bessie looked at him curiously.

"I, uh, well, that is," Hugh blushed even more brightly. "I thought that you'd had an awfully hard day," he struggled to explain. "I thought some flowers might brighten things up for you."

Bessie was touched beyond words. She took the flowers from Hugh and was annoyed to find tears in her eyes.

"Thank you so much," she managed to choke out before turning away and taking several deep breaths in an attempt to regain her composure. Doona came forward, chattering excitedly and filling in the uncomfortable silence.

"What a beautiful bouquet," she enthused. "Did you get it from that new flower shop in Lonan? I don't know how they expect to do any business out in the middle of nowhere like they are, but they sure do have beautiful flowers. Let me get them in a vase. Oh, and they've included a packet of cut flower food, very nice of them. I hope they last a good long time. The last time I got flowers from ShopFast they were brown and horrible in only a few days. But these are so lovely, I'm sure they will just last and last."

While she wittered on about nothing, she filled a vase with water, added the flower food and put the bouquet into it. Hugh finally stopped blushing once the flowers were safely settled into the middle of the kitchen table, and Bessie had managed to compose herself as well. She shot Doona a grateful look as she heard more tires crunch on the ground outside.

By the time she had the door open again, Inspector Rockwell was out of his car and heading towards the door. He had something in his hands as well, and Bessie could only hope that it wasn't more flowers. She definitely didn't want to cry in front of the inspector and it felt as if her emotions were somewhat close to the surface tonight.

"When Doona said you were cooking, I thought the least I could do was bring pudding," John Rockwell announced as Bessie showed him in. He handed Bessie the bakery box that he had been carrying. She said a polite thank you as Doona nearly snatched the box from her hands.

"Oooh, what lovely thing have you brought?" Doona cooed as she put the box down on the counter and peeked inside. "It looks choco-latey," she said excitedly as she turned back towards the others.

Bessie chuckled at her friend and then put the pasta into the now boiling water. The foursome ate their salad while the pasta cooked and then Bessie served up steaming plates of it, smothered in sauce, with the toasty hot garlic bread. While they ate, everyone seemed determined to keep the conversation away from the recent murders.

Instead, Inspector Rockwell entertained them all with funny stories from his days in police training and on the force in Manchester. It was only over pudding, a rich chocolate cake, that the conversation finally came around to what they had all come together to discuss.

"This is delicious," Bessie said as she dug into her cake.

"It's amazing," Doona moaned. "Where did it come from?"

Rockwell named a small bakery in the centre of Ramsey. "I had to go back into Ramsey to meet with Inspector Kelly and some others just before I came here, so I grabbed the cake while I was there," he explained.

"That's lots of running up and down the coast for you," Doona remarked.

"I don't mind," he told her. "I had a forty-five minute commute in Manchester and that was on a good day. Anyway, it was important to talk to Aunt Bessie again."

Bessie shook her head. "Inspector Kelly didn't seem to think so," she said.

"We have very different approaches to investigation," Rockwell replied mildly. "And we have different theories as to what happened."

"So what's your theory, Inspector?" Doona asked.

The man smiled at her. "While we're off-duty, I think you can all call me John," he said. "But just because we are off-duty doesn't mean I'm going to start talking out of turn. My theories are only that, theories, and while I can't prove anything, it would be irresponsible of me to discuss them."

"So what did you want to talk to me about?" Bessie asked.

"A couple of things," he told her. "Firstly, when you found Daniel Pierce's body, did you happen to see a mobile phone anywhere around? Maybe lying on the sand or sitting on a rock nearby?"

Bessie shook her head. "It wasn't exactly the brightest of mornings," she reminded the man, "but I didn't see anything like that. If there was one around, it would have been ruined in the wind and the rain, surely?"

"Possibly," Rockwell shrugged.

"Wouldn't he have kept his phone in his pocket?" Bessie asked.

"It's not his phone I'm interested in," Rockwell answered.

Bessie shuddered as she remembered the gruesome appearance that Samantha's face had taken on when lit only by the flickering bluish light of a mobile phone.

"Who was ringing Samantha?" she demanded. "I keep remembering that ringing phone and wondering who was ringing her."

"Donny Pierce," Hugh answered. "He was trying to reach both

Samantha and Vikky to tell them that it was time to head back to the cottage."

Bessie nodded. "I suppose that makes sense," she said slowly.

"Here's what doesn't necessarily make sense," Rockwell told her. "And I'm telling you this in total confidence. The phone that was with Samantha's body wasn't hers. No one seems to know where Samantha's phone is now."

"But if it wasn't her phone, how could Donny ring her?" Bessie asked, feeling confused. Then her eyes grew wide. "It was Vikky's phone?"

Rockwell nodded. "The phone found with the body was Vikky's. But Vikky claims that she gave it to Daniel on Sunday afternoon. His battery was running low and he needed to run to the store for something. Vikky lent him her phone and she claims she never got it back from him. Presumably it was still in his coat pocket when he went out for his walk on the beach later, but it wasn't found on or near the body."

Bessie shook her head. "I'm confused," she admitted.

"I think we all are," Hugh told her. "But it does tie the murders together."

Rockwell frowned. "Anyway, you didn't see anything on the beach when you found Daniel. I'm assuming you only saw the one phone when you found Samantha?"

Bessie closed her eyes and tried to remember exactly what she had seen. "It was so dark. The only light came from the phone." She shook her head. "I only saw the one phone," she said finally.

"As expected," Rockwell told her.

"Was there anything else?" Bessie asked, hoping the answer would be no.

"I've been over your statement several times, comparing it with the one that Donny Pierce gave us," the Inspector replied.

"I should hope that they agree," Bessie said sharply.

"For the most part," the man answered. "He gave us far less detail about your conversation and, when pressed, claims he doesn't remember exactly what you two talked about."

Bessie opened her mouth to argue, but Rockwell held up a hand. "I'm happy to believe your account of the conversation," he told Bessie. "At any rate, you both agree that he mentioned that his brother had a drug problem and that he felt the murder had something to do with a drug deal gone bad. That's the line of inquiry that Inspector Kelly is pursuing."

Bessie nodded. "I suppose that was the most important part of the conversation I had with the man," she said.

"The question becomes, therefore, what did a drug deal gone bad have to do with Samantha Blake?" Rockwell asked.

"I didn't even remember her last name," Bessie said sadly. "Did Donny have any suggestions about it?"

"If he did, he didn't share them with me," Rockwell answered. "Inspector Kelly is looking into how well Samantha and Daniel knew each other. He's thinking that she might have been his connection to a supplier or something." The man shook his head. "I can see why Donny Pierce is such a fan of the theory. Anything that shifts suspicion from his family has to appeal, but I can't see why Inspector Kelly is so convinced."

"Kelly sees drugs under every rock on the island," Hugh told them all. "I heard a rumour that one of his kids got caught with something and now he's decided that the island is overrun with drugs. He takes every opportunity to pursue every possible lead in any investigation that could possibly have any connections to drugs."

Rockwell held up a hand. "I shouldn't have made that last remark. It was unprofessional and out of character," he told them all. "We shouldn't speculate about Inspector Kelly or his investigation. Let's focus on our own investigation instead of worrying about anything else."

Doona grinned. "Don't worry, boss, none of us is going to repeat anything said here. We don't gossip when we shouldn't."

The man smiled back at her. "I certainly hope that Aunt Bessie gossips now and again. I'm counting on her to fill me in on what's really going on around here. I'm just hoping she won't be talking about me when she's talking about the murders."

Bessie was quick to reassure the man. She had no intention of doing or saying anything that might get him into trouble.

"So, what we really need is inside information about the Pierce family," Rockwell said eventually. "Any idea how we can get it?"

"I know exactly how to get it," Bessie answered. She told him about Bahey and her years with the Pierce family. "We're having lunch together tomorrow," she told him. "I'm sure I'll know a lot more after that."

"I don't think anyone has interviewed the woman," Rockwell said with a frown. "Perhaps we should have, but she wasn't in Laxey when the first murder took place. Someone should have talked to her for background information, though."

"I took her statement this afternoon, after Samantha's body was discovered," Hugh told his boss. "She was at the house all day, mostly sitting with Mrs. Pierce. The security folks were able to alibi both Bahey and Mrs. Pierce for the day. There's no way they had anything to do with Samantha's death."

"What about Mr. Pierce?" Doona demanded.

"He left the house around the same time as his son and the two women," Hugh answered. "He told Bahey he needed some fresh air. He took the keys to one of the family's cars with him. In his statement originally, he claimed that he was home all day, but when challenged, he admitted to going out for a short time. He claims he went for a drive along the coast road and back. Unfortunately, there are no witnesses."

"And now we're teetering on the brink of talking too much about things that should be confidential," Inspector Rockwell broke in. "I'm sorry to say that this isn't really a two-way street," he told Bessie. "I'm hoping you will gather information for me, but I can't offer you much, if anything, in return."

"I'm not interested in hearing the latest skeet on the murders," Bessie replied. "I just want to see the murderer behind bars."

"Don't we all?" Doona said emphatically.

"While we're talking about alibis," Bessie said slowly. "Does anyone at Thie yn Traie have one for the first murder?"

Inspector Rockwell shook his head. "Tomorrow's paper will cover the fact that the coroner's office is having a hard time determining even an approximate time of death," he told them all. "With the wild weather and the tides coming in and out, all they can offer is a fairly broad window from around nine Sunday evening, which is when the Pierce family agrees that Danny left the house, until three or four the next morning. He was dead at least three to four hours before you found the body. No one at Thie yn Traie is able to provide a water-tight alibi for that entire stretch."

"No pun intended," Doona suggested.

Rockwell smiled. "Indeed, no pun intended."

The dinner party broke up soon after that, with everyone agreeing to meet again the following evening to discuss whatever Bessie could learn from Bahey. Inspector Rockwell walked Doona to her car. Hugh was kind enough to help Bessie with the dirty dishes, gobbling up the rest of the cake as his compensation once they'd finished.

"I'll just say good night, then," Bessie told the man as she finished tidying up from his second pudding.

"I hope you'll sleep well," Hugh told her, giving her another hug. "Try to think about happy things."

Bessie nodded and headed for the stairs. She was surprised at how kind and understanding young Hugh was turning out to be. Perhaps Doona was right to think so highly of him.

In bed, she tossed and turned for a while, struggling to find a comfortable position while she listened to Hugh as he got ready for bed. When the last light was finally switched off downstairs, she had nearly given up and climbed back out of bed. Now, unwilling to disturb her guest, Bessie burrowed down under the covers and tried to force herself to sleep. Tomorrow was going to be a busy day and she needed to be well rested if she was going to find out anything useful for the investigation.

For once her sleep was restless and disturbed, and more than once Bessie considered getting up and reading instead of lying in bed feeling wide-awake. Her new books were all in the sitting room, where Hugh was snoring loudly on the couch. She wondered, briefly, how likely he was to actually wake up if she walked down to get one. She had plenty of other books in the office next door to her bedroom, of course, but nothing appealed to her overtired and overwrought brain. She felt like she had been pummelling her pillow all night as she flipped it around and around, trying to make it comfortable enough to tempt her into sleep. Finally, the clock rolled around to six and she felt like she could get out of bed.

# CHAPTER 8

*T*hursday morning was clear and noticeably warmer. Bessie smiled, in spite of her tiredness, as she looked out her bedroom window. For the first time in ages, she might actually enjoy her morning walk. After a quick shower, she dressed and went down for some breakfast. Hugh was still snoring loudly and she wondered just how much noise pollution the young policeman was causing.

After tea and toast she headed out for a short walk before Hugh was even awake. This time she walked towards the police crime scene tape, stopping just short of it. She frowned as she studied the scene in the dimly lit dawn. With the fluctuating tides of the last several days it was impossible to tell exactly where Daniel Pierce's body had been. Any evidence that had been missed was, no doubt, long gone as well. Bessie breathed in deeply, pulling fresh salty air into her lungs. In spite of everything that had happened this week, she still loved the island.

With Hugh up and fed and off to work, Bessie tidied her cottage and then spent the rest of the morning working on her research paper. She hadn't done anywhere near as much as she would have liked over the last few days. Bahey was picking her up at half-eleven, so at eleven she shut her computer off and stretched.

"I'm getting old," she sighed to herself as an entire range of muscles complained when she got to her feet. In her bedroom she changed into black trousers and a lightweight lilac-coloured sweater. Her hair needed a quick brushing after that and she even took the time to add a touch of colour to her cheeks and lips.

"Not so old that you still don't look good," she grinned at herself in the mirror. She gathered up her handbag and checked that her mobile was charged. Until the murderer was safely behind bars, she didn't want to take any chances.

On the dot of eleven-thirty a fancy black car pulled up outside Bessie's cottage. As Bessie opened her door, Bahey rolled her window down and shouted to her.

"Hello, Aunt Bessie, hop in."

Bessie locked up her cottage. When she turned around, the car's driver had climbed out and he was now holding the car door open for her. She flushed as she slid past him into the car. Such fancy treatment wasn't what she was used to. There had been a time, many years ago, when taxi drivers sometimes afforded the same courtesy, but the practice seemed to have died out. Some days Bessie felt as if her taxi driver thought he was doing her a favour by simply slowing down when she was ready to get out.

The luxury car slid smoothly along the road as Bahey fussed over her. "Fancy you finding two dead bodies," she prattled. "I mean, finding Danny must have been awful, but then to go and find Miss Samantha as well? I can't imagine what that must have been like."

When she paused for a breath, Bessie just murmured a vague reply. She was happy for Bahey to keep talking, no matter what the subject. Something interesting might just come of it.

"Not that I was a huge fan of Miss Samantha," Bahey continued. "But she was much better than that Vikky person, anyway. Honestly, those boys were raised well, but neither one of them has any sense at all when it comes to women. Daniel chased after everything in a skirt. I was amazed when he actually got married to one of his 'girls,' and Donny, well, don't even get me started on Donny."

Bessie smiled to herself. This was going to be an interesting afternoon.

Bahey took a deep breath and then launched herself into a long and rambling story about how she had come to work for the Pierce family in the first place. The story filled the rest of the drive to Foxdale. While it was somewhat interesting, Bessie wasn't especially interested in hearing it. Over lunch she would have to make sure to get Bahey talking about the murders again. It was probably best to have that conversation somewhere that the Pierces' driver couldn't overhear, anyway.

Joney Kelly's husband had passed away many years earlier and her son had moved off-island. That was the explanation that Bahey gave for the rundown state of the house where she and Bessie were dropped off.

"She just doesn't have the energy to keep the place up like she should," Bahey tutted. "And she doesn't have the money to get a man around to take care of things either. That husband of hers left her just enough to make ends meet, but not a penny more." Bahey sighed. "And that son of hers doesn't visit often enough to see what she needs."

"Maybe you should get her to move to Douglas with you," Bessie suggested tentatively.

"Ha, that'll never happen." The woman who had opened the door to Bahey's knock glared out at Bessie. "Move to Douglas? Why on earth would I want to do that?"

Bessie smiled at Joney, hoping to disguise her surprise at the other woman's appearance. Joney had been "the pretty one" in the family, but the years had not been kind to her. She now looked substantially older than her younger sister and, Bessie flattered herself, even older than Bessie herself. Of course there were only about seven years between them, but Bessie fancied that she looked much better than the thin and pale woman who stood in the doorway.

"Will you be moving into Douglas some time soon, then?" Joney demanded of Bessie.

Bessie laughed. "Of course not, I'm staying in my home until the last, and I imagine you are, too."

Joney nodded emphatically. "They're going to have to carry me out of here," she told her. "This was home from the time I was twenty-five and I don't intend to be moving out of it now I'm a bit older."

"A lot older," Bahey snorted. "And I'm happy for you to stay here. I just wish your William would help you out a bit with the expenses. The house needs a good coat of paint, inside and out; the garden is overgrown and…."

"Yes, yes, yes," Joney interrupted her sister. "If you're done complaining about my home, maybe you want to come in and have lunch? If you can stand the idea of spending time in my falling-down wreck, that is."

Bahey laughed. "I'll try to stand it for today," she said in a teasing tone, "but next time lunch is at my place."

Joney made a face behind her sister's back as she stepped aside to let the other women into the house. "At your fancy condo-minimum, huh, where everything is all slick and shiny and new? I suppose I could just about have lunch there one day."

Bessie smiled at the pair and their good-natured bickering. She felt a small sadness as she thought about her own sister, whom she had last seen when she was only a teenager. Katherine had stayed in America when Bessie and her parents returned to the island. She had chosen to marry the man she loved and remain with him. She and Bessie exchanged frequent letters over the years until Katherine's death, but spending time with Bahey and Joney reminded Bessie of what she'd missed by not having her sister around.

She shook her head to clear the thought from her mind. Everyone had to make his or her own choices in life. Katherine had made hers and, by all accounts, she had lived happily with her husband, eventually raising ten children with him. Bessie had taken a different path, and while she sometimes indulged in a bit of "what if" with herself, she never regretted any of her decisions.

"What must you think of us?" Bahey now said to Bessie. "We don't always argue, just usually."

Bessie just grinned and then stepped into the house. Bahey was right; it did need a coat of paint. The formal sitting room that the entryway opened into also needed dusting and a good run through with a vacuum cleaner. Bessie wrinkled her nose as she inhaled a good portion of dust with her first breath. The house smelled musty and damp and Bessie wondered how often Joney's son did visit. Surely, if he had been there recently, he must have noticed that his mother was no longer keeping the house as she should.

"Please pardon the dust," Joney announced. "I don't use this room often, so I don't clean it as much as I should." She looked around the room, her face surprised as if she, too, were seeing it for the first time. "Well, my goodness, it has managed to get itself into a state, hasn't it?" she sighed. "I suppose I should have taken the time to clean it yesterday."

"It might have been nice," Bahey told her. "I assume you managed to clean the kitchen, at least?"

Joney laughed. "The kitchen is as spotless as ever," she answered. The remark worried Bessie. Just how spotless did the woman usually keep her kitchen, she wondered.

She needn't have worried, however. While the kitchen wasn't exactly spotless, it was clean and tidy. Joney ushered the other two women into the spacious kitchen that took up the entire back of the house.

"We remodelled everything about ten years ago, just before my husband passed on," Joney told Bessie. "This was a small kitchen and a small dining room, so we knocked them together and put the new kitchen in. Then we tacked on the little conservatory."

Bessie followed her through an open sliding door into the glass-walled room that jutted out into the garden. It was small, but it was cosy, clean and comfortably furnished with overstuffed couches.

"Have a seat," Joney offered. "I've a lasagne in the oven; it won't be long now."

Bessie sat down tentatively on one of the couches and then smiled and slid back into the seat. It was at least twice as comfortable as it looked.

It wasn't long. Bessie was loath to give up her seat in the sunny conservatory only a few moments after she had sat down. The delicious smells that filtered in from the kitchen, however, had her quickly changing her mind.

"I hope everyone likes red wine," Joney said, as she poured some into glasses that were already in place around the small kitchen table.

"Sounds good to me," Bessie answered. Bahey looked at the bottle's label and frowned, but she didn't complain. Joney caught the look and smiled at her sister.

"Sorry sis, I'm sure you're used to much nicer stuff at the Pierces', but this is what I can afford."

Bahey took a sip and smiled at her sister. "Actually, it isn't bad," she admitted. "It's not a brand I've heard of, but it tastes okay."

Joney laughed. "I just buy whatever's on offer at ShopFast," she told them. "This was last week's special purchase. If you bought two bottles, you got a third one free. I thought if it was horrible I could just cook with it."

The conversation over lunch wandered through the threesome's shared past and then into each woman's individual life story. Bessie heard all about Joney's long teaching career and her wonderful son who was something important in London. She was more interested in hearing about Bahey's life with the Pierce family, but those stories revealed nothing she thought was relevant to the murders. After sharing a few stories from her own past, Bessie decided that it was time to shift the conversation back to what she really wanted to discuss.

"I'm sure Mr. and Mrs. Pierce must be ever so pleased that you're there for them in their time of need," she said to Bahey as Joney passed around profiteroles and chocolate sauce.

"Well," Bahey said slowly, "I suppose they are." She shrugged. "It's hard to tell what they're thinking. I think they're just so upset that they aren't really thinking at all."

"Well, at least Donny must be happy to have you around," Bessie persisted. "Especially now that he's lost Samantha."

Bahey snorted. "Ha, I can't say he's all that broken up about that," she replied. "More like now he has plenty of room to move in on our Miss Vikky."

Bessie tried to look as shocked as Joney did. "He wouldn't chase after his own brother's widow, would he?" Joney asked.

"He's chasing, all right," Bahey answered grimly. "And she isn't exactly trying to run away, if you know what I mean."

Bessie shook her head. "I thought she was really devastated by her husband's death," she said sadly.

"She's just looking out for number one," Bahey told her.

"What I don't understand," Joney chimed in, "is why she's acting so posh and snobby. She's a Foxdale girl, after all."

"She is?" Bessie gasped.

Joney and Bahey both nodded. "I thought I recognised her when I first got to the house, so I took a few photos to show to Joney," Bahey told Bessie.

"I recognised her right away," Joney picked up the story. "She was born and raised right here. I even had her in my class when she was about seven or eight. She was always looking for the easy way out, even back then," Joney said in a disgusted voice.

Bessie frowned. "Well, she certainly acted like she'd never been on the island before when I met her."

"The family moved to Liverpool before she hit her teens," Joney told her. "I suppose she might not really remember much about the island."

"And she was awfully upset, that first time I saw her," Bessie added.

"Yeah, because her meal ticket had just run out," Bahey said caustically.

"Bahey!" Joney said sharply. "I know you don't like the woman, but give her credit for some feeling. She'd just found her husband's body, after all."

"Unless she was the one who stabbed him. If she was, then she'd just rediscovered her husband's body," Bahey countered.

"Surely if they got into a fight, the man was strong enough to get the knife away from her?" Bessie asked.

"If they were fighting," Bahey answered. "But what if they were having a nice romantic stroll and then she just snuggled up to him and shoved the knife in?"

Bessie shuddered. "I suppose that could have happened," she said.

"Besides, I overheard Inspector Kelly telling Mr. Pierce that his son was pretty heavily drugged when he died. The Inspector seemed to be suggesting that anyone could have killed him; Daniel was barely conscious and certainly not in any state to fight back."

Bessie drew a sharp breath. That was something she definitely hadn't known. No wonder Inspector Kelly was so focussed on the drug angle.

"Did he take drugs often?" she asked.

"Not when I was living with them," Bahey replied. "Neither of my boys was dumb enough to get mixed up with anything like that while I was around. But I can't say as I know what's happened since I left."

"So the murder could have been related to drugs?" Joney asked.

"I suppose," Bahey shrugged. "But I still think they should start by looking close to home."

"And the widow is your favourite suspect for the murders?" Bessie asked her friend.

"Either the widow, or...." Bahey paused and then looked around furtively. After a long and, to Bessie, overly dramatic pause, she continued. "I do wonder a bit about Donny's wife."

"Donny's wife?" Bessie said questioningly. "He wasn't married to Samantha, was he?"

"No," Bahey said excitedly. "He couldn't marry Samantha, even if he'd wanted to, and he can't marry Miss Vikky, either. He's already got a wife."

"What you are going on about?" Joney asked.

"Donny is already married," Bahey repeated herself. "He got married here, on the island, about two days after his eighteenth birthday."

Bessie frowned. Now that Bahey mentioned it, she had a very vague recollection of some sort of rumours from back then about the Pierce family.

"He eloped with the oldest Kelly girl," Bahey reminded Bessie. "She was nineteen and already had a reputation for being, um, fast."

"The oldest Kelly girl?" Bessie was putting two and two together quickly. "That would be Inspector Patrick Kelly's older sister?"

"That's the one," Bahey nodded, glancing around again as if she was worried someone would overhear her.

Her sister laughed. "We're all alone in my house," she teased. "Who are you looking for?"

Bahey frowned. "I really shouldn't be talking out of turn," she said slowly. "Mr. and Mrs. Pierce would probably never forgive me for talking about them like this."

"But they'll never know," Bessie soothed. "And you can't stop now. You have to tell me what happened to Maeve Kelly."

"That was her name," Bahey beamed at Bessie. "You are so much better at remembering things than I am. I had forgotten her Christian name. Of course, it was never, ever, to be said in the Pierce household, so maybe that isn't surprising."

"Finish the story," Joney demanded, pouring the last of the wine into their glasses.

Bahey flushed. "Well, the pair ran off and got married in Port Erin, I think it was. Mr. Pierce and young Daniel went after them, and when they caught up with them at some cheap bed and breakfast down there, they brought Donny to their London townhouse and left Maeve there. No one ever talks about it."

"What happened to Maeve, then? Are you sure they're still married? There must be more to tell." Bessie threw out questions as her thoughts tumbled over themselves. Bahey had to know more.

"Well," Bahey said slowly, "I was something of a confidante of young Donny back then," she told the others. "He told me that he made his father set up a trust fund for Maeve so that she was 'looked after.' He also told me that he wasn't ever planning to divorce her. He was hoping, at least then, that when his father died, he could win her back. Of course, that was nearly twenty years ago; he may well have changed his mind."

"And divorced her," Joney added.

"Oh no, I know they aren't divorced. Maeve rang right after Danny was killed and wanted to talk to Donny. I, um, overheard a bit of the conversation, and Maeve made it clear that they were still legally married. From what I heard, neither of them ever felt the need to make their split legal, although Maeve is clearly the chief beneficiary of their staying together."

"If Donny had been the one who died, I could see Maeve being a suspect," Bessie said slowly. "She must have some right to make a claim towards his estate if she's been his legal wife all these years. But she couldn't possibly have had any claim on Daniel's fortune. Why would she kill him?"

"Well," Bahey answered. "From what I, um, accidentally over-heard...." she paused, blushing, but Bessie simply smiled at her encouragingly. "I mean, there could be lots of reasons. All I know for sure is that she's definitely on the island, even though when I talked to her mother recently she said Maeve hasn't visited her for years. I actually saw Maeve in Douglas last week when I was shopping. She ignored me, but I'm sure it was her."

"I still don't see any clear motive," Bessie answered after a moment's thought.

"What if she thought she was killing old man Pierce instead of young Daniel?" Joney suggested. "Or maybe she's planning to kill Donny as well but she wanted to make sure Donny inherited all of Daniel's money first. Or...."

Bahey held up a hand. "That's enough melodramatic plotting," she said. "I just think it's interesting that Donny's wife is on the island but nobody seems to have questioned her."

"Perhaps Inspector Kelly questioned his sister himself," Bessie suggested.

"Whatever happened with Daniel, she certainly had a motive for killing Samantha," Bahey added.

"Why?" Bessie asked. "Was Donny getting serious about Samantha?"

"I doubt it," Bahey replied. "But Maeve may not have known that."

"Anyway, she had more motive for killing Samantha than she did for killing Daniel," Bahey continued.

"I don't think she had any motive for killing either of them," Joney interjected. "I still think it was that Vikky that did it."

"So neither of you believes it was drug-related?" Bessie asked.

Bahey shook her head. "I can't see the Daniel I knew getting mixed up in something like that," she told Bessie.

"People do change," Joney said with a sigh.

"You were surprised that he got married," Bessie added. "Perhaps he'd changed more than you realised."

Bahey shrugged. "I don't know. You may be right," she told her. "The whole family seems to have changed in the last three years. Mr. Pierce is drinking all the time. Mrs. Pierce is keeping herself medicated to the eyeballs. Daniel married that gold-digging hussy. Now Donny barely speaks to anyone other than his dead brother's wife."

She sighed deeply. "I'm sorry now that I offered to help out. They all insist they want me there, but no one seems to know what I should be doing."

"So leave," Joney suggested. "You have a life of your own now. You're not dependent on them like you were all those years. Tell them you're going back to your own life."

"It isn't that easy," Bahey sighed. "I don't want to leave them until Daniel and Samantha's killer is behind bars. Leaving them in the middle of this crisis feels wrong. They were like family to me for so many years."

"Are you sure the same person killed them both?" Bessie asked another question that occurred to her.

"I don't know," Bahey's head sank into her hands. "I can't work out any motive for anyone to kill either of them, let alone both of them."

"Well, I certainly hope the same person killed them both," Joney said stoutly. "One murderer running around on the island is more than enough!"

Bessie nodded her agreement and then changed the subject. Bahey looked exhausted and upset and Bessie didn't feel as if she should push her any further. The afternoon had already given Bessie lots to talk about with Inspector Rockwell and the others later.

A short time later Bessie glanced at her watch and was amazed to see that it was nearly five o'clock. The afternoon had flown past.

"What time did you say you had to be back by?" she gently reminded Bahey.

"Oh. good heavens," Bahey exclaimed. "I told Mr. Pierce that we would have his car and driver back by five. I'd better ring the driver. Hopefully, we won't be too late."

Moments later the fancy black car was back and Bessie and Bahey wasted little time with goodbyes.

"Thank you for a lovely afternoon," Bessie called to Joney as she climbed into the car. "We must do it again soon."

"Yes, I'd like that," Joney answered.

Then they were on their way, sweeping out of Foxdale and heading towards Laxey before Bessie could collect her thoughts.

"That was very nice," Bahey said, as the pair settled in for the twenty-minute journey.

"It was lovely," Bessie replied. "Your sister's home is very nice and she's a wonderful cook."

"Next time you'll have to come to my flat," Bahey told her. "I'm a pretty good cook too and I buy better wine."

Bessie laughed. "I'm sure I won't be able to tell the difference," she said, "but I hope we can do it again soon."

The pair lapsed into silence for a short while, each lost in their own thoughts.

"Bessie?" Bahey broke the silence.

"Yes?"

"I'm really worried about Mrs. Pierce. She seems so upset about Daniel's death, but she seemed weirdly pleased when the police told her that Samantha had been killed. I know she didn't like the woman. She's never liked anyone her sons have brought home. But she seemed, well, off somehow."

"You said the doctor is keeping her medicated," Bessie said soothingly. "She's probably just a little bit out of touch with reality, that's all."

"I don't know," Bahey said doubtfully. "She told the police she was home all day yesterday, but I know she went out for a little while. I didn't see her leave, but I saw her when she was coming back in. She said she'd just gone for a little walk, but she was all windblown and wet as if she'd walked a long way or something."

Bessie was silent as she thought about the "something" that Mrs. Pierce might have been doing.

"She wouldn't have killed her son," Bahey said. "But if she thought Samantha had something to do with his death..." she trailed off, looking at Bessie with an anguished expression.

Bessie patted her hand, trying to reassure her friend. "Look," she said finally, "Hugh is staying with me at the moment. Why don't I mention all of this to him, and he can work it all out?"

Bessie wasn't sure why, but she didn't feel like mentioning that she would also be talking to Inspector Rockwell about everything she had learned that afternoon. Perhaps that was because Bahey knew Hugh. She expected that the other woman would feel more comfortable with the idea of Bessie talking to someone she knew, rather than to the inspector from "across."

Bahey sighed. "I don't want to get Mrs. Pierce into any trouble," she told Bessie. "But I do think her behaviour has been rather odd since Danny died."

Bessie nodded. "I'll talk to Hugh tonight," she promised.

The few minutes that were left in the journey passed silently. Back at her cottage, Bessie was quick to thank both Bahey and the driver before they headed back to Thie yn Traie.

Inside her little home, Bessie checked her answering machine. She listened to the ten messages, most of which she immediately deleted. The few that mattered were quickly dealt with, including a call to Doona to confirm the plans for later.

Apparently Inspector Rockwell was bringing dinner and pudding tonight. Doona told Bessie to expect them all around seven. Remembering the dust and disorder at Joney's house, Bessie spent a few minutes tidying her kitchen before sinking into a comfortable chair with another book from her latest shipment. Time flew past as she lost herself in the pages and before she knew it the doorbell was ringing.

# CHAPTER 9

"I brought Indian food," Inspector Rockwell announced as Bessie showed him and the others in. "I got a bunch of different things, so hopefully there will be something here that everyone likes."

Bessie pulled out plates as the inspector began to pull box after box of food from the bags he had brought in with him.

"Did you invite the rest of the constabulary to join us?" Doona joked as Rockwell ran out of counter space with two bags still unopened.

"Just pile the rest on the table," Bessie suggested. "We can fill our plates and then move the boxes."

Hugh's eyes lit up when he saw the generous spread. "Wow, I've only tried about half of these before. This is great."

Rockwell frowned at the man. "Just remember that this meeting is totally off the record," he told him sternly. "If word gets out at the station that I'm buying dinner for certain members of my staff after hours, I could find myself in trouble."

"Why don't Hugh and I contribute towards the meal?" Doona offered. "Surely there's nothing wrong with us all going in together to get some food after a long day's work?"

Rockwell hesitated and then nodded. "I didn't mean for you guys to chip in, but it might make things less complicated if you paid for part of it."

Doona and Hugh were both quick to offer some cash to the inspector, who pocketed it with obvious reluctance.

"Shall I contribute as well?" Bessie asked.

"Doona's more than paid for your share," Rockwell answered with a grin. "You can take that up with her."

Bessie smiled at her friend, who quickly waved away any notion of Bessie giving her money. When plates were filled, Bessie and Hugh moved the now nearly empty boxes from the table and the foursome sat down to eat.

"Did this come from the new Indian place in Laxey?" Bessie asked.

"Yes," Rockwell answered. "I thought it would be best to get dinner from somewhere close by so it would be good and hot when I got here. No one I talked to knew anything about the place, though, so I wasn't sure what we would be getting."

"They've only been open a few weeks," Doona told him. "I had lunch there last week one day and it was pretty good. So far everything I've tried tonight has been excellent."

"It's really great," Hugh agreed, talking around a mouthful of food.

"Don't talk with your mouth full," Bessie told Hugh, almost without thought. Manners these days were so neglected.

"Sorry," Hugh answered, ducking his head when he realised that his mouth was still full.

Doona choked back a laugh as Bessie rolled her eyes. In spite of the huge amount of food on offer, it was only a short time before all of the boxes were emptied and only scraps remained on plates. Hugh had done most of the work, eating as if he hadn't seen food in weeks, but Bessie had found that in spite of her large lunch she was starving.

"My hands were so full that I had to leave pudding in the car," Inspector Rockwell told them as he rose to his feet. "I'll just go and collect it."

While he was gone Doona and Hugh cleared the table. Doona

made Hugh start on washing up the dishes while she dug out clean plates for pudding.

"I'm not an invalid," Bessie had protested as Doona waved her back into her seat.

"But you have opened up your home to us for three nights in a row," Doona answered. "The least we can do is a bit of washing up."

The inspector had brought apple pie and custard for pudding, and Bessie dug in with an enthusiasm that surprised her. She shouldn't have been hungry after everything she had eaten earlier. Perhaps all the unaccustomed excitement was making her body crave food. She wasn't the only one who enjoyed the pie. Hugh stopped just short of licking his plate as he finished not one, but two slices of pie, both topped with generous dollops of custard.

"Right," Inspector Rockwell smiled as Bessie served everyone tea. "That was very nice, but now I'm afraid we have to get down to business. I'm really hoping that you found out something interesting at lunch today," he told Bessie.

"I found out several things that I found interesting," she answered. "Let's see what you think."

"Don't tease," Doona urged her friend.

Bessie smiled. "So first of all," she began, "did you know that Donny is married?"

Doona's jaw dropped and she gasped. "Not to Samantha?" she asked.

"No," Inspector Rockwell supplied the answer. "He's actually married to Inspector Kelly's sister."

Now it was Hugh's turn to gasp. "How come I didn't know that?" he demanded.

Rockwell frowned. "Inspector Kelly isn't exactly bragging about it," he told the others. "He told me about the connection when we found Daniel Pierce's body, but as it seemed highly unlikely that his sister had anything to do with the murder, he remained on the case."

"Why is it 'highly unlikely' that she's involved?" Doona demanded.

"She moved off the island only a few years after the wedding and hasn't been back since," Rockwell answered.

"Bahey saw her last week in Douglas," Bessie informed him.

Rockwell frowned. "Is she sure about that?" he demanded tensely.

"She said that Maeve ignored her, so I suppose it might not have been her, just someone who looks like her, but I think it's something that needs looking into," Bessie answered.

"Oh, definitely," Rockwell answered, writing furiously in his small notebook. "And soon."

"What else did you learn?" Doona asked excitedly.

"Bahey doesn't believe that Daniel was taking drugs," Bessie shrugged. "But she hadn't seen him in three years, and people change."

"We're checking very carefully into the man's recent past," Rockwell informed her. "If he had developed a drug habit, we should be able to find traces of it. At the moment all we have to go on is what Donny told us."

"What did Vikky say when you asked her about it?" Bessie asked.

"You know I can't repeat what was said in interviews," Rockwell answered. "Let's just say that, no matter what she said, we're taking the allegations very seriously."

"The only other interesting thing from this afternoon is that Bahey is worried about Mrs. Pierce," Bessie told them all.

"Worried, why?" Hugh asked.

"She's upset and acting out of character," Bessie answered. "I understand she went out for a walk yesterday and when the police questioned her, she said she'd been in the house all day. Things like that."

Rockwell flipped back through his notebook, checking something. "I'll have to have another little talk with Mrs. Pierce, I think," he said, almost under his breath.

"She couldn't possibly have killed her own son," Bessie said firmly. "I saw how devastated she was after he died."

"We can't rule anyone out based on how you feel, Aunt Bessie." Rockwell's smile softened the words. "Anyway, it's always possible that we're dealing with two different murderers."

Doona gasped again. "Like I wasn't having enough trouble sleeping when I thought there was one running around?"

Rockwell patted her hand. "We do think the same person killed them both, but we can't be sure," he told her. "I'm trying to keep an open mind about every possibility."

"Maybe Samantha killed Daniel and then Mrs. Pierce killed Samantha," Hugh suggested.

Rockwell held up a hand. "We could start speculating now and be here all night coming up with increasingly crazy solutions. I would rather gather evidence and testimony before I start trying to assign labels to the players."

Bessie grinned. While she really agreed with the Inspector, it was sort of fun throwing out all of the different ideas that were bouncing around and seeing how they sounded. It was almost like trying to solve the murder in one of her books before the detective managed it.

"What about alibis?" Bessie asked. "I know we talked about them before, but surely some of the suspects must have alibis for one or the other murder?"

Rockwell shook his head. "The Chief Constable gave an interview today with the local press. He told them that, actually, no one in the family has an unbreakable alibi for the first murder. We had ruled Mrs. Pierce out for Samantha's death, but now, based on what Bahey told Bessie, that might be questionable."

"So none of them can be ruled out for either murder?" Bessie questioned.

"Not really. Mr. and Mrs. Pierce have alibied each other for the first murder, but we don't usually put much faith in spouses supporting one another. There wasn't any staff staying in the house before Daniel was killed, and from what I've heard everyone else was up and down and all over the place during the night that Daniel died. Add to that the fact that everyone was asleep for at least some of the relevant period and wouldn't necessarily have noticed where anyone else was and it all adds up to no alibis."

"Vikky said that she and Daniel had a fight," Bessie said. "She told me that he had taken off somewhere."

"Theirs wasn't the only fight," Rockwell remarked.

"You'd think, with all that money, that they would be happy," Doona sighed.

"Money attracts its own troubles," Bessie told her friend.

"I suppose I should stick to poor but happy," Doona laughed.

"Surely there's a much smaller time frame for the second murder?" Bessie asked.

"Much smaller," Rockwell agreed. "But that doesn't mean that anyone can prove they didn't do it. Vikky and Donny are obvious suspects; we know that they were there, but Mr. Pierce was out for a drive and could have stopped anywhere. As I said, we thought Mrs. Pierce was accounted for, but perhaps not. Even most of the staff at the house seems to have been in and out for much of the afternoon, although none of them appear to have any motive for killing either of the victims, at least not at this point. Unfortunately, Thie yn Traie is close enough to the Laxey Wheel that someone could have driven over, killed Samantha and returned almost without their absence being noticed."

"Bahey doesn't drive," Bessie told the inspector.

"And she's the only staff member who the security team has said was definitely in the house all day. Of course, they said the same about Mrs. Pierce, so now I've got to consider that they were lying or weren't keeping track of people as carefully as they claim."

"Oh, I almost forgot," Bessie remembered. "Did you know that Vikky grew up in Foxdale?"

The Inspector tilted his head and Bessie could almost see him searching through his memories. After a moment he flipped through his notebook, examining several pages carefully.

"Well, now," he said eventually, "that seems to be something that must have slipped her mind when we spoke."

"I think they moved when she was still pretty young," Bessie told him. "Maybe she didn't think it was relevant."

"It's relevant," Rockwell answered. "And it might even be important."

"So what do we do now?" Bessie asked after a sip of tea.

"'We' don't do anything," Rockwell answered. "This investigation is police work. I appreciate everything you've done so far, but now the Isle of Man Constabulary need to do their job and solve these murders."

"I assume you don't have any objection to my visiting Thie yn Traie again?" Bessie asked. "I really should pay my respects for Samantha."

Rockwell frowned. "I don't think that's a good idea," he told Bessie. "Two people in that house have been murdered in the last week. I would think it would be best to stay well clear of it."

Bessie thought for a moment before she answered. "I understand what you're saying," she told the inspector. "But I really feel as if I should pay my respects. Besides, I might be able to find out more about Maeve and Donny and Vikky's past there. And I can see how Mrs. Pierce is really doing. I'm sure they'll tell me things they would never tell you."

The inspector shook his head. "It might be dangerous," he told Bessie. "Going to pay your respects is one thing, but going to snoop is another. And I'm not comfortable with you doing either at this point."

Bessie smiled at him. "What if I promise not to snoop?" she asked. "I'll just go and do the polite thing and then leave. At least I might get to see Mrs. Pierce and get an idea of how she's doing."

Rockwell sighed. "I can't stop you, of course," he said slowly. "And it might be helpful if you can see Mrs. Pierce. When I went to see her after Samantha's body was found, her doctor wouldn't allow me to speak to her for more than a few moments. Of course, that was when we were told she had an alibi."

"Well, I'm glad that's settled then," Bessie told him. "Tomorrow morning I'll walk over and have another little chat with Mr. and Mrs. Pierce and whoever else is at home."

"And tomorrow night we'll hear all about what they said," Doona added.

"Of course," Bessie said. "I think it's Hugh's turn to bring the food."

Hugh blushed. "Is pizza okay with everyone?" he asked hopefully.

Everyone laughed, but then agreed that pizza was fine.

"I'll bring pudding," Doona offered. No one objected.

Minutes later Inspector Rockwell was escorting Doona to her car and Bessie and Hugh were getting ready to turn in for the night.

"I hope you sleep well," Hugh said politely to Bessie.

"I always do," Bessie answered him, choosing to ignore her difficulties from the previous evening.

But when she got into bed a short while later, she again found herself unhappily tossing and turning. As Hugh's snores began to make their way up the stairs she found that once more sleep was being evasive. She sat up and grabbed a nearby book that she had deliberately brought up the stairs with her for just such an eventuality. She read several chapters before she finally felt sleepy enough to turn out the light. Once she settled in, much later than normal, she happily fell asleep almost immediately.

# CHAPTER 10

The next morning Bessie was shocked awake by Hugh's alarm, ringing loudly from the floor below her. Her own internal alarm had missed six and she had slept right through until seven. She frowned as she threw back the covers and climbed into her robe. She would get Hugh and herself some breakfast while he was in the shower and would take her own shower later, she decided. It seemed like the most sensible solution to her over-sleeping.

Hugh's incessant whistling while in the shower didn't improve Bessie's mood. By the time he'd had some breakfast and headed off to work, Bessie felt like crawling back under the covers and simply waiting for the weekend from under there.

After a shower that quickly ran cold thanks to Hugh's earlier ablutions, she dressed and then headed out for a short stroll, hoping some fresh air might improve her mood. Just steps away from her door, the skies opened and Bessie got thoroughly drenched as she turned and walked back to her cottage as quickly as she could.

"Well, really," Bessie said as she slammed her front door. "Can anything else go wrong today?" She quickly tapped on her wooden table to stave off any bad fortune that might follow such a pronouncement, and then she dragged herself into the nearest bathroom to try to dry off.

The phone was ringing its annoyingly insistent tone as she gave up and headed up the stairs to change. She hesitated on the third step, wondering if it was worth turning around or not. Doona's voice on the answering machine answered the question.

"Bessie, are you there?" Doona asked. "If you are pick up quick, otherwise, ring me when you get this message."

Bessie grabbed the receiver and switched off her answering machine. "I'm here," she said, a bit breathlessly.

"I can't say much," Doona sounded excited, "but there's about to be an arrest in the murder cases."

Bessie felt a sharp pang of something like disappointment. She had been enjoying the investigation more than she had realised. She frowned at herself as she replied to Doona. "Who's about to get arrested?" she demanded.

"Ah, arrested is probably too strong a word," Doona backtracked. "Someone is about to be brought in to, um, help with our inquires."

"But who?" Bessie said impatiently.

"Jack White," Doona whispered.

"Who is Jack White?" Bessie asked, confused.

"You know, if you think about it," Doona answered.

"Stop teasing," Bessie said frustrated. Then she snapped her fingers. "The Laxey and Lonan chemist?" she asked. "What on earth does he have to do with the murders?"

"Well," Doona began. "It looks as if, um, yes, well, if you turn off at the last junction and then take the second left, we're the first building on the right."

"Pardon?"

"Yes, that's fine. You can come in any time and report your missing cat," Doona rattled on at her. "We're happy to take your statement and, obviously, we will do our best to help you find little Fluffy."

Bessie laughed. "Fluffy? Come on, if I did have a cat I would give it a much better name than that. I take it someone has just walked in and you can now be overheard?"

"Absolutely, madam," Doona answered.

"Can you ring me back later?" Bessie asked. "When it gets quieter?"

"Certainly, madam. I'd be happy to do that."

Bessie sighed after they had said polite goodbyes and she'd hung up her phone. She had been planning on walking over to Thie yn Traie this morning, but what with oversleeping and then the rain, the plan was less appealing now than it had been last night. Besides, it would probably be best to see what Doona had to report before she went to see the Pierce family. If Jack White was the killer, that would certainly put a different spin on her visit.

While Bessie waited for Doona to ring her back, she tried to remember everything she knew about Jack White. It wasn't much. She knew he had moved to the island only six months or so earlier, replacing the retiring John Corkill as the dispensing chemist at the small Laxey branch of the local chain.

He was much younger than the man he'd replaced, somewhere in his late-thirties, she reckoned. He was much more attractive than the portly and balding man he had replaced as well. Bessie remembered dark brown, almost black, hair and vivid blue eyes. He was almost exactly what Bessie had always pictured when people spoke of someone "tall, dark and handsome." There had been some gossip when he first arrived about his behaviour with young and pretty female customers, but that had died down fairly quickly.

Last month, the chain had been purchased by a large British company, and the hours at the Laxey branch had been cut as Jack White began to split his time between there and an even smaller store in Lonan.

Bessie wasn't fond of putting chemicals into her body unnecessarily, so she rarely needed the services that chemists like Jack offered. There had only been one occasion since the man arrived when Bessie had needed a course of antibiotics for a particularly nasty throat infection. In her brief visit to his shop, Bessie had found the man to be perfectly pleasant to deal with.

The obvious inference to make from the news of his arrest was that he was the local source for Daniel's drug supply. Bessie frowned as she considered it. Surely it wasn't good business practice to kill your customers, she mused. There had to be more to the story than she knew.

She frowned at her silent phone and then paced a few times around her kitchen. The rain had slowed to a miserable drizzle, at least temporarily, but she didn't dare go for a walk and risk missing Doona's call. As she frowned at the phone again, it rang, startling her.

"Okay," Doona didn't bother with preliminaries. "All I know is one little thing and it's going to be part of a press conference in a few hours, so I'm not telling tales. Just don't repeat this until after four. Apparently Jack White was supplying prescription drugs to someone in the Pierce household. Unfortunately for Mr. White, he was doing so without a prescription."

"What does that have to do with the murders?" Bessie asked.

"Maybe nothing," Doona admitted. "But it's enough to get the man arrested and for Inspector Kelly to get all the credit."

"So what happens now?" Bessie asked.

"Inspector Kelly has been questioning Mr. White all morning," Doona told her. "He only stopped when Mr. White's advocate arrived and insisted on a break. The Inspector and the Chief Constable are giving the press conference I mentioned to talk about this latest break in the murder investigation."

"Do they really think he's the killer, then?"

"It sounds like it," Doona answered. "I don't know all of the details, but we'll all know more after four o'clock."

"Maybe I should get over to Thie yn Traie before that, then," Bessie said thoughtfully. "I can see if they've heard about the arrest and let them know about the press conference."

"And poke around a bit," Doona added.

"Well," Bessie said, "I'm curious how they'll take the news, that's for sure."

"I'm not sure that's a good idea," Doona told her friend. "Inspector Kelly might be convinced that Jack White is guilty, but there are still several other suspects and they all live at Thie yn Traie."

Bessie sighed. "I wish I could be a fly on the wall while they're questioning Jack White. I'd love to know what he's telling them."

"I don't know anything else, and I couldn't tell you if I did," Doona answered her. "I only found out that little bit because I overheard a phone call that I shouldn't have. Inspector Kelly isn't talking to anyone except the Chief Constable. Even Inspector Rockwell got told that he has to wait for the press conference if he wants to know anything."

"I'll bet that didn't go over well," Bessie chuckled.

"He wasn't pleased," Doona told her. "But he stayed polite about it anyway. I suggest you just sit tight and wait and see what I can tell you tonight. We'll meet at seven as planned and by then everything that the police are willing to release will be public knowledge. And maybe Inspector Rockwell will know even more."

Bessie sighed. "I suppose I can wait to pay my respects until tomorrow," she said slowly. "It's a miserable day anyway. Walking to the Pierces' doesn't really appeal to me."

Bessie ate a quick lunch and then curled up with a book, frowning at the steady rain that was falling outside her window. A nice hot cup of tea took the chill off, in spite of the dampness. She was so deeply involved in her fictional tale that she barely registered the ringing telephone.

It rang half a dozen times before Bessie really heard it. She sighed when she remembered that she'd turned off her answering machine when Doona had rung earlier. If she hadn't, the machine would have picked up by now and she would have been able to completely ignore the whole thing.

After ten rings she decided she had better answer the call. Anyone that was willing to hang on that long deserved an answer. She walked as quickly as she could to the phone and grabbed it after more than a dozen rings.

"Hello?"

"Oh, you are there." The slightly breathless voice was familiar, but Bessie couldn't place it immediately. "I thought I needed to let it ring a whole bunch so you had plenty of time to get yourself up and answer."

Bessie frowned. Vikky Pierce, as rude as ever. "What can I do for you, Mrs. Pierce?" Bessie said coolly.

"Oh, well, the thing is, like, the police have just rung," Vikky told her. "It seems likely that we're going to be allowed to leave tomorrow, which is great. I can't wait to get off this island."

"Leave tomorrow?" Bessie echoed. "I suppose that means that they've found the murderer?"

"I suppose," Vikky said vaguely. "I didn't talk to them. It was the Chief Constable what rang, and he talked to Mr. Pierce. I only know what Mr. Pierce told us all. Which is what I just said. We're going to be allowed to leave tomorrow."

"I see," Bessie said, trying to keep her surprise out of her voice.

"Anyway," Vikky continued. "I went up to pack and then I realised that I still have your clothes. I mean the staff washed them and every-thing, but I never got around to returning them to you. I just wanted to tell you that I'm going to give them to Bahey and she can get them back to you. Is that okay?"

Bessie thought quickly. "Actually," she told the woman, "I'd rather just pick them up this afternoon if I might."

"I suppose." Bessie could almost hear Vikky's shrug. "I mean, I'll be here if you want to stop by."

"I do," Bessie said firmly. "I wanted to come by and pay my respects for Samantha anyway, and it sounds as if I need to do that today or else you'll all be gone."

"Well, yeah," Vikky answered. "We're all eager to get out of here. This hasn't been the most pleasant visit ever for any of us."

"No, of course not," Bessie agreed. "I'll walk over now. It should take me about twenty minutes to get there, as I still have to come along the road."

"Okay, I'll tell everyone you're coming. It will make a nice break from sitting around and staring at each other, I suppose."

Bessie hung up the phone and then thought about picking it back up. She probably ought to let Doona know where she was going, espe-cially since Doona had tried to talk her out of this visit.

Her hand hesitated over the receiver and then she changed her mind. Doona would try to persuade her not to go and she didn't want to take the time to have that argument. Bahey would be at the Pierces'; she would keep an eye on things.

Bessie pulled on her waterproof coat and Wellington boots for the walk. The rain was steady, but there wasn't much wind, so she added an umbrella to her outfit. "Here goes nothing," she muttered to herself as she locked the door to the cottage behind her.

The walk along the road felt longer than ever as she stomped through puddle after puddle in the pouring rain. At one point, behind the cottages, she stopped for a second and then leaped into one particularly impressive puddle with both feet. She laughed like a small child as the water splashed up around her. She was already soaked; she might as well have some fun.

The crowd of reporters in front of the Pierce cottage had now dwindled down to a single car with a man and woman sitting inside. Bessie frowned at them as she walked past, but they were both busy on their phones and barely glanced at her. At the gate she pushed the call button, and a moment later Robert Clague emerged from the garage door. He grinned at Bessie as he approached the gate.

"Nice to see you again, Aunt Bessie," he greeted her.

"You too, Robert," she answered. "But I don't think I need security this time. There are only a few reporters left and they don't seem interested in me."

Robert chuckled. "You can never be too careful," he told Bessie. "If we just buzzed the gate open, those two might just charge forward and be in the house before we could stop them."

Bessie looked back over her shoulder as she walked through the gate. The two reporters were still on their phones and neither seemed to have even noticed the activity at the gate. She shrugged. "I shouldn't complain if the Pierces want to keep paying you, should I?"

"Nope," Robert grinned again. "I'm happy to have the work. We were told this was our last day about two hours ago, and then about ten minutes ago they said we would be needed at least until after the weekend. I'm not sure what's going on."

Bessie frowned. "That's strange. I talked to Vikky a short time ago and she said they were all heading back across tomorrow."

"I think that was the plan, but something has come up," Robert shrugged. "It's not really my place to question it, or even talk about it, really."

Bessie patted his arm as he escorted her to the door. "Don't worry, I'm sure Bahey will tell me absolutely everything." Robert smiled and then took her umbrella from her hand and folded it neatly for her.

"I'll leave this just inside the door," he told her as she entered the house. "Don't forget it on your way home."

Bessie thanked him quickly as Bahey rushed up to give her a hug. She stopped short when she saw that Bessie was dripping wet.

"Let me take that coat," Bahey told her, holding out a hand.

Bessie was happy to slip off the sodden and heavy coat.

"I'll just hang it by the door for you," Bahey told her. After she did so, she returned to Bessie's side and gave her the hug that had been delayed.

"Oooo, Aunt Bessie, I didn't know you were stopping by," Bahey told her. "I was just thinking about you."

"I hope you were thinking nice things," Bessie replied.

"Oh yes, well, I was planning our lunch for next week, you see," Bahey replied. "Mr. Pierce told me that they were all heading home tomorrow, so I thought I could start planning a day to have you and Joney over. But then, just when I had the menu all arranged in my head, he called me back in and said that they are staying until Monday. Now I'm all out of sorts."

Bessie smiled at her friend. "Never mind, I'm sure it will all be worked out quickly enough," she said reassuringly. "In the meantime, I came to see Vikky. She rang and said she had my things to return."

"Is she the only one you want to see?" Bahey asked.

"Well, I suppose I should pay my respects in regards to Samantha as well," Bessie answered. "So I suppose a few minutes with Donny would be useful as well. I imagine he's the right person to pay my respects to in this case."

Bahey nodded. "Let me tell them that you're here. You can wait in the great room."

Bahey walked Bessie down the now familiar hall and pushed open the great room door. She flipped on several lights in the dark and empty room.

"I still don't like this room," Bessie remarked, more to herself than Bahey, as she walked towards the windows.

"Oh aye, it's just not a welcoming space, is it?" Bahey replied as she left to find the others for Bessie.

"No, it most certainly isn't," Bessie said emphatically to no one. She stood at the windows and watched the rain that was still falling steadily. She sighed and turned away from the view as the door behind her opened.

"Hey, Aunt Bessie," Vikky called as she bounced into the room with a plastic shopping bag in her hand. "How are you? It's filthy out there, isn't it? I wish I'd known that the police were going to change their minds and keep us here a couple more days. I wouldn't have bothered you today."

"It doesn't matter," Bessie answered. "I didn't have any other plans and I often walk in the rain. But why have the police changed their minds?"

Vikky shrugged and looked out the window. "I don't think they can prove that the guy they arrested actually did it, at least not yet. Anyway, here, and thanks."

Vikky handed the bag she was carrying to Bessie, who glanced inside at her clothes. "You're welcome," she said formally.

"Anyway," Vikky told her. "I can't wait to get out of here and back home. I hated the island when I was a kid, and I hate it even more now."

"And yet your husband loved it," Mrs. Pierce said sternly from the doorway. "And if you had made any effort to be a good wife to him, you would have tried to love it for his sake."

Vikky rolled her eyes at Bessie before turning to her mother-in-law. "I did try," she said with tears in her voice. "I tried everything I could to be a good wife for the few short days that Danny and I had together."

Mrs. Pierce just looked at her and then turned to Bessie. "It's kind of you to pay another visit," she said. "Bahey said you wanted to pay your respects for Samantha."

"Yes, that's right," Bessie answered. "I don't know anything about her family, but Donny's the closest thing she had to family on the island. It seemed appropriate to offer him my sympathy, especially since I talked to him just that afternoon."

"I'm sure he'll be down shortly," Mrs. Pierce said. "I'm sorry my husband won't be joining us. He's started taking long drives around the island lately and he doesn't let the weather stop him."

Bessie nodded slowly. That was what he was meant to be doing when Samantha was killed. "I understand that you were planning to leave tomorrow, but that's changed?" she asked the other woman.

Mrs. Pierce sighed and made her way into the room. She headed towards the bar, but at the last minute she turned and took a seat in a small seating area just in front of it instead. "Please, join me," she said.

Bessie walked across and tentatively took a seat on the couch opposite the one where Mrs. Pierce was sitting. "You have a lovely view," she remarked politely, unable to think of anything else to say.

"I always loved it," Mrs. Pierce replied. "But now, every time I look out there, I see the spot where my son died."

Bessie winced. "That must be very painful," she murmured.

"We'll be selling the house," Mrs. Pierce told her. "I expect someone will turn it into a bed and breakfast or something."

"It's awfully isolated isn't it?" Vikky asked as she flopped down into a chair between the others. "I mean, who would want to stay all the way out here?"

Mrs. Pierce and Bessie both bristled at the comment and when their eyes met a rare moment of understanding passed between them. Neither bothered to address Vikky's remark.

"I'd love to see another family buy it," Mrs. Pierce said. "It was a great summer home for the children."

"I'm sure it was," Bessie answered.

The conversation was interrupted when the door suddenly burst open and Donny came crashing into the room. Bessie could tell at a glance that he'd been drinking heavily.

"Hey, Aunt Bessie, my Laxey Wheel buddy, how the blazes are you?" he asked, sliding onto the couch next to her.

"I'm fine," she answered primly, pulling her knees to the side away from the man who was now sprawling across most of the couch.

"Good, good, good," he muttered. "I'm not so good, you might have guessed."

"I'm very sorry about Samantha," Bessie answered.

"Oh, thank you, yes," the man's face reflected his struggle to try to work out what he should say next. "That is, thank you for your simmm, er, shimm, er, sympathy."

"Donald, you're drunk," his mother said sharply. "I don't think you should be spending time with guests right now."

Donny rolled his eyes at Bessie. "I'm not drunk," he whispered loudly to her. "I just had one little drinky to help me forget about Sam and Danny. Just the one, or maybe it was two. I forget."

Mrs. Pierce shook her head. "I apologise for my son's behaviour," she said tartly. "He hasn't been himself since Samantha died."

"I'm sure it was a huge shock to you all," Bessie replied.

"Shocking," Donny agreed. "Simply shocking."

Mrs. Pierce frowned at her son. "Donny, why don't you go and lie down for a little while?" she asked. "I think you could do with some rest."

"Have to get packed," Donny told her. "Police said we can go tomorrow. I need to pack my things."

"Haven't you heard?" Vikky drawled. "They've only gone and changed their minds. We're stuck here until Monday, earliest."

Donny's face went pale for a moment then he sat up and glared at Vikky. "You're lying," he said harshly.

"I'm afraid she isn't," Mrs. Pierce interjected smoothly. "Apparently the police haven't yet received all of the information they need. We have been asked, politely, to stay here for just a few more days."

Donny sank back in his seat, an angry look on his face. "What do you know about this?" he demanded of Bessie. "I see the police going in and out of your cottage all the time. What's going on? You have to tell me."

Bessie shook her head. "I don't know anything," she said truthfully. "I came over because Vikky said you were leaving and I wanted to get the things I'd loaned her back and pay my respects."

"But I thought the police arrested someone," Donny said.

"They have," Vikky answered. "Some chemist who was dealing drugs on the side. They seem to think that Danny was taking drugs and his murder was a drug deal gone bad."

"Preposterous," Mrs. Pierce erupted. "My son did not take drugs," she said insistently. "And I won't hear anyone say otherwise."

Bessie glanced over at Donny, but he was staring at his mother intently. Bessie gave a mental shrug. She wasn't going to tell Mrs. Pierce where the police first got the idea. The family had enough problems without Bessie suggesting that Donny knew about Danny's drug issues.

Mrs. Pierce looked over at Bessie. "I know that when you were here a few days ago I was a little bit out of it," she told Bessie. "But you need to understand that when they told me about Danny, I, well, I suppose I sort of lost control." The woman frowned and looked away for a moment.

"You don't need to explain anything to me," Bessie began, but Mrs. Pierce held up a hand.

"I feel that I do," she told Bessie. "We, as a family, have always been passionate opponents of the use of illegal drugs. We aren't even that fond of legal ones. I take headache tablets rarely, and my husband hasn't taken anything in years. The doctor who treated me when I found out about Danny gave me something strong to help me get through the first few days. I was very tempted to keep taking them. Forgetting my pain had a certain appeal, but that would have been cowardly. So I stopped taking them, and I shan't take them again."

Bessie nodded at her. "You're a strong woman," she told her.

"In spite of all the money and the trappings that go with it," Mrs. Pierce waved an arm to encompass the house and surroundings, "my husband and I have had to deal with our share of misfortune and even tragedy. And we've done so without medicating ourselves. Oh, yes, Mr. Pierce likes a few fingers of whisky now and then and I love a good glass of white wine, but we've never gone beyond that and we've always insisted that our children stay clear of such temptations as well."

Bessie nodded, feeling at a complete loss as to what to say.

"Now you can run home and tell your police friends everything my mother has said," Donny said angrily. "Then they'll have to take another look at me and Vikky as suspects, I suppose. Too bad I didn't have any motive."

Vikky sat up and gave him a dirty look. "What the hell is that supposed to mean?" she demanded.

Donny passed a hand over his face. "Nothing," he muttered.

Vikky glared at him. "Just because I knew Jack White before he came over here, doesn't mean that I had anything to do with anything," she said angrily.

Bessie looked over at her in surprise and then bit her tongue. She was finding out much more than she bargained for already. If she started asking questions she might make people go quiet.

"Exactly how well did you know him?" Donny sneered at her.

Vikky shook her head. "He was friends with a friend of mine," she sighed. "We went through all this when he was arrested," she said. "I told you everything then."

"Well, whatever your friend Mr. White is telling the police, it obviously means they suspect one of us. Otherwise, why wouldn't they just let us go?" Donny sounded a good deal more sober suddenly.

"Maybe you should ask her," Vikky suggested, pointing at Bessie. "You seem to think she has connections to the police."

"I know she does," Donny replied. "So, tell us, dear Aunt Bessie, what do the police think we're guilty of?"

Bessie shook her head. "I don't know anything." She was sure she was repeating herself. "Doona is an old friend who visits often and Hugh has been sleeping at my place because he's worried about my being on my own with a murderer running around. Neither one of them has told me anything about the case. Doona did mention Jack White's arrest, but that was all she was able to tell me."

Donny stared at her for a moment and then slumped back on the couch. "Never mind," he said softly. "I'm a little drunk and a lot fed up and I'm looking for someone to blame. I can only assume that Jack White is trying to save himself by telling all sorts of lies and that the police have to work out if there's any truth in them before we can go."

"I'm sure you're right," Mrs. Pierce told her son soothingly. "Why don't you go up and have a nap? I'll have Bahey call you for dinner in a little while. I'll see if she can make you one of your favourites."

Donny smiled at his mother. "I'm really okay," he told her gently. "But I think a nap might do me some good." He stood up and smiled at them all. "Sorry for my outbursts," he said to them all before he turned to Bessie. "I do appreciate your taking the time to visit," he told her. "I didn't realise how much Sam meant to me until she was gone."

Bessie nodded. "That's often the case," she said softly. Donny nodded and then walked slowly to the door.

"Thanks again," he said softly, looking back at Bessie with tears in his eyes.

As the door shut behind him, Mrs. Pierce let out a sigh of relief. Bessie looked over at her.

"He's suffering so much," Mrs. Pierce told her sadly. "He idolised his big brother and he was really falling for Samantha. It's been so very hard on him."

"It must be very hard for all of you," Bessie said sympathetically. "I wish there was something I could do...." she trailed off, unable to think of anything to offer.

"You can tell your police friends to let us go," Vikky suggested grumpily. "Tell them that you're sure we're all innocent."

Bessie just barely held back a sigh. "I wish, for your sake, that I had that sort of influence with them," she lied politely. "Unfortunately, they aren't interested in my opinion."

Vikky shrugged. "I think I'll go and have a cup of tea with the security guys," she said as she climbed to her feet.

Mrs. Pierce watched her go with a sad look on her face. "I wish I could say that I thought she was suffering as well," she told Bessie as the door swung shut behind Vikky. "But I'm not sure that she really cared about my son at all."

Bessie reached across and patted the other woman's arm. "I'm so sorry," she muttered, feeling ineffectual.

"Thank you my dear," Mrs. Pierce answered, giving Bessie a forced smile. "And now I must ask you to excuse me. I think that all this talking about naps has made me tired. I'm going to go and rest for a short time."

"That sounds like a good idea," Bessie told her as she and the other woman both rose to their feet. "I hope you feel better after some rest. And I hope you have a safe journey home on Monday."

"I just hope they let us leave on Monday," Mrs. Pierce said tiredly. "I think we'll all feel better getting away from here. And we have a funeral to plan as well," she sighed. "That doesn't even bear thinking about."

Bessie patted her arm again and then, with the younger woman leaning heavily on Bessie's arm, the pair made their way to the door. Bessie watched as Mrs. Pierce made her way down the hall, further into the house. Bessie could see that she was struggling to maintain her self-control as she turned a corner and disappeared from view. The sound of a tiny sob reached Bessie's ears as she turned to walk back to where her coat and umbrella had been left.

# CHAPTER 11

"*D*id you have a nice visit, then?" Bahey asked Bessie, appearing at Bessie's side from somewhere in the depths of the house after Bessie had taken only a few steps away from the great room.

Bessie paused. "I wouldn't call it nice," she answered sadly. "The whole family seems so shattered."

"Aye, they are at that," Bahey told her. "And from what I'm hearing, it's going to get worse."

"What have you heard?" Bessie asked, trying to keep excitement from her voice.

Bahey looked around to make sure they couldn't be overheard. The pair made their way slowly towards the back door as Bahey spoke. "Mrs. Pierce was on the phone to the Chief Constable earlier, before you came," Bahey whispered. "I was just taking her up a cup of tea and I couldn't help but overhear. She always puts her calls on the speaker because she has trouble hearing and she finds that easier."

Bessie held back a grin. She had no doubt that Bahey could have helped it if she'd actually wanted to. "So what did you hear?"

"Mrs. Pierce was asking why they couldn't leave. She's really desperate to get off the island now," Bahey told her sadly. "Anyway,

143

apparently Jack White has been telling the police all sorts of things. I think the police have plenty of evidence that proves he was selling drugs, but nothing that ties him to the murders. Now he's afraid they're going to try to pin the murders on him, so he's talking fast and implicating everyone from Mr. Pierce himself to the men who empty the dustbins!"

Bessie shook her head. "No honour among thieves, I imagine," she said. "Still, I suppose we should be happy if he can help the police find the murderer. Assuming he really didn't kill the victims himself."

"The Chief Constable told Mrs. Pierce that there's a witness who saw Jack on the beach that night," Bahey hissed.

Bessie gasped. "Has he admitted to being there?" she asked.

"Apparently, he told the police he was meeting Vikky," the other woman said.

"Meeting Vikky? Why?"

"I assume he was the old boyfriend who sent the racy text message," Bahey told her. "I've heard that he and Vikky used to be a couple. But the police aren't sure if Vikky got the message or not. Vikky claims that Danny took her phone away before Jack sent the message, so she never went to meet up with him."

"And what did Jack say to that?"

"I don't know," Bahey said frustratedly. "Mrs. Pierce didn't ask that."

Bessie frowned in disappointment. "Did you hear anything else?" she asked.

"The rest of the call was all about how Danny couldn't possibly have been doing drugs," Bahey sighed. "As if he were always the perfect child."

"And he wasn't?" Bessie asked.

"Oh, he wasn't too bad, I suppose," Bahey said with a shrug. "He was never as bad as his brother, anyway. But they both had their share of teenaged, well, hijinks might be the right word. They both snuck drink out of their parents' liquor cabinet on more than one occasion and I'm pretty sure they both at least tried drugs more than once or twice. I'm not suggesting that either of them got hooked on anything, but they weren't as sweet and innocent as their mum thinks, either."

Bessie nodded. What Bahey was saying made sense. In her experience, few children were ever as perfect as they appeared in their mother's eyes.

"Anyway," Bahey continued, "it seems that Jack White is busy pointing fingers in every possible direction and the police aren't willing to let the family go until they've checked out what he's saying."

"No one seems happy about that," Bessie said.

"No, I expect no one is happy," Bahey agreed. "It's hard to tell with Mr. Pierce. He just keeps wandering off on his own. Mrs. Pierce doesn't seem to know what to do with herself. Mr. Donny is devastated and drunk most of the time and Miss Vikky just keeps behaving like a spoiled child." Bahey sighed.

"What about the staff?" Bessie asked, remembering that Inspector Rockwell had mentioned them as possible suspects.

"What about them?" Bahey echoed. "I don't really know any of them. They were all hired locally, just for this visit. Apparently there's a service in Ramsey that dealt with it all. I think the girls all come up from Douglas during the day, and I know the driver does. None of them are staying here, although the security team is working twenty-four hours a day, of course."

"Doesn't the family usually bring their own staff with them?" Bessie asked.

"When I worked for them, I always went wherever the family went, but the housekeeper who replaced me had to have an emergency appendectomy the day before they left. Her husband, who usually does most of the driving and errands, obviously stayed behind to be with her." Bahey shrugged. "I can't imagine any of the temporary help having any reason to kill Danny or Samantha."

Bessie sighed. "If Jack White isn't the killer, then it must have been one of the family," she said quietly.

Bahey shook her head. "It weren't," she said emphatically. "It had to be something random if it wasn't Jack White. I bet Danny saw the text from Jack and went out to confront him. Either Jack killed him or he was doing a drug deal and Danny interrupted and the other guy killed him. That could have happened."

Bessie nodded. "Yes, I suppose you're right," she agreed. "But what about Samantha?"

"Maybe she followed Danny on the night he died and saw him get murdered. I don't know, maybe she was trying to blackmail the killer or something."

Bessie nodded again, this time with less certainty.

"Anyway, I just know it wasn't anyone in the family," Bahey told her. "I've known them my whole life; they aren't killers, none of them."

"You haven't known Vikky your whole life," Bessie pointed out.

"Aye, but it's just too sad to think of her killing her own husband only days after their wedding," Bahey answered.

Bessie thought about arguing with her friend but decided against it. In a way, Bahey was right. It was sad to suspect the young widow of killing her husband while on their honeymoon. Still, whatever Bahey thought, Bessie wasn't ruling Vikky out as a suspect.

"I'd better get back to the kitchen," Bahey told Bessie. "I promised I'd make one of Mr. Donny's favourites tonight to try to cheer him up. Their temporary cook doesn't much like it when I'm in the kitchen, but tonight she's going to have to deal with it."

Bessie grinned at her. "Have fun," she said. "I've got a long and cold walk back along the road to home to get through before I get my dinner."

Bahey disappeared back towards the kitchen as Bessie set the bag that Vikky had given her down and put her still damp coat back on. She buttoned it up tightly and then grabbed her umbrella from the corner where Robert had left it. With a resigned sigh, she pulled open the door and looked out at the relentless rain.

"The police have taken down the crime scene tape." The voice was completely unexpected and it made Bessie jump.

"I didn't mean to startle you," Robert Clague told her. "I noticed you were getting ready to leave and I wanted to tell you that the police have finally taken down the crime scene tape. You can walk home along the beach now. That has to be faster."

Bessie smiled at him even as she wondered how long he had been standing near her. She certainly hadn't noticed his approach. How much of her conversation with Bahey had he overheard?

"That's good to know," she told him. "It's definitely faster, once I find my way down to the beach."

"It isn't hard," the man laughed lightly. "There are a series of short flights of stairs down to the sand. I'll take you down," he offered.

"That would be great," Bessie replied. She stepped outside and popped her umbrella up. Behind her Robert followed, pulling the door shut as he took her arm.

"Be careful," he counselled. "Everything is probably slippery with all this rain."

Bessie took his arm gratefully as they made their way along the driveway beside the house. After a short time, a path that skirted along behind the house appeared.

Robert stopped as something buzzed in his pocket. "Hello?" he said into his mobile phone that he struggled to shield from the rain. He sighed deeply and then disconnected the call.

"I would love to be able to walk you the rest of the way," he told Bessie, "but I've got to get back and deal with an, um, issue that's come up. If you follow the path behind the house, after a short while it branches off down towards the beach."

"I'm sure I'll find it," Bessie told him, nearly shouting to be heard over the heavy rain that was pounding on her umbrella, the house roof and the ground around them.

"No doubt," Robert said. "Take care of yourself," he told her before he dashed away, presumably wanting to get out of the rain as quickly as possible.

"Can't say as I blame him," Bessie said to herself as she followed the path. It insisted on winding around in a pointlessly circuitous fashion that was probably charming on a warm spring day, but was simply unnecessarily torturous in the heavy rain. The noisy banging on her umbrella began to make Bessie's head ache.

Finally, she came to a split in the path, with one fork clearly heading off towards the expanse of beach below. Bessie couldn't help but take a minute to admire the view, which was striking in spite of the weather. As she started down the first short flight of stairs, she paused. Could she hear footsteps behind her?

She turned cautiously, peering around her oversized umbrella. There was no one there. She continued down the steps, shaking her head at how her mind was playing tricks on her. As the first flight ended, she thought she heard another sound behind her. Again, carefully, she turned around. Again, she could see no one.

She sighed at her own jumpiness and took off down the short and winding path that led to the next flight of stairs. Again, she paused briefly to admire the view. Although she wasn't that far from her own cottage, the view of the sea seemed completely different from here.

The next flight of stairs was longer, maybe twenty steps, and it was steeper as well. Bessie grabbed the handrail tightly with the hand that was also carrying the bag that Vikky had given her. Holding the railing felt awkward as she started down the steps.

After two steps she heard yet another sound that seemed to come from behind her. She paused, wondering if it was worth turning around yet again. She listened intently but could only hear the drumming rain. She started down the next step, sliding her hand down the railing, trying to keep a firm grip on the slippery wet metal.

Suddenly two strong hands pushed her from behind. She grabbed at the railing, but couldn't hold on. The bag slipped from her grip and the umbrella flew from her other hand as she grasped at thin air. She felt herself tumbling downwards, out of control and unable to stop.

# CHAPTER 12

*E*verything hurt. Bessie winced as she wiggled a single toe and a stabbing pain shot through her leg. She moaned softly.

"Oh, Bessie, are you awake?"

Bessie heard Doona's voice, but she didn't feel like answering. She could tell that she was in a bed somewhere and from the noises she could hear she reckoned it must be a hospital. She sighed to herself as she realised that her nose was so itchy she was going to have to move.

Cautiously, she opened her eyes and looked around. The first thing she spotted was Doona's worried face.

"Oh, Bessie, you're awake then," Doona said happily. "Let me get the doctor. I'll be right back."

Before Bessie could speak Doona had leapt up and run to the door. Bessie could hear her talking excitedly to someone in the hallway.

"The nurse is going to get the doctor," Doona announced when she returned to Bessie's bedside. "He wasn't expecting you to wake up until at least tomorrow."

As Bessie took a mental inventory of her aches and pains she thought that perhaps the doctor was right. Perhaps she would've been better off sleeping until the next morning.

"Everything hurts," she said softly. "And the end of my nose is itchy."

Doona chuckled as she reached over and gave Bessie's nose a quick scratch. "Your nose is one of the few spots that isn't bumped and bruised," she told Bessie as she patted her arm.

Bessie cautiously tried moving first one arm and then the other and was relieved to find that the pain was mostly bearable. She shifted her legs back and forth a little bit and again felt satisfied that there would be no lasting damage.

"What happened?" she asked Doona.

"Well, that's what we all want to know," Doona told her. "Hugh found you at the bottom of the stairs leading from Thie yn Traie to the beach."

Bessie nodded slowly. "Someone pushed me," she said.

Doona drew a sharp breath. "Are you sure?"

"I'm positive," Bessie answered. Before she could go any further the door swung open and a man, who looked all of fifteen to Bessie's eyes, strolled in casually.

"How are we feeling, then?" the man said to Bessie, patting her hand and then taking her pulse.

"I'm feeling pretty miserable," Bessie told the man with sandy-blonde hair and a very boyish face.

"That's hardly surprising. You took a nasty tumble down those stairs," the man replied. "With your age I was expecting quite a few broken bones when they brought you in, but it appears you've escaped with only minor bumps and bruises."

Bessie bristled at the reference to her age, but held her tongue. "It's all pretty painful," she said.

"We didn't want to fill you up with pain medication until you regained consciousness," the man told her. "I'm Dr. Mark Cannell, by the way. I'll be looking after you this evening."

"How long do I have to stay?" Bessie asked.

The doctor laughed. "Why does everyone always want to leave as soon as they arrive?" he asked, not expecting a reply. "I want to keep you overnight for sure. We'll see how you're feeling in the morning before we decide anything past that."

Bessie frowned but then realised that she was in too much pain to argue. "One night," she told Dr. Cannell firmly. "I'm going home in the morning."

"We'll see in the morning," the doctor answered her cheerfully, his clear green eyes meeting her pain-filled ones. "For now, I'll send the nurse in with some pain medication and maybe something to eat as well. The police are waiting to take a statement, but I suggest you have me tell them that they have to wait until tomorrow."

Doona had slipped out of the room while the doctor was checking Bessie over; now she returned and grinned at her friend.

"Who's here waiting to see me?" Bessie asked her.

"Inspector Rockwell and Hugh," Doona told her with a grin.

"I'll see them tonight," Bessie told the doctor. He looked as if he might argue with her, but then shook his head and left the room.

A few minutes later Hugh and Inspector Rockwell stuck their heads around the door to Bessie's small room.

"How are you?" the inspector asked as he entered.

"Confused," Bessie answered slowly. "Before I answer your questions, you need to answer mine."

"Certainly." The inspector smiled at her and then pulled up a chair from along the wall. He sat down next to her bed and patted her hand gently. "Go ahead, then; what do you need to know?"

"Well," Bessie sighed. "For a start, where am I? If I had to guess, I would say Ramsey Cottage Hospital, but I thought I knew all the doctors there and this Mark Cannell is a stranger."

Doona smiled. "You are at Ramsey Cottage Hospital," she told her friend before Inspector Rockwell spoke. "Dr. Cannell transferred here from Noble's last month. He's replacing Dr. Martindale, who's moved back across to somewhere near Leeds."

"Ah," Bessie smiled. "I never liked that man anyway, so good for us and good luck Leeds."

Doona laughed. "I don't think anyone liked him," she remarked.

"He had no idea about bedside manner. Why, my neighbour brought her...."

Inspector Rockwell coughed softly. "I hate to interrupt, but I still have some murders to solve here and every reason to think that the murderer is someone at Thie yn Traie. If we could focus on that for just a few minutes, I'll get out of your way and leave you to your chat."

Doona looked apologetically at the man. "Sorry, I forgot," she muttered.

"It's fine," Inspector Rockwell told her with a smile.

"So how did I get here?" Bessie interjected her next question. "I remember talking to Bahey and then Robert showing me around the back of the house. I was walking down the steps and I could hear someone behind me, but every time I looked back, there wasn't anyone there."

"The paths and stairs wind around a great deal," Rockwell told her. "And there are plenty of trees and shrubs and other landscaping to hide behind as well. Doona said you thought you were pushed when she came out to see me."

"I was definitely pushed," Bessie said firmly. "I heard someone behind me again just as I started down the long flight of stairs. I was debating whether I should turn around or not when, suddenly, two hands gave me a shove from behind."

Doona gasped again, as if she were hearing it for the first time. Bessie shot her an exasperated look. "What I want to know," Bessie said, "is what happened next."

Hugh cleared his throat self-consciously. "I think that's where I come in," he told Bessie as he approached the side of her bed. "I was down on the beach, taking down the rest of the crime scene tape. Well, actually, first I was taking it down and then I was putting it back up." He sighed.

"Inspector Kelly and I had something of a difference of opinion as to whether or not it was time to take the tape down," Inspector Rockwell said smoothly. "He gave orders for the tape to be removed, and then I suggested that it might be best if we left it up for just a short time longer."

"Aye, and you could hear his 'suggestion' from about a mile away," Doona told Bessie with a chuckle.

Inspector Rockwell flushed. "Poor Hugh was stuck out in the rain almost all afternoon, taking down and then replacing the tape."

"And it's lucky I was," Hugh returned to his story. "I was just about finished when I looked up and saw you walking down the steps towards the beach," he told Bessie. "Of course, I didn't know it was you. I just saw someone walking down the steps. I thought it was one of them Pierces and I was going to have to tell them that the beach was still a crime scene and they couldn't walk on it. But then," he paused dramatically, "I spotted someone coming up behind you. Well, I thought they were just going to catch up to you for a chat or something, and I got on with what I was doing, but the next time I looked up, you were in a big heap at the bottom of the stairs."

"So you didn't see me get pushed?" Bessie asked in a disappointed voice.

"No, sorry," Hugh said. "I had no reason to think you were going to get pushed," he tried to explain. Bessie could tell that he felt terrible.

"Of course you didn't," she answered, taking his hand and giving it a squeeze.

"Well, anyway, once I realised that you'd fallen, I rang the ambulance crew and I ran over to you. I was scared, when I saw it was you, that you'd broken your neck or something. I tried to wake you up, but I couldn't." He stopped and Bessie could see how upset he had been by the look on his face.

"But I was okay," she reminded him. "I think the fall just knocked the wind out of my sails."

"The doctor said you were amazingly lucky," Doona told her. "Somehow you managed to fall at just the right angle to protect your head and not break any bones. It helped that you landed in sand, rather than anything harder."

"I don't feel so lucky right now," Bessie admitted. "I ache everywhere."

A middle-aged nurse, with black hair that was obviously coloured, chose that opportune moment to peek her head in. "Are we ready for a wee pain tablet now?" she asked in a cloying voice.

"I suppose so," Bessie said reluctantly. "I don't really like to take such things," she told the nurse.

"Now, now, doctor's orders," the nurse clucked. "We wouldn't want to make nice Dr. Cannell unhappy, now would we?"

Bessie bit back a dozen replies and simply swallowed the medicine she was offered.

"Can I get you some toast or a cup of yoghurt?" the nurse asked. "Are you hungry at all?"

Bessie shook her head. "I'm fine, just very tired."

"Well now, in that case, I think it's time to chase away your visitors so you can get some rest," the nurse told her.

"We still have some unfinished business," Inspector Rockwell told the woman. "We won't stay long."

The nurse clucked again. "Make sure that you don't. This patient needs a lot of rest." Disapproval was evident in every word, even as she smiled ingratiatingly at the handsome inspector.

"Ten more minutes," Rockwell promised her.

"If you must," the nurse answered, giving Rockwell a wink, before she swept out of the room.

"She's fun," Doona drawled as the door swung shut.

Bessie laughed and then stopped. "Oh, don't make me laugh," she moaned. "It hurts to laugh."

"No worries, that 'wee pain tablet' will sort you out," Doona said with a laugh.

Bessie smiled at her friend. "So Hugh rang an ambulance and they brought me here," she picked the story back up where Hugh had left off.

"Yes, and he rang me as well. I met the ambulance in Accident and Emergency, where the doctor checked you over and said nothing was broken, but you might not come around until morning," Doona told her.

"Hrmph," Bessie said. "Shows what he knows." Doona and the others laughed.

"I just have one question for you, then, before the nurse comes back and throws us out," Inspector Rockwell told her. "Who pushed you?"

Bessie shook her head slowly, trying to think. The painkiller was already starting to cloud her thinking, but even before she had taken it she had been trying to work out the answer to that question. "I have no idea," she finally admitted. "It could have been just about anyone from the house. Did you get to question them all?"

"We did," Inspector Rockwell answered. "Although we didn't know then that you were pushed. Regardless, they were all here, there and everywhere, and they all claim they didn't see or hear anything out of the ordinary."

"Why am I not surprised?" Doona said dryly.

"Did you get any impression of the size of the person or whether it was a male or female?" Rockwell pressed Bessie for more.

"He or she was a few steps above me," Bessie told him. "I got the impression that they were tall, but that could just be because of the steps. They also seemed strong to me, but they wouldn't have needed much strength to push me off slippery steps in the rain. I wasn't holding the railing properly because I was carrying the bag that Vikky gave me," she sighed. "I'm sorry, but I'm fading away here. That tablet must have been quite strong."

Inspector Rockwell nodded. "I'll be back in the morning to talk to you again," he told Bessie. "I want to know what you said and did at Thie yn Traie that might have made you a target."

Bessie frowned and tried to think, but the medication made her head feel fuzzy and she couldn't focus. "I'll try to remember," she promised.

"In the meantime, we've insisted on a private room for you. I hope you enjoy it. I'm going to leave Hugh here to keep an eye on you," Rockwell told her. "Someone was trying to get rid of you and I want to make sure that whoever it was doesn't get a second chance."

Bessie nodded sleepily. She tried to thank the inspector, but actually making words felt like a huge effort. She stretched her legs and various pains shot through her, momentarily shocking her awake. A moment later, however, the drugs overcame everything and she sank into a deep and necessary sleep.

The first thing she saw the next morning when she opened her eyes was Bahey Corlett's worried face.

"Ah, Bessie, you're awake then," Bahey stated the obvious. "I was so worried when the police started arriving at the cottage saying something about someone falling down the stairs to the beach. What on earth made you try to get home that way, anyway? It was too dark and rainy to be trying to get down those stairs safely."

Bessie smiled at her friend. "Good morning, Bahey," she said softly. "It's kind of you to take the time to visit."

"Of course I came to visit, as early as I could," Bahey answered stoutly. "I feel almost guilty about the whole thing, though I don't know why I should. I never told you to go home that way."

Bessie shook her head. "No, Robert Clague suggested it," she told Bahey. "He thought it would be faster so that I could get out of the rain more quickly."

"But those steps are a hazard," Bahey said. "Even the family don't try to use them when it's raining. They're strictly for nice bright sunny days when you can actually go and enjoy the beach."

"I expect Robert didn't know what they were like. I doubt he's had any reason to use the steps while he's been working at the cottage."

Bahey nodded slowly. "I suppose you're right," she said grudgingly. "But I still blame him. If he were going to suggest you go that way, he should have seen you safely to the bottom."

Bessie thought about arguing, but decided against it. Bahey had a valid point. "Anyway, I'm fine, really," she told Bahey. "Just a little bit banged up and bruised."

"And thank goodness for that," Bahey sighed. "They wouldn't tell me anything about your condition yesterday and I got really scared."

"I'm fine," Bessie repeated.

"I still can't get over you slipping and falling down those steps," Bahey told her. "Robert Clague is going to get an earful when I get back to Thie yn Traie. He should have seen you down."

"He said he had to see to some 'issue,'" Bessie recalled.

"Aye, that'll be Miss Vikky pitching a fit," Bahey rolled her eyes.

"What happened?" Bessie asked.

"Oh, Miss Vikky got this idea that she needed a walk to clear her head. Like there's anything in there to clear," Bahey scoffed.

Bessie grinned. "She certainly wasn't thinking about a walk the last time I saw her."

"Yeah, well, whatever, she got it in her head that she wanted to get out of the house, so she took off towards the front gate. Of course the reporters that were left jumped on the chance to ask her a few questions. Apparently, within minutes it had turned into a shouting match and the security guys had to break it up. I gather your friend Mr. Clague spent the night in gaol, having 'accidentally' broken the video camera that one reporter was using to capture the incident for posterity."

Bessie sighed. "I hope he doesn't lose his job over that."

"Are you kidding?" Bahey asked her. "Mr. Pierce gave him a huge bonus and sorted it out with the reporter so that all of the charges were dropped. Mr. Pierce would not have been happy seeing footage of his daughter-in-law fighting with reporters splashed all over the telly."

"Can't say as I blame him for that," Bessie said.

"No, I suppose not," Bahey answered. "Still, I'd like to see Mr. Clague fired for letting you fall."

"He didn't 'let me fall,'" Bessie told her. "I was pushed."

Bahey drew a sharp breath and then sat back in her chair. "Pushed?" she choked out. "By who?"

"I have no idea," Bessie admitted.

Bahey looked as if she wanted to say something, but Bessie could see indecision wavering in her eyes. After a moment she looked down at the ground. When she still didn't speak, Bessie did.

"I don't suppose you saw anyone following me out of the house yesterday?" she asked.

"No," Bahey answered too quickly. "I didn't see anything."

"I know the police have been asking as well," Bessie told her. "But apparently no one saw anything."

"The police just asked about everyone's whereabouts," Bahey shrugged. "They didn't say anything about you being pushed. In fact, I got the feeling, from what they said, that they thought you'd just slipped and fallen."

"They didn't know I was pushed until I woke up," Bessie told her.

Bahey shrugged. "I suppose that makes sense," she said. "Anyway, I need to get going. After the incident with Vikky and your fall yesterday, Mrs. Pierce is in a bad way. I want to keep an eye on her."

She was up and out the door in seconds, leaving Bessie convinced that she knew something she didn't want to talk about. Bessie pondered whom Bahey would be willing to lie to protect, but the answer didn't help her much. There was no doubt in Bessie's mind that Bahey would do anything to protect the entire Pierce family, probably even including Vikky. Bessie sighed and snuggled back under the covers. It was only seven o'clock; Bahey had been an early bird.

Bessie had slept well enough, only being woken twice to take additional tablets to help with the pain. She had briefly considered arguing against taking them. Surely, if she were able to sleep, she didn't need any more pain medicine. She had been too tired in the night to argue, but now that it was morning, she decided that she would refuse to take anything else. Her mind made up, she let herself drift back off to sleep.

She was rudely awoken a short time later by a nurse's aide bearing a breakfast tray.

"Well now, what we have here?" the very young and almost pretty aide asked perkily as she set the tray down in front of Bessie.

"It looks like runny oatmeal and burnt toast," Bessie said dryly, as she inspected the meal that had been put in front of her.

"I'm sure it's all super yummy and it will do you a world of good," the aide told her with a bright artificial smile.

Bessie raised an eyebrow, but didn't answer. After the aide bustled out, she added some milk and sugar to the cup of tea that was the only thing on the tray that looked even remotely appealing.

It was cold and she took only a single sip before she put it back on the tray and pushed the tray table away from her bed. She sighed deeply and wondered what to do next.

"Here we are with another nice wee tablet to make us feel all better," the same night nurse burbled as she came into the room. "Giving you your tablet is my last job for the morning," she told Bessie. "Then I can get off home and get some rest myself."

"Yes, well, I think I have enough painkillers for now," Bessie told her.

"Doctor's orders," the nurse said with a forced grin.

"Then I'll just take it up with the doctor when I see him," Bessie answered back. "Thank you anyway."

The nurse frowned and glanced at her watch. "Well, if I can't change your mind..." she trailed off and looked at her watch again.

Bessie steadfastly remained silent, smiling politely at the woman.

"I really must be going," the nurse said at last as she spun on her heel. "I shall tell the doctor that you refused the last tablet," she said over her shoulder as she left the room.

Bessie sank back into her pillow, more tired than she ought to have been from the short encounter.

When the door swung open again, Bessie braced herself for another argument with the nurse. Instead Doona's smiling face appeared at the door.

"Yuck," Doona said as she took in the contents of Bessie's breakfast tray. "Good thing I brought breakfast," she told Bessie as she began to open the bags she was carrying.

Moments later Bessie was feasting on a still warm and decadently delicious chocolate chip muffin from Ramsey's premier bakery. She took a swallow of the hot milky tea that Doona had also provided.

"That's much better," she told Doona a short time later. "I feel almost human again."

Doona laughed and then frowned. "How's the pain?" she asked seriously.

"It's bearable," Bessie answered. "At least for now. I had tablets overnight, but I refused to take any more this morning. We'll see how I feel as they start to wear off."

Doona nodded. "I know you don't like to take stuff," she told Bessie, "but it's better than suffering."

Bessie nodded reluctantly. Doona was probably right.

"What does the doctor say?" Doona asked.

"He hasn't been in yet," Bessie told her. As if on cue, the door swung open yet again and the smiling face of the young doctor peeked around it.

"How are you this morning?" he asked Bessie with a cheery smile.

"I'm not too bad," Bessie said cautiously. "Obviously, I'm in some pain, but it's bearable so far."

The doctor nodded and checked something on the chart he was carrying. "Amy, the night nurse, tells me that you didn't want to take your pain medicine this morning," he remarked casually.

"The tablets just make me sleepy," Bessie told him.

"They're supposed to," he smiled at her, and then frowned.

"Seriously, though, your body had a huge shock and some considerable trauma yesterday. The more rest you can give it the better at this point. You can be strong and tough early next week when you've made a good start on healing."

Bessie frowned. "I would really rather not take drugs I don't absolutely need," she insisted.

"And I suppose you'll be wanting to get out of here as well," the doctor sighed. "I work hard on my bedside manner," he teased, "but no one ever wants to stay here for more than a day or two."

Bessie smiled, finding herself liking the man in spite of herself. Now if he could just do something about the nurses, she thought.

"I'll tell you what," Dr. Cannell said to Bessie. "I'll let you go home this afternoon if all of your vitals are good and you promise to have someone stay with you for a few days." Bessie nodded at his words.

He held up a hand. "But," he continued, "you go home with two prescriptions, one for the same painkillers that we gave you overnight and a second one for something not quite as strong. You can choose which to take when, but I want you taking something every four hours or so throughout the day, and I want you to promise to take the stronger ones at bedtime until at least Monday.

The best thing you can do for your body right now is let it rest and recover."

Bessie nodded, willing to agree to just about anything if it would get her home. Hospitals had bad food, funny smells and old and dying people in them; she hated being there.

"Don't worry, Doctor," Doona told the man. "I'll make sure she behaves."

Bessie rolled her eyes at Doona behind the doctor's head, which made Doona snicker. The man fussed over Bessie for a few minutes, checking this and that and asking terribly personal questions before he finally gave her hand a pat.

"Dr. Quayle will be in to check on you after lunch," he told Bessie. "Assuming all your vitals are still good, you'll be free to go."

"He's awfully cute," Doona remarked as the door closed behind him.

"He's awfully young," Bessie answered her.

"Hmm," Doona said thoughtfully. "I've never dated a younger man."

Bessie shook her head. "I'm so glad my misfortune has given you an opportunity to brush up on your flirting," she said sardonically.

Doona just laughed. She was still sitting with Bessie a short time later when Inspector Rockwell arrived.

"I hope you had a good night," the inspector told Bessie as he handed her a small vase full of flowers. "And I hope these brighten your room."

"They're lovely, and I shall be very happy to take them home with me later today," Bessie told him.

"They're letting you go home, then?" he asked.

"After lunch, if all my signs are good," Bessie replied. "And not a moment too soon."

Rockwell smiled. "I'd love to think that I'll have the killer locked up before you get out of here, but that isn't looking very likely at the moment."

Bessie frowned. "I was hoping you'd have better news than that," she told him.

"You need to tell me what happened at Thie yn Traie," Rockwell told her. "Who did you see and what did you say? Something had to trigger the attack on you."

Bessie shook her head slowly. "I've been trying to think it through," she told the inspector. "I had a short visit with Mrs. Pierce, Vikky and Donny and exchanged a few words with Bahey. That was about it."

Inspector Rockwell took her through her entire visit slowly, having her recount every conversation as close to verbatim as possible. Halfway through the recitation, a different nurse came in to offer Bessie something for pain, and she took it reluctantly.

"This one won't make you sleepy," the pleasantly plump nurse, who had to be in her sixties, assured Bessie. "It'll just take the edge off."

Bessie wasn't sure that the nurse had been telling the truth half an hour later when she finally finished going through her previous afternoon. She felt exhausted.

"I've already told you how Robert showed me to the stairs and then left," she told Rockwell. "And how I started down and then got pushed from behind."

The inspector nodded. "I don't know," he told her. "There doesn't seem to be anything in there that would trigger an attack on you." He gave a frustrated-sounding sigh. "Perhaps the killer thought you were someone else."

"Who else would be climbing down those stairs?" Bessie asked incredulously.

"No one," Rockwell admitted. "At least no one that I can think of." He sighed again. "I have to get back to my office. The Chief Constable has called a meeting this afternoon so that we can get together and compare notes. I know Inspector Kelly is convinced that he's got everything wrapped up. I just hope the Chief Constable agrees that the attack on you is connected to the murders."

"I think you need to get some sleep," Doona told Bessie, after the inspector left. "I'll just sit here and read quietly. You shut your eyes for a bit."

Bessie was going to protest, really she was, but she fell asleep before she managed to do so.

A different, but still terribly young nurse's aide with a lunch tray woke her. "Here we are then," the woman smiled at her. "I've brought you some nice lunch."

Bessie looked down at the tray and grimaced. Nothing looked particularly tasty and much of it appeared almost inedible. She gave the aide a pained look. "Would you eat that?" she asked.

The aide chuckled. "No Miss Cubbon," she told Bessie. "I bring my lunch in from home every day. I've yet to see anything sent up from that cafeteria that looks edible. Most days I carry trays back down just as full as the ones I brought up."

Bessie laughed. "Well, I certainly don't want that," she told her. "I don't even know what it is."

"It's, um," the aide reached into a pocket and pulled out a sheet of paper. Bessie could see the words "Today's Menu" across the top. "Chicken and rice in savoury gravy with mushy peas and mashed potatoes. Pudding is cinnamon spiced apple sauce with cream."

Bessie looked again at the tray. "If you say so," she said doubtfully.

The aide shrugged. "I'm supposed to leave it with you for at least ten minutes," she said apologetically. "At least a few patients end up getting desperate enough to eat some of it."

Bessie nodded. "Go ahead and leave it, then, but I won't be eating a single bite. I'm supposed to go home this afternoon, anyway. I can wait until I get there to get some lunch."

The aide nodded and then bustled out again, back to her trolley full of meals. Bessie pushed her tray table away and then frowned. Doona had obviously gone, and now she felt wide-awake and bored. She thought about trying to get out of bed, but that had been such a chore when the nurse had helped her to the loo before breakfast that she decided to stay put. If she were going home later, she would have plenty of opportunity to push her damaged body then.

She didn't have much time to get bored, however. Doona rushed in only a few moments later. She was carrying several bags and struggling to catch her breath.

"I was supposed to be back half an hour ago," she gasped at Bessie.

"No worries," Bessie grinned. "I'm not going anywhere in a hurry."

Doona smiled back at her. "Yeah, but I was supposed to relieve the guy on door duty," she told her friend. "Anyway, at least I brought enough lunch for you and me and poor Nigel on the door. I've given him his sandwich and a piece of cake and sent him away."

As she spoke, Doona moved Bessie's lunch tray off the small table and set it just outside the door. Then she pulled sandwiches and packets of crisps from one bag and bottles of juice from another. In minutes she had an appetising lunch laid out in front of Bessie.

"Door duty?" Bessie said in a confused voice as she watched Doona work.

"Yep, Hugh was here until three in the morning and then Nigel took over for him. I was supposed to relieve him at midday and I'm late," Doona explained as she pulled another sandwich from a bag and took a big bite.

"Really? Does Inspector Rockwell genuinely think I'm in danger?" Bessie asked in surprise.

"We all do," Doona answered after a sip of her juice. "Well, all of us except Inspector Kelly. He thinks you fell down the stairs and are claiming that you were pushed because you're embarrassed about it."

Bessie stared at her friend, too angry to speak for a moment. "He actually said that?" she asked.

"Well, not in so many words," Doona admitted. "But that was what he meant."

Bessie shook her head. "Just wait until I see his mother the next time. She and I will have a long chat."

Doona laughed. "Don't let it bother you," she soothed. "Inspector Kelly is just eager to get the case solved and get the Pierce family off the island. I gather the whole situation with Maeve has been causing him trouble."

"What is the situation with Maeve?" Bessie asked.

Doona shrugged. "I've only heard bits and pieces," she told Bessie. "She and Donny are still married, but apparently they haven't seen each other in a long time. According to Maeve's statement that she gave to the papers, their both being on the island right now was a total coincidence."

"She made a statement to the papers?"

"Oh, indeed," Doona answered. "She held her own little press conference yesterday afternoon, right before the one the police were giving and just in time for today's local paper. She got a fair bit of coverage from the papers in the UK as well, which I suspect was her real aim."

"Why?"

"She's looking for her fifteen minutes of fame, I imagine," Doona said. "She got all dramatically teary-eyed and weepy as she recounted how she had been cruelly dragged away from her first and really, truly, only true love." Doona scoffed. "By the time Donny got ahold of her, she'd already been through half a dozen 'true loves,' if my sources are anything to go on."

Bessie shrugged. "All of that must have happened in Douglas," she remarked.

"Well, yes, mostly, I suppose," Doona answered. "The Kelly family was living there at that point and from what I gather, young Donald was spending as much time in the 'big city' as he could when the family was here on holiday."

"What else did she tell the press?"

"How worried she is about 'her' Donny now that he's caught up in a murder investigation and how surprised she was to learn that he was here when she arrived for a short visit with her dearly loved mother. I know her little brother is technically my boss, but I didn't believe a word she said."

Bessie sighed. "Even if she was lying through her teeth, though, what possible motive could she have had for killing Danny or pushing me off the steps yesterday?"

Doona shrugged. "I don't know, but I don't trust her. Eat your lunch."

Bessie sighed. "Yes, mother," she said mockingly. Then she took a bite and gave Doona a smile. "This is delicious," she told her friend.

"I bought all the ingredients and then ran home and made the sandwiches myself," Doona told her. "That way I could be sure to put together exactly what I know you like."

Bessie thanked her again. The sandwiches and crisps disappeared quickly and Bessie found that she felt much better once her tummy was full. She obediently took yet another pain tablet when the nurse popped in while she was eating her pudding and then settled back into the bed.

"Thank you again," she told Doona. "I'm sure I wouldn't feel nearly this good if I'd eaten the stuff the hospital kitchen sent up."

Doona laughed. "I'm sure."

"Unfortunately, I'm afraid you're right." The voice in the doorway startled Bessie.

Dr. George Quayle walked into the room and smiled at her. "It's always nice to see you, Aunt Bessie," he told her. "Even under less than ideal circumstances."

Bessie was pleased to finally see someone that she knew. While he wasn't her usual doctor, he occasionally filled in at her surgery when one or another of the physicians needed a holiday. She noted that, even though he had to be pushing sixty, he still had a full head of the snow-white hair that had started changing from its original brown when he had still been in his twenties. His eyes were a shade of brown that had once matched his hair perfectly. He'd put on a few pounds since Bessie had last seen him, but he was still in reasonable shape and he appeared to be full of energy.

The pair chatted easily while the doctor ran a few quick tests. "Well," he said after a moment, "all of your vital signs are excellent. I think you're in better shape than I am."

Bessie glanced down at the man's emerging potbelly and bit her tongue. He followed her eyes and laughed.

"Anyway, Dr. Cannell left a note that I'm meant to let you go home this afternoon if your signs are good," he told her. "But before I do that, I want to make sure you'll be able to get around on your own."

Bessie opened her mouth to protest, but the doctor held up a hand.

"Don't argue," he said. "Even if you have someone staying with you, you'll need to get to the loo and the kitchen and whatever. I'm not asking you to race me up the corridor, I just want to see you shuffle from here to the loo and back."

Bessie gave him a determined smile and then, hesitantly, swung her legs out from under the covers. There was no denying that the movement was painful. She got her feet to the floor and then sat on the edge of the bed for several minutes, breathing steadily.

"Bessie?" Doona asked nervously.

"I'm okay," Bessie insisted. "I'm just taking it slowly."

"I'm here until six," the doctor told them both. "No need to rush."

Bessie rolled her eyes at him and then slowly got to her feet. With slow and deliberate caution, she began to shuffle forward. Doona was quick to take her arm. The pair made their way across the room to the small, attached loo. Bessie tapped on the door and then unhurriedly turned around. The walk back to the bed felt shorter and Bessie was relieved to find that her muscles seemed to loosen up slightly the more they were used.

"Okay?" the doctor asked.

"I think so," Bessie replied. "It wasn't as bad as I thought it might be."

"Just remember that you're taking pain medication right now. Dr. Cannell said that he gave you instructions for that; make sure that you listen to him. No sense suffering unnecessarily."

Bessie nodded. "Does that mean that I can go home?"

Dr. Quayle winked at her. "Yes, you can go home."

"Hurray," Doona cheered as Bessie sank back down on the bed, feeling quite worn out by her short stroll.

"You may as well lie back down and rest," the doctor told her. "It's going to take me at least an hour to sort out all of your paperwork so you can leave."

Bessie smiled at him. She wasn't sure she believed him, but she was grateful that she could rest for a while and not feel guilty about it.

In the end, it was nearly three o'clock before all of the necessary paperwork was completed and Bessie was wheeled out of the hospital in the required wheelchair. Doona brought her car around to the entrance and Bessie struggled into the passenger seat with a sigh.

"I hope these bruises start healing fast," she told Doona, as she gingerly fashioned the seatbelt around herself. "I'm already tired of being in pain all the time."

"Maybe you should take another tablet?" Doona suggested.

"You know me better than that," Bessie replied.

The drive back to Bessie's didn't take long, but Bessie still nodded off for a moment. She awoke with a start when the car stopped.

"Oh, goodness," she exclaimed. "I didn't mean to fall asleep."

"Your body needs the rest," Doona told her.

"I'm getting tired of hearing that," Bessie snapped back. Then she sighed. "Sorry, I shouldn't take it out on you."

"It's fine," Doona told her. "I'll just ignore you."

Bessie had to laugh at that. She unhooked her seatbelt and carefully exited the car.

"You know," Doona told her as she made her way towards the door, "you can always come and stay with me for a few days, if you want."

"I would rather be in my own home," Bessie answered. "I'm just hoping that Hugh will stay for another night or two. The doctor said I'm not to be alone."

"If Hugh won't, I will," Doona assured her.

Once inside, Bessie was eager to change. She was wearing the clothes that she had lent to Vikky. In their plastic bag, they had survived the fall much more successfully than the outfit that Bessie had been wearing. Now she wanted out of the skirt and sweater that were too warm for today's nice weather. The outfit held uncomfortable memories for Bessie, as well.

She made her way carefully up the stairs and changed into a little-worn pair of sweatpants and a T-shirt. She put the outfit she now thought of as "Vikky's" into her laundry pile. Perhaps once they were washed in her own machine with her usual detergent they would feel less foreign. Really though, she doubted if she would ever wear them again.

The trip back down the stairs took almost as long as the climb had taken, but the stairs were too narrow for Doona to walk alongside her to help. Doona was ready at the bottom, however, to help her into the sitting room.

"Now you just sit down and rest yourself for a bit," Doona insisted as she helped Bessie into a chair. She fetched Bessie's latest novel and a blanket, "just in case you get a chill," and then left Bessie on her own. Bessie could hear Doona moving around in the kitchen as she drifted off to sleep yet again.

# CHAPTER 13

$\mathcal{W}$hen Bessie woke up a few hours later, it was to an unexpected smell. She sniffed the air and frowned, taking a moment to place the aroma.

"Is someone eating pizza?" she demanded loudly, as her brain finally cooperated.

Doona stuck her head into the sitting room and smiled. "Aye, and there's plenty for you, too."

Bessie smiled. It had been some time since she'd had good pizza. She got shakily to her feet. Doona was quick to step to her side and offer some support. As Bessie walked the handful of steps to her kitchen, she realised that she was overdue for another pain tablet, and she was more than ready to take it.

She was surprised to find Hugh and Inspector Rockwell in the kitchen. "You've all been very quiet," she said as a greeting.

"We didn't want to wake you," Hugh told her, rising to his feet and giving her a gentle hug.

"Well, I'm glad I'm awake now. That pizza smells fabulous."

"Doona had me bring it when I brought your prescriptions," Hugh explained.

"Which reminds me," Doona interjected. "I think you're overdue for a tablet."

Bessie nodded. "And I won't complain about having to take it, either," she told Doona. "Everything hurts."

Doona nodded and got Bessie a glass of water and the required medication. "This is the light one," she told Bessie. "I assume you'd rather save the more powerful ones for bedtime."

Bessie hesitated for a moment. She was in a lot of pain. But she also wanted to chat with Hugh and Inspector Rockwell and she knew that if she took the stronger drugs she wouldn't be able to stay awake to do that. She took the tablet that Doona offered. Hopefully, it would be enough to get her through until bedtime.

"We were just talking about the case," Hugh told Bessie.

"We've all got our own pet theories as to what happened," Doona added.

"But we don't have enough evidence to prove any of them," Inspector Rockwell said gloomily.

Bessie finished her slice of pizza and grabbed a second before she spoke. "I'm assuming the murderer is someone from the family," she said once she'd taken yet another bite. "No one else could have pushed me off those steps."

"You can't rule out the staff," Hugh argued. "Everyone from Bahey Corlett through Robert Clague had the same opportunity as the family to give you that shove."

Bessie shrugged. "But none of them had any reason to try to kill me."

"Why did anyone have a reason to try to kill you?" Rockwell asked. "That's what I can't seem to make sense of in all of this."

Bessie shook her head. "Maybe we should start back at the beginning," she suggested. "Look at motive and means and opportunity for the first murder and then work forward."

"We were going to do that once we finished the pizza," Doona told her. "Well, after the ice cream."

Bessie smiled. "There's ice cream?" she asked, feeling like a ten-year-old child again.

Doona was just digging out giant scoops of the promised pudding when Inspector Rockwell's phone rang. He glanced at the display and then sighed.

"I need to take this," he told the others.

He stepped into Bessie's sitting room to get some privacy and the others dug into their ice cream as snippets of conversation drifted past.

"You know I'm working…."

"That isn't what I meant…."

"I'm in the middle of a murder investigation, remember?"

"I don't care what your mother…."

The others ate their ice cream in silence, exchanging glances as the words streamed by. After a few minutes, they heard nothing but silence before Inspector Rockwell stormed back into the room.

"I need to leave," he said tersely, his face flushed. "Hugh, I expect a full report from you Monday morning, covering everything that's discussed after I'm gone."

"Yes, sir," Hugh said smartly.

"And remember what should and shouldn't be discussed with a civilian," he added, shooting Bessie a look she couldn't read.

"Ah, yes, sir," Hugh repeated himself.

Rockwell shook his head. "Sorry, I'm not, that is…." He shook his head again and then grabbed a spoon. He dug it into the tub of ice cream that was still sitting on the counter and scooped out a generous mouthful. Bessie watched him curiously as his agitation seemed to dissipate as the ice cream melted in his mouth.

"Ah, that's better," he sighed. "I'll see you all on Monday. I hope you feel better by then." The last remark was directed at Bessie and she smiled in lieu of a reply. The reply would have been wasted anyway, as the inspector had quickly let himself out and within seconds they could all hear his car engine starting.

"Well, that was weird," Doona complained as she got up to put the ice cream away.

"That had to be his wife," Hugh told her. "From what I've heard, she's finding it hard to adjust to life over here. I think this murder investigation is pushing her over the edge."

Bessie resisted the urge to comment. She was just starting to like the inspector. She hoped his wife wouldn't drag him back to Manchester.

"Before we do anything else, what happened at the news conference yesterday?" Bessie asked.

"Not a whole lot," Doona shrugged. "Inspector Kelly announced that he'd arrested Jack White for dealing in illegal drugs, or rather for providing legal drugs without a prescription, and that was about it."

"He didn't say anything about the murders?" Bessie asked in surprise.

"Nope. The press tried to get him to answer questions, but he kept dodging everything and talking about not being able to discuss active investigations. I overheard a few reporters complaining that they'd wasted their time in even bothering to attend," Hugh told her.

"So let's talk about means, motive and opportunity," Doona suggested after the ice cream bowls were empty.

Hugh started. "The problem is everyone in that family had the means and opportunity, but to hear them tell it, none of them had any motive, at least not for both murders."

"So let's assume, just for a minute, that Samantha was killed only because she knew who killed Danny," Bessie suggested. "That means that we only have to consider who might have had a motive for killing him."

"That's easy," Doona answered. "Vikky!"

Hugh shook his head. "I know you'd like to get her put away for a long time," he told Doona, "but from everything we've discovered, she didn't have much motive for killing her brand-new husband."

"Except lots and lots and lots of lovely money," Doona argued.

"Not really that much," Hugh replied. "A lot of the family money is tied up in complicated trusts and stuff. I don't understand any of it, but even if Vikky inherits everything that she's meant to according to Danny's will, she won't get anything like what the family is worth.

And according to my sources, Mr. Pierce is fighting the will anyway. It's likely she won't get much of anything."

"Maybe she didn't know about the family trusts and stuff," Doona suggested. "Maybe she thought she was going to get tons."

"She certainly didn't mention any family trusts when I talked to her after I found the body," Bessie interjected. "She said she was Danny's heir and she seemed to think she was going to be very rich indeed."

"I still find it hard to believe that she could kill her husband only two days after their wedding," Hugh asserted.

"And I still think she's the best suspect," Doona replied.

"What about Mr. or Mrs. Pierce?" Bessie asked.

"I can't see Mrs. Pierce killing her own son," Doona said. "I saw her at the station the afternoon after the body was found. She seemed like she was genuinely devastated."

"I'd be inclined to agree with that," Bessie said. "I saw her at the house the next day and she was still barely functioning."

"She might have killed Samantha, though," Doona suggested.

"Let's focus on Danny's murder for now," Bessie said. "I think we can agree that Mrs. Pierce didn't kill him. What about Mr. Pierce?"

"It's hard for me to imagine any parent killing their child," Doona said with a sigh.

"I know," Bessie told her, "but I can picture him doing it far more easily than I can see his wife being involved."

"I sat in when Inspector Rockwell was interviewing him," Hugh told them. "I can't tell you anything that was said, but I can tell you the impression I got of the man. He's a hardheaded businessman who got where he is today by stepping on whomever he needed to on his way up. While I can't see him getting his own hands dirty, I can see him ordering someone else to get rid of anyone he thought was in his way."

"Even his own son?" Doona asked incredulously.

Hugh hesitated. "Maybe," he finally answered, uncertainly. "It would depend, I think, on what his son did that upset him."

"It isn't like there are killers for hire roaming around the island, though," Bessie argued. "Where would he find someone to do the job?"

"It would be easy enough for someone to come across, do the job and be on the next plane out," Hugh told her. "And he might have deliberately planned it for here, assuming his position would impress a small island force more than a big city one."

"If Mr. Pierce hired someone to kill his son, then who killed Samantha?" Doona asked.

"A different goon?" Hugh speculated. "As soon as Danny was killed, Mr. Pierce hired security round the clock. Who's to say what else the security firm might handle?"

"Hugh Watterson, you are not seriously suggesting that Robert Clague and his associates at Manxman Security are assassins for hire," Bessie exploded.

Hugh frowned. "You were the one that kept pointing out how Robert always seemed to be sneaking up on you," Hugh reminded her. "And we know he had plenty of opportunity to push you down the stairs."

Bessie shook her head. "That's crazy," she told him. "Robert Clague ate shortbread at this very table. He would never try to kill me."

Hugh shrugged. "I'm sure old man Pierce has plenty of underground connections. It would have been easy for him to get someone over here to get rid of Samantha if he wanted to. Both murders took place in public spaces where strangers might not have been noticed."

Bessie wasn't sure she agreed, but she moved on. "What about Donny?" she asked.

Hugh shrugged. "As far as we can tell, he didn't have any real motive. Everyone I've talked to has told me that the brothers were close and got along well. I haven't found anyone that overheard any arguments between the two. Donny claims that he was upset with his brother over his drug use, but no one else seems to have noticed the tension. And all the money is tied up in those trusts, so Donny won't gain anything financially from Danny's death."

"Maybe they were fighting over Vikky," Doona suggested.

Hugh shrugged again. "The way I was told, Donny introduced the two of them. Surely if he was interested in her, he would have just asked her out himself, rather than set her up with Danny."

"But he had the means and the opportunity," Bessie said. "And he might have had a motive for killing Samantha."

"What motive?" Hugh asked. "If they'd had a fight, he could have just broken up with her. He didn't have to kill her."

Bessie sighed. "Maybe my first assumption was correct, then," she said. "Maybe Samantha saw Danny's killer and that's what got her killed."

"Or Samantha killed Danny and someone killed her for revenge," Doona suggested.

"Well, she did have means and opportunity," Hugh told them. "Just like everyone else."

"But what could have been her motive?" Bessie demanded.

"If she didn't know about the trusts either, maybe she thought she'd get Donny a fortune if she killed Danny," Doona speculated.

"Seems a bit extreme, killing someone to help out your boyfriend," Bessie said thoughtfully. "Samantha didn't seem stupid to me. If she was going to kill Danny for Donny's benefit, I think she'd have made sure she married Donny first."

"Just for the record," Hugh inserted, "Samantha had the best alibi for Danny's murder. She wasn't feeling well at dinner and went straight to bed afterwards. Danny went out for his walk about an hour later and by that time Samantha had already asked one of the maids to bring her some headache tablets due to a severe migraine. Assuming she took the tablets they gave her, it's a fair bet she was fast asleep all night. While it's just possible that she was faking it and managed to sneak out, murder Danny and then sneak back in, it seems pretty unlikely."

"What if," Doona said excitedly, "Samantha was the real target and Danny's killing was just meant to distract us?"

"That seems a little farfetched," Bessie answered.

"But it's possible," Doona insisted.

Hugh shook his head, but Bessie spoke first. "Ok, if we assume that Samantha was the real target, who had a motive?"

The three looked from one to another.

"From what we've uncovered in the investigation to date," Hugh said finally, "I don't think anyone had much of a motive."

"Vikky did," Doona asserted. "She was after Donny and Samantha was in the way."

"Maybe," Hugh said, doubt obvious in his tone. "But only after Danny was dead."

"I'm getting awfully tired," Bessie told the others. "Before I fall asleep in my chair, what has Jack White been saying?"

"As I understand it," Hugh answered, "he's been saying plenty, but only to Inspector Kelly and the Chief Constable and they surely aren't talking."

Bessie sighed. "Inspector Rockwell probably knows what he's said, as well. It's too bad he had to leave."

"He wouldn't have told us anyway," Doona said. "Remember what he said about talking to civilians."

Bessie sighed again. "I still wish I knew what our friendly neighbourhood chemist had to say."

"Let's think about the attack on you," Doona suggested.

"Must we?" Bessie asked.

"Yes," Doona said firmly. "Clearly everyone had the means to carry that out. We don't have any one-armed suspects. As I understand it, none of the usual suspects has anything like an alibi, either." She looked questioningly at Hugh.

Hugh shrugged. "Everyone claims they were doing this or that, but any one of them could have slipped out, given you a shove and got back inside without anyone else noticing."

"What about Mr. Pierce?" Bessie asked. "He was out taking a drive while I was there."

"Actually, he arrived back home just before Vikky's shouting match with the reporters at the gate. His arrival was what had them out of their car in the first place. You heard Robert getting called in to deal with the matter, so we know that Mr. Pierce was home before you fell."

"But surely that means that Robert couldn't have done it, if he was dealing with Vikky. And it must let Vikky off the hook as well?" Bessie asked.

"Inspector Rockwell drew up a comprehensive timeline of events for the afternoon. According to that, no one is in the clear," Hugh told her.

"But," Bessie began, but Hugh held up a hand.

"Robert's phone shows that he was rung at fifteen-twenty-seven, but he didn't show up on the security camera at the gate until fifteen-thirty-five. He can't seem to account for the discrepancy. As for Miss Vikky, as soon as Robert showed up, she ran off sobbing. She would have had just about enough time to get around the back and give you a push. Unfortunately, I can't be exact enough about the time you fell to narrow the suspects down any further."

"Never mind that," Bessie patted his hand. "What sort of mood was Mr. Pierce in when you talked to him after you found me?"

"I'm not sure that drunk to nearly incapacitated is a mood," Hugh answered, "but that was what he was."

"I thought he went out for a drive," Bessie said.

"He did; I just wish one of our patrols had seen him go by and stopped him. No doubt his hotshot advocates would have got him off, but we might have been able to make him sweat a bit. There's no way he should have been driving, although I gather he'd welcomed himself home with another double whisky before I got there."

"Maybe I'm just overtired or over-medicated," Bessie told the others, "but I'm feeling befuddled."

"We need to let you get some sleep, then," Doona said. "Let's get you up to bed and all tucked in."

Bessie was in too much pain to argue. She let Doona lead her up the stairs, climbing slowly with one hand firmly gripping the handrail. In spite of her protests that she could manage, Doona insisted on helping her change and supervised her while she brushed her teeth and washed her face.

"Honestly, I'm not five years old and I'm not an invalid," Bessie grumbled as Doona helped her climb into bed.

"You snuggle down," Doona said soothingly. "I'll go and get your painkillers."

Bessie was still struggling to find a comfortable position when Doona returned. She swallowed the proffered tablet without complaint.

"I'll be sleeping in the spare room," Doona told Bessie as she tucked the covers around her. "Hugh will be on the couch. Just shout if you need anything."

"You both don't have to stay," Bessie said. "I'm sure I'll be fine."

"Yes, well, we're staying and there's no point in you arguing."

Doona started to leave, but Bessie caught her hand. "Thank you," she said softly.

"You're very welcome," Doona replied, giving Bessie's hand a gentle squeeze before she left, softly pulling the door shut behind her.

Bessie was vaguely aware of Doona checking on her once or twice in the night. She obediently took a second pain tablet at some point as well.

The sun was shining at her window when Bessie finally woke up properly the next morning. Doona was sitting in a chair next to the bed.

"What time is it?" Bessie croaked through dry lips.

"Nearly nine," Doona answered. "If you're ready to get up now I'll help you through the shower."

Bessie wanted to argue, but as she struggled out of bed she realised that Doona was right. She was going to need a helping hand this morning.

Doona was brisk and efficient as she helped Bessie through her morning routine, an attitude that did much to assuage Bessie's embarrassment as they went along. In less time than she thought possible, Bessie was showered and dressed and on her way down the stairs for some breakfast.

As the two women reached the bottom of the steps, they looked at each other and giggled. Hugh's loud snores were nearly shaking the cottage's foundations.

"I almost took one of your tablets to help me sleep," Doona told Bessie. "That snoring kept me awake all night."

"I don't understand why it doesn't keep him awake," Bessie replied.

"I suppose he's used to it," Doona shrugged. "I feel sorry for any woman he gets involved with, though."

Bessie grinned at her friend and the pair headed into the kitchen. Doona popped the kettle on and plugged in the toaster.

"If you want anything more exotic than toast or cereal," she told Bessie, "you'll have to wait and see if Hugh can make it. I don't cook in the morning, not even when I'm looking after my friends."

"Toast and some juice is fine with me," she told Doona. "I'm not a big breakfast eater really, but I know I'm supposed to eat something, so I always force myself."

The ladies were on their second cup of tea when Hugh finally appeared in the doorway, scratching his head and frowning. "I meant to be up hours ago," he said apologetically. "I know it's Sunday, but it feels like we should all be up and doing something."

Doona smiled. "I've been thinking that same thing," she said. "I think we need to set a trap for the killer."

Hugh raised his eyebrows as he made himself some tea. "That sounds dangerous."

"It won't be," Doona promised. "Look, we know the killer is someone at Thie yn Traie, right?"

"I'm not sure 'know' is the right word," Bessie answered. "I mean, we don't know what Jack White has been saying. Inspector Kelly seems to think that he's the guilty party."

"If they were sure he was guilty, they would have already made a big announcement about his arrest," Doona replied. "I'm sure he's guilty of lots of other things, but they can't have found any evidence to tie him to the murders or else we would all know about it. No, the murderer has to be someone from the Pierce family circle."

"Even if we agree with you, so what?" Hugh asked as he buttered himself four slices of toast.

"Whoever it is, they already tried to get rid of Bessie once. I think we should give him or her another chance."

"Pardon me?" Bessie said sharply.

"We won't really let you get killed," Doona assured her.

"Oh, well, thanks very much for that," Bessie said sarcastically.

Doona laughed. "No, really, what we need to do is tell everyone at Thie yn Traie that we have to leave you alone for a short time. Hopefully, the murderer will see that as his or her chance to finish you off. Hugh and I will really be here the whole time, of course. We'll be able to stop whoever it is before you get hurt."

Hugh shook his head. "Too dangerous," he said firmly. "Bessie's already all beat up. I don't want to put her in any more danger."

"But this could be our chance to catch the killer," Doona argued. "It would be good for your career, besides getting a killer locked away."

"My career isn't as important as Bessie's health," Hugh said testily. "Your proposal is too risky."

As Doona started to speak again, Bessie held up a hand. "Stop arguing about this like I'm not even here," she said. She took a sip of tea, glaring at each of them in turn when it looked like they might try to speak.

"Right, then," Bessie said eventually. "Let's talk about this like adults, instead of squabbling like children." She held up a hand as both Doona and Hugh opened their mouths.

"Don't argue," she said. "Doona, I think your idea has some merit, but Hugh, I also understand your concerns. Let's see if we can come up with a way to put the plan into place while minimising the risks, shall we?"

"I don't like it," Hugh muttered.

"I don't like it, either," Bessie answered. "But I also don't like trying to sleep at night knowing that there is a murderer out there somewhere, probably close by. I'm sure that Inspector Rockwell will work it all out eventually, but if we can take a shortcut somehow, it may be worth it."

"Maybe we should ring Inspector Rockwell and see what he thinks of the idea," Hugh suggested.

"I don't think we should disturb the inspector on a Sunday," Doona said. "Let him have some time at home with his family. If we can pull this off, we'll have to ring him later, anyway."

"That is such a big 'if,'" Bessie sighed. "Wasn't it you who warned me about getting all caught up in being Miss Marple when this all started?" she asked Doona. "Now who's trying to play at being the detective?"

Doona blushed. "I know it sounds kind of crazy," she admitted. "But I'm tired of sitting around waiting for someone else to solve this case. I just keep thinking that we have everything we need to get the killer to walk right into our trap."

"What do we have?" Hugh asked.

"Well," Doona blushed again. "Bessie."

Bessie laughed. "That's it? You think I'm enough of a temptation?"

"Whoever it was, they already tried to kill you once. I bet they'd like another go. Presumably, they thought you were a threat or they wouldn't have pushed you in the first place. We have to assume that they still think that."

"But surely they should expect that I've told the police everything I know by now," Bessie argued.

"We could say that you're still dazed and confused. We can tell everyone that you don't remember much of anything from the last week or so," Doona suggested.

"Who exactly are you planning to tell all this to?" Hugh asked.

"Well, um," Doona shook her head. "I thought Bahey would be the best place to start," she said finally. "I haven't thought it all the way through yet."

"I don't know whether I should stay and try to talk you out of this or leave now before I get fired for taking part in your crazy scheme," Hugh complained.

"If you don't want to get involved, we understand," Doona told him. "I would hate for you to get fired over this."

"And yet, if I leave, you'll still go through with your plans, won't you?" he challenged. "And when the murderer kills you both, I'll have to live with knowing I could have stopped it."

Doona laughed. "No one is going to kill anyone else," she said firmly. "Whether you help us with the plan or not."

Hugh sighed. "Why do I know I'm going to regret this?" he asked rhetorically. "Okay, let's see if we can come up with a plan that we think might work but that doesn't put Bessie in any danger. If we can do that, I'll think about helping."

Doona smiled. "It's going to work, you'll see," she insisted.

An hour later, after many more cups of tea and two entire packets of biscuits, the trio had hashed out a rough plan.

"I don't think we're going to get anything better than that," Doona said, sitting back with a sigh.

"I'm still not convinced that this is a good idea," Hugh sighed.

"It's not a bad idea," Bessie remarked. "But maybe I just think that because I'm full of drugs."

They all laughed at that, but there was tension in their laughter. Bessie had taken one of the lower-strength tablets as soon as she woke up, and it wouldn't be long before she would need another.

"So are we actually doing this?" Doona asked.

Hugh opened and closed his mouth about ten times before he actually spoke. "As I see it, I suppose there isn't any reason not to try. It seems like there are so many places where it could all fall apart that Bessie probably won't be in any danger."

Bessie nodded. "I sort of agree," she told the others. "We're relying on a lot of little things that have fall into place in order for this to work. Chances are something will go wrong along the way. At least if it goes wrong and the killer doesn't fall into the trap, we haven't messed up the whole case or anything."

Hugh nodded. "I think I might even get to keep my job," he said.

"So when should we ring?" Doona asked.

"How about right after lunch?" Hugh suggested. "I'm getting hungry, and we'll all perform better on full stomachs."

"You just ate over a packet and a half of biscuits," Doona pointed out. "How can you possibly be hungry?"

Bessie just laughed. "It's nearly midday," she pointed out. "Hugh's right, we should have some lunch and then Doona can ring."

"I brought bread and sandwich fixings," Doona told the others. "Let's make ourselves some sandwiches and then we can go over the plan one more time."

Bessie sighed. "I don't want to talk about it anymore," she said.

"Just thinking about it is making me nervous. Let's talk about something else while we eat."

Sandwiches ready, the threesome settled down and discussed recent island events.

"I don't know, it seems like all these banks and insurance companies are expanding and bringing all of their staff in from across. House prices are going crazy," Hugh said.

"I'm glad I bought my house when I did," Doona replied. "I couldn't afford it anymore on what the Isle of Man Constabulary pays."

"I don't reckon I'll ever be able to afford to buy," Hugh shrugged. "Good thing I like my little flat."

Bessie let the discussion wash over her as she nibbled on a sandwich. After taking that last tablet she had been left feeling slightly detached from everything. The feeling was pleasant, but somehow it left the nagging dread in the back of her mind untouched. After lunch they were seriously considering trying to trick a murderer into trying to kill her. That was nothing short of crazy. Perhaps she wouldn't have agreed to the plan without the drugs in her system.

With lunch finished and the dishes washed, Doona helped Bessie into the sitting room, where she settled into her favourite chair. Doona found her the book she was in the middle of and stuffed pillows and a blanket around her until Bessie insisted that she was as comfortable as she could possibly be.

"Enough fussing," Bessie said. "If we're going to do this, we need to do it now, before I lose my nerve."

"Now don't do that," Doona replied. "We've been over it enough. The worst thing that can happen is that the murderer doesn't fall into the trap. If that's what happens, no harm done."

Bessie nodded. "Okay, then, go ahead and ring," she said.

"Are you sure?" Hugh asked. "We can forget about the plan and just have a nice quiet afternoon at home if you want," he told Bessie.

"I want the murderer caught," Bessie said quietly. "If this actually works, it will have been worth it."

Doona gave Bessie a long and serious look and then headed into the kitchen to take the first step in the plan.

# CHAPTER 14

*H*ugh and Bessie sat together in the sitting room, listening to Doona's phone call.

"Oh hello, yes, is that Bahey Corlett?" Doona's voice floated through the room. "Oh yes, this is Doona Moore, Bessie Cubbon's friend?"

After a short pause, Doona's voice carried on. "I was just ringing to ask you for a huge favour," she said. "I've been staying with Bessie since her fall, you see, and now I have to run out and get some shopping in, both for me and for Bessie."

Another pause and then Doona continued. "Yes, Hugh Watterson is here as well, but he's actually got to work this afternoon. In fact, he's already going to be late for clocking in."

That was Hugh's cue and he almost missed it. "Are you sure?" he hissed to Bessie.

"I'm sure; just go," she whispered back.

She watched him walk into the kitchen and heard him calling loudly as he went. "Okay, then, Bessie, you get some rest," he shouted. "Doona? I've got to go now."

Bessie could hear her front door opening and closing, and as Doona spoke again she heard Hugh's car start.

"Anyway," Doona was saying, "I've got to go and do some shopping and I was hoping you might come and sit with Bessie while I'm out."

Another pause. "Not until four?" Doona sighed deeply. "I suppose that's fine," she told Bahey. "The thing is, though, I need to get to the bakery by half-two. Maybe I can leave Bessie alone for just that little while. She's so out of it anyway, it isn't like she'll notice I'm gone."

Bessie frowned. Even though she knew Doona was lying, the remark still annoyed her.

"I know she seemed fine yesterday morning, but today she's very confused. The police are actually waiting to interview her tomorrow, after she's had some rest. I just hope she's more herself by then and can answer their questions."

Bessie forced her lips together to keep from talking out of turn. Even though Doona knew she was listening, it felt like she was over-hearing unpleasant gossip about herself.

"She said she thought she was pushed?" Doona was talking again. "She didn't tell me that," Doona lied through her teeth. "I think the poor dear is even more confused than I realised."

After another short pause, Doona wrapped up the conversation. "Well then, I'll just pop out now and grab what I need. It's getting on towards two already. If you can get over here before four, that would be wonderful, but I suppose whenever you arrive should be fine. I expect I'll be back around five, maybe a bit later. I'll leave the door unlocked. It isn't like anyone's likely to break in, not here."

Only a week earlier, Bessie would have agreed with that senti-ment; now she was sad to find that she no longer felt safe behind unlocked doors.

"That went well," Doona said when she rejoined Bessie. "I was worried that she'd just drop everything and head over, but not being able to get here until four gives us lots of time."

"I told you she would need time to sort out a ride," Bessie replied.

"Well, I didn't think it would take her that long."

"I do think you laid it on a bit thick, the bit about me being 'out of it,' I mean," Bessie said.

"We want her to think that you haven't given a statement to the police yet," Doona reminded her. "That way the killer will think you're still a threat."

"Now we just have to hope that she actually tells everyone at Thie yn Traie what's going on," Bessie sighed.

"Maybe we should have filled Bahey in on the plan," Doona said. "She could have made sure to tell everyone whatever we wanted."

"No," Bessie said. "I think it's best if as few people as possible know about the plan." Bessie couldn't shake the feeling that Bahey knew more than she was letting on. Telling her the plan might have spoiled the whole thing.

"Right, well, I've got to go now," Doona told Bessie. "I'm going to drive straight over and park out of sight at the cottages. Hugh should already be there. If it takes Bahey five minutes to talk to everyone at the house, the soonest the killer should get here is still at least fifteen minutes away. He or she will have to drive because the police tape is still blocking the beach. I can't see any of them choosing to walk over along the road, not with the reporters sitting at the gate."

Bessie nodded. They had been all through this, but that didn't make her any less nervous.

"Hugh and I will both be back and well hidden before anyone else gets here," Doona said reassuringly.

Bessie nodded and settled comfortably into her chair. "Off you go," she said, a touch of excitement in her voice. Really, in spite of the danger, she was curious to see if they could flush out the killer.

She listened as Doona walked through the kitchen. A moment later Bessie heard her door open and close and then she heard Doona's car roar to life. Bessie sighed and closed her eyes. In ten minutes both Doona and Hugh would be back and they could all wait and see if the killer turned up.

Bessie's eyes flew open a moment later when she heard an unexpected noise. Her front door was opening again. Doona and Hugh were going to use the back door from the beach so as not to be spotted by anyone approaching from the road. Could Bahey have found a ride over already?

"Hello, Aunt Bessie." The voice was cold, and Bessie pulled the blanket across herself more tightly as a chill ran through her.

"Donny, what brings you here?" she asked, her voice shaking only slightly.

"I wanted to see how you were doing," Donny answered with an amused grin. "How are you doing?"

"I'm fine," Bessie answered, her mind racing. "How are you?"

Donny laughed harshly. "Oh, I'm just fine as well," he answered. He sat down on the couch across from Bessie and studied her for a moment.

"How long are your minders going to be gone for?" he asked eventually.

"Not long," Bessie answered. "And Bahey is on her way. Didn't she tell you?"

"Bahey?" Donny frowned. "I haven't seen her all day. I've been hanging out on the beach since early this morning, hoping you might be left alone for a minute or two."

And there was the obvious fault in their plan, Bessie thought. They hadn't expected the killer to be watching Bessie's cottage. "What did you want to talk to me about?" Bessie asked, struggling to keep her voice calm. She needed to drag the conversation out until Hugh and Doona got back.

"Nothing really," Donny shrugged. "You know I killed Danny and Samantha, so now I have to get rid of you as well."

"I don't know any such thing," Bessie replied.

"No? I thought I was your chief suspect."

"Not at all," Bessie lied. "I thought, that is, I still think, that Vikky killed Danny and probably Samantha as well."

Donny shook a finger at her. "Now, now, Aunt Bessie, I just said that I did it, didn't I? It's no good pretending you didn't hear me."

"But why?" Bessie asked. She had to keep the man talking.

"Why don't you guess?" Donny suggested.

Bessie frowned and tried to think. "Maybe, when you talked about Danny's drug problems, you were really talking about yourself?" she began hesitantly.

"Very good," Donny answered.

"I assume that Danny found out and tried to get you to stop," Bessie continued.

"Oh yes, he was such the good big brother," Donny said. "He offered me all sorts of help and promised not to tell the folks. I knew he was lying, though. He was just waiting for the right moment. I found out he'd been talking to his solicitors. He seemed to think he could break up the trust if I was arrested for some drug offense."

"That's terrible," Bessie said as sympathetically as she could.

"It is, isn't it?" Donny mused. "He was suspicious of Jack White. He knew that I knew him from across and I think he thought Jack was my local source. I wasn't dumb enough to leave things to chance like that, though. I don't trust Jack White, not one little bit. I brought more than enough with me to get through the long and boring family weekend, even if I did have to use a few tablets here and there for other purposes. Of course, now it's dragging on and on. If we don't get to leave tomorrow, I'll start worrying about running low."

Bessie thought about pressing him for more information about Danny's murder, but she wasn't sure she could stomach the details. "What about Samantha?" she asked instead.

"Ah, the lovely and misguided Samantha," Donny laughed harshly. "She wasn't feeling well that night and she went to bed early. If she'd stayed in bed, she would still be alive today."

"What happened?" Bessie had to ask.

"Talking to you is cathartic," Donny answered. "I thought that at the top of the Laxey Wheel as well."

"I'm glad," Bessie murmured. What else could she say?

"My dear sweet Samantha was already suspicious," Donny told her. "She saw a bottle of tablets in my suitcase when we were unpacking. I told her they were mild stuff for my back problems, but I don't know if she believed me or not. Anyway, as I said, the night that Danny died she went to bed early with a headache. But a few hours later, when she started feeling better, she decided to come and find me."

He stopped there, his unseeing eyes gazing at the wall behind Bessie.

"And where did she find you?" Bessie asked after a moment.

"I was just coming back in," Donny answered. "She was surprised that I had been out walking on the beach in the dark. It was raining as well, and I was carrying my coat, not wearing it." He shook his head.

"I made up some story about a fight between Danny and Vikky. Said that I went out to try to find Danny and calm him down, but I couldn't find him. Then I got her back to bed with one of my special tablets. In the morning I insisted that she must have dreamt it all. She was still so groggy from the tablet that I thought she believed me."

He fell silent again, and this time Bessie left him to his memories. She wasn't in any hurry for the conversation to finish, after all. After a brief period, he shook his head and then smiled eerily at her.

"It wasn't long before she started making little comments that spooked me, though. She was going to try to blackmail me. Would you believe that she wanted me to marry her?"

"No," Bessie said softly. "Not if she actually suspected you of murder."

Donny shrugged. "I couldn't marry her anyway," he continued. "I've already got a very convenient wife."

"What does that mean?" Bessie asked.

"It means I can date lots of women and when they start whining about wanting a commitment I've got the perfect excuse to dump them," Donny chuckled. "All men should marry young and inappropriately."

Bessie shook her head. "What's Maeve getting out of the relationship?" she asked curiously.

"Money, what else?" Donny told her. "As long as we're legally wed, she gets a monthly stipend that means she doesn't have to work. Why would she rock the boat? Besides, we still hook up once in a while. She's a great girl, lots of fun to spend time with, especially in bed."

Bessie blushed, which made Donny laugh. "Sorry, I suppose that isn't really an appropriate comment to make in front of an old spinster lady."

Bessie bit her tongue. The man was already planning to kill her; she didn't want to argue with him.

"Anyway, Samantha was starting to get on my nerves, and she knew too much. It was easy enough to get her fighting with Vikky so that Vikky took off as soon as we got to the wheel. Then I just had to follow Sam into the mine. There wasn't anyone else around; I was surprised at how easy it was, actually."

"Why did you leave Vikky's phone with the body?" Bessie didn't really care, but it was another topic for discussion. Hugh and Doona must be at the cottage by now.

"That was a mistake," Donny shrugged. "I meant to leave Sam's phone with her, but she was taking pictures with it when I stabbed her and she dropped it. I picked it up and tucked it in my pocket while I put her body in the cart and then I grabbed the wrong phone out of my coat. Danny had Vikky's phone in his possession. That's how he saw the sexy text from Jack White, and then he actually used it to record his conversation with Jack. In the recording, Jack was dumb enough to admit that he used to be my supplier before he moved to the island."

Donny shook his head. "I'd happily kill him, too, if I could get near him, just for being so stupid. The police have him wrapped up tight, though."

Bessie thought she heard a sound outside the sitting room window. She tried to look towards it casually, but from where she was sitting she couldn't see anything but beach and sky. Donny didn't seem to have heard anything.

"What about Vikky?" Bessie asked. "How does she fit into all of this?"

"Dear, sweet Vikky," Donny shook his head. "She really is nearly as dumb as she seems. She was seeing Jack White when I met her and I was able to tempt her away from him by suggesting she go after Danny instead. She's just another gold-digging slut, but Danny was too taken with her to notice."

"And that was to your advantage?" Bessie wondered.

"Sure, she was able to keep track of Danny for me. She was the one who let me know that Danny was talking to solicitors about breaking the trust because of my drug use. I told her to hurry up and marry him before the trust got broken."

"And she did just that."

"Yep, I'm not sure how she managed it, but she did it, and then I killed Danny and put her in line for a nice little inheritance. Of course, my father wasn't going to sit back and let her collect a penny, but I sorted that out as well."

"Did you?"

Donny grinned nastily. "Just last night I got Miss Vikky to sign a bunch of papers rescinding any claim to Danny's estate."

"Why would she do that?"

"Because she knew she'd have a huge legal battle on her hands if she refused." Donny held up one finger and then a second as he counted the next reason. "Because we offered her what she thinks is a generous settlement to get her to sign." He smiled and held up a third finger. "And because she thinks I'm going to marry her once all the dust has settled."

"But you're not?" Bessie kept the questions going.

Donny shrugged. "I might, you never know. She isn't bad-looking and she could be fun, for a little while anyway. I'll have to get rid of Maeve first, though."

Bessie shuddered as she wondered exactly how Donny would 'get rid' of his first wife. "Vikky doesn't know about Maeve?"

"Nope. Samantha didn't know about her either. It's helpful that my parents refused to let her name be spoken in their house," he smirked.

"So why did you push me down the steps?" Bessie had to ask.

Donny shrugged. "I was a little bit drunk and decided to go out and get some fresh air," he explained. "I saw you talking with Robert and decided to follow you, just because I could. Then, when you were walking so carefully down those slippery steps, I just couldn't stop myself. Killing gets easier and easier, you know. Especially if you start by killing someone that you love."

Bessie's blood ran cold as he finished speaking. She swallowed hard and tried, desperately, to work out what to say next.

"Anyway, I suppose I'd better get the job done and get back home,"

Donny told her, rising to his feet. "I've really enjoyed our talk. It's been nice to have someone to talk to about it all."

Bessie couldn't even begin to frame a reply to that.

Donny tilted his head as he studied her. "What do you think?" he asked. He pulled a huge knife out from his coat pocket. "It's another one from the set that my parents bought Vikky and Danny," he explained. "It's a really nice set and the knives are really sharp."

He took a step towards Bessie, twirling the knife in his hand lightly. "I thought the police would confiscate the rest of the set after I killed Danny, so I grabbed a couple of spares before they got to Thie yn Traie. I used another on Samantha, and that left this one for you."

Bessie frowned. "You don't have to kill me," she said, surprised at how loud and shaky her voice sounded.

"Oh, but I do," Donny told her with an evil grin. "The question is, how should I do it? As nice as these knives are, I'm getting bored with them. Maybe it's time for something a little bit different."

"Variety is always nice," Bessie said inanely, struggling to keep the man talking. Hugh and Doona had to be somewhere nearby. Why weren't they interrupting?

"I don't suppose I could persuade you to just swallow the whole bottle of tablets that you're meant to be taking for pain?" Donny asked her.

"I'd rather do that than be stabbed."

"Yes," Donny frowned. "But if we do it that way, I'd have to sit here and wait for the tablets to work. I've got better things to do with my time."

"Oh, goodness, don't let me inconvenience you," Bessie said crossly.

Donny laughed, a hollow sound that seemed to echo through Bessie's small cottage.

"No need to get grumpy," Donny told her.

Bessie just stared at him.

"You know what?" he asked Bessie as he took another step towards her. "I think I'll just hold a pillow over your face. It'll be pretty quick and if I do it right, it might even look like natural causes. That'd be pretty good, and it will be a lot less messy. Danny ruined my favourite coat. This one doesn't fit nearly as well. I was lucky that Sam was wearing a raincoat herself; I was able to keep her blood off me that time."

"How nice for you," Bessie muttered.

"Anyway, if I suffocate you, there won't be any blood to worry about."

"Then what?" Bessie asked. "Do you just go back to Thie yn Traie and have dinner?"

"Pretty much," Donny shrugged. "The police are supposed to be letting us go tomorrow. Once I'm off the island, I think I'll just take a long holiday somewhere warm and then return home once things have died down a bit."

"Holiday where?" Bessie struggled to keep the man talking, expecting someone to burst in at any time.

"Oh, I don't know," Donny waved the hand that still held the knife. "Somewhere that I can live quietly with my millions, I imagine."

"I thought all of your money was tied up in trusts?"

"It's complicated," Donny admitted, "but I've no doubt my father will be happy to fund my 'retirement.'" Donny made quotation marks in the air around the word retirement, nearly dropping the knife in the process.

"Why?"

"Because he suspects I killed Danny. Actually, he probably knows I did it, but he'd rather play dumb than see his only remaining son in prison."

Bessie shook her head. "That doesn't make sense," she said.

Donny shrugged again. "You'd have to know my father."

"I think I'm glad I don't," Bessie shot back.

Donny chuckled. "Okay, then, let's get this over with. I've been away too long as it is. Someone might notice my absence."

"You really don't have to kill me. I won't say anything to anyone. If you leave me alone, you should be able to leave tomorrow. If I turn up dead, the police are going to start asking questions all over again and they aren't going to let you go for ages."

"My father has it all sorted. No matter what happens in the next twenty-four hours, we're getting off this godforsaken island tomorrow. If they don't let us go, the police know they'll have a lawsuit on their hands."

Bessie looked desperately towards the window as Donny advanced towards her, but she could see nothing but sea and sky.

"This will be easier if you don't struggle."

Donny set down the knife and picked up one of the pillows that Doona had so thoughtfully arranged for Bessie.

"I'm not interested in making things easier," Bessie told the man.

As Donny lowered the pillow, Bessie lashed out, clawing desperately at his face and hands.

"Ouch!" Donny shouted as she dragged her nails down one of his cheeks. "Cut that out before I get really cross," he told Bessie.

He pushed the pillow over her face. Bessie tried to kick him, but her legs were tangled in the blanket that was tucked around her.

This was not in the plan, Bessie thought as she struggled against the man. Slowly, the world went dark.

# CHAPTER 15

"This is all your fault," a loud male voice was shouting. "I told you this was a bad idea."

"It isn't all my fault," a second voice, this one female, responded. "You were supposed to be back here in ten minutes."

"I got an emergency call," the man answered. "I had to answer it."

"Enough." The third voice was also male. It was quieter, but authoritative. "Shouting at each other isn't going to help."

Bessie sighed as she opened first one eye and then the other. She was flat on the floor in her own sitting room, with an oxygen mask pinching into her face. She pulled the mask off and breathed deeply.

"Miss Cubbon, you really should leave the mask on," a man wearing a white uniform and sitting next to her on the floor said.

"Nonsense," Bessie answered. "I'd rather breathe sea air anytime. Help me up, please."

The man frowned. "We have a doctor on his way to check you over," he told her. "Apparently you had a bad fall yesterday and now I've been told that today someone's tried to kill you." He looked a bit incredulous as he spoke.

Bessie glared at him and struggled into a sitting position without his help. She looked over at Doona, Hugh and Inspector Rockwell who were still arguing and hadn't noticed her return to consciousness.

"I can just about understand how Doona came up with this crazy scheme," Rockwell was saying to Hugh, "but I can't believe that you were foolish enough to go along with it."

"Oh, for heaven's sake," Bessie exploded at them. "I went along with it as well, you know."

"Bessie? You're okay?" Doona was on the floor next to her in seconds, tears falling as she hugged her friend. "I would have never forgiven myself if you weren't okay," she sobbed.

"I suppose it's a good thing that I'm fine, then," Bessie told her. "Now, someone needs to help me up."

"I wouldn't advise that," the paramedic said.

Bessie rolled her eyes at him. Hugh and Inspector Rockwell got on either side of Bessie and slowly brought her to her feet. She took a couple of cautious steps and then sank down in what used to be her favourite chair.

"I think I'll replace this chair," she said softly. She couldn't help but feel that now it would always remind her of Donny Pierce and his attempts to kill her.

"I'll buy you a new chair," Doona told her. "It's the least I can do after putting you in all that danger."

"Before we talk about how it all went wrong," Bessie said. "What's happened to Donny?"

A sharp knock on the door interrupted the conversation. A uniformed constable standing in the doorway opened the door and allowed Dr. George Quayle to enter.

"I wasn't planning on seeing you again so soon," he told Bessie. "What's this I hear about attempted murder?"

Bessie started to explain, but the man waved away her story. "I haven't really got time to hear it all now," he told Bessie apologetically.

"Mrs. Christian is in labour and I need to get over there. She's insisting on another home birth and the midwife can handle it, I'm sure, but her husband is quite excitable. When she had her last one, she ended up delivering the baby herself while the midwife dealt with him. He was so nervous that he tripped over the birthing pool and fell and knocked himself out. I promised the midwife I would be there this time to keep Mr. Christian out of the way."

Five minutes later he'd checked all of Bessie's vital signs. "Well, you don't seem any worse for whatever happened here tonight," he told her. "The good news is that you still have plenty of tablets left from yesterday's misadventure, so I don't need to prescribe anything else. The tablets should be strong enough to let you sleep without any nightmares, as well."

Bessie shivered as she thought about trying to sleep. Every time she closed her eyes she could see Donny Pierce looming over her with the pillow. That pillow was something else she suddenly wanted to replace.

Doona noticed the shiver and squeezed her hand. Inspector Rockwell followed the doctor out, talking quietly with him as they left.

When the inspector returned he smiled at Bessie. "Well, it looks as if you're going to be just fine in spite of everything. You're tougher than you look."

Bessie smiled at him. "You bet I am."

Hugh sank down on the couch opposite Bessie and gave her a huge smile. "I was so worried," he told her.

"You need to tell me what happened," Bessie said.

"Tomorrow," Inspector Rockwell insisted. "Dr. Quayle was quite clear that what you need now is a good night's sleep. We can all have breakfast together and go through the whole thing in the morning."

Bessie wanted to argue, but she was overcome by a sudden wave of exhaustion. Tomorrow would be soon enough to hear all of the details, she decided, but there was one thing she needed to know immediately.

"Where's Donny?" she asked.

"Locked up tightly," Rockwell assured her. "He won't be able to try to hurt you again, not tonight or ever."

Bessie stood up shakily and gave both Hugh and the inspector quick hugs.

"I'll see you both at breakfast, then," she told them. Doona helped her make her slow progress up the stairs. Once she was in her night-gown and tucked into bed, Doona brought her a tablet that Bessie took gratefully. Dr. Quayle was right; she slept deeply and dream-lessly, waking feeling amazingly refreshed in the morning.

Doona was already up and dressed and sitting by Bessie's bedside when she awoke. "Good morning," she told Bessie. "Are you ready for some breakfast?"

"I've just realised that I never got any dinner last night," Bessie answered. "I'm starving."

Doona laughed and then helped Bessie out of bed. In spite of the previous day's events, Bessie found that she was feeling less stiff this morning. She managed to shower on her own and only needed a minimum of assistance in getting dressed. Doona still walked in front of her down the stairs, holding tightly to Bessie's arm.

Bessie was shocked to find that Hugh was already up as well. "What time is it?" she demanded.

"Just before seven," Hugh answered. "Inspector Rockwell will be here any time now so that he can get your statement."

Doona made tea and toast. "I'd make a proper breakfast today, if I could," she said apologetically. "Unfortunately, I didn't think to get eggs or bacon at the store yesterday."

"Toast is fine," Bessie assured her. "I told you I'm not much of a breakfast eater."

She changed her mind a few minutes later when Inspector Rock-well arrived bearing bags crammed full of muffins and pastries.

"This is delicious," she said around a mouthful of chocolate crois-sant. "Thank you."

"I thought it was the least I could do," Rockwell answered with a grin. "Especially since now I have to ask you to relive everything that happened here yesterday."

Bessie closed her eyes and breathed deeply. "I know you need a statement," she told him. "I'll do my best."

The inspector had her start from the time she left the hospital, slowly taking her forward until her confrontation with Donny Pierce. Bessie did her best to remember everything as clearly as she could.

She was interrupted the first time when she explained Donny's entrance.

"He was watching the cottage and waiting for us to leave?" Doona demanded. "That sneaky little, well, I don't like to say what he is. I can't believe we didn't think about that when we made our plans. We thought we had at least fifteen minutes for Bahey to tell everyone what was happening and then for the killer to get over here. If he was just waiting for us to leave, that means he was here for a lot longer than I realised."

"It felt like he was here for a very long time," Bessie told her with a shiver.

Doona got up and gave her a warm hug. "I feel as if I can never say 'sorry' enough."

"It isn't your fault," Bessie insisted. Doona stayed on her feet, with her arm around Bessie as Bessie continued with her story. When she got to the part where Donny complained about the blood on his favourite coat, the inspector interrupted.

"He actually told you that?" Rockwell shook his head. "Once we had him on attempted murder charges, we were able to get a search warrant for his suite at Thie yn Traie in spite of his father's connections. We found the coat he must have been wearing rolled up in a ball in the back of his wardrobe. We're having the stains on the coat checked out, but it sounds as if they'll come back as a match for Danny's blood type."

"Did you find anything else interesting?" Bessie asked.

"We'll talk about that once you've finished your statement," was all that she could get out of the man.

He didn't interrupt again until she mentioned how she had scratched Donny's face when he first approached her.

"That was very clever of you," he said. "He gave me three different excuses for how his cheek got scratched when I questioned him, but none of them were believable."

Doona was in tears when Bessie finished talking.

"And to think, you could have died," she said sadly. "It would have been all my fault."

"I'm fine," Bessie replied. "Don't fuss."

Rockwell laughed and closed his notebook. "I think that's all I need from you," he told Bessie. "I suppose you have a few questions for us, though."

Bessie shook her head. "A lot more than a few," she told him.

"In that case, I suggest we get another round of tea and pastries."

A few minutes later they were all settled in with their second lot of breakfast.

"Okay," Bessie said. "Off you go. Tell me what happened from where Hugh left onwards."

"I suppose I'd better start, then," Hugh told her. "You heard me leave. I was just going to drive straight over and park at the cottages, but then there was a car crash on the coast road and I got tagged to head over and help sort things out. It wasn't much more than a fender bender, really, but one of the cars was pretty much inoperable and blocking the road, so it took a while to sort through. I think it was probably getting close to an hour before I got back to the cottages. Doona's car was there, but she wasn't, so I parked up and walked across as quickly as I could. I got here just in time to see Doona and Inspector Rockwell going in the back door."

"My turn," Doona picked up the story. "I followed Hugh out and drove over to the cottages, but I took a roundabout route, stopping at the corner store to grab a few things. The whole journey took a bit longer than I expected. I got caught behind a bus after the shop and it stopped on every single corner. I couldn't get around it, either."

Now Bessie patted Doona's arm as she heard the frustration in her voice. "Really, it's okay," she assured her friend. "I'm sure you did your absolute best."

"I didn't really rush," Doona said apologetically. "I assumed that Hugh would be in place and I thought we had lots of time. When I got to the cottages and Hugh's car wasn't there, that's when I started to worry."

Hugh got up and poured everyone another cup of tea. Doona was obviously finding telling her story difficult and everyone welcomed the distraction. As Bessie stirred a second spoonful of sugar into her cup, she patted Doona's arm again.

"You really must stop blaming yourself for what happened," she told Doona. "Firstly, I'm absolutely fine, and secondly, if you want to blame someone, blame Donny Pierce. He's the one who turned out to be a murderer, after all."

Doona nodded and then sniffed loudly. "I'm sorry, I just keep remembering seeing him standing there with that pillow...." she trailed off and drank the rest of her tea. Then she took a deep breath.

"Okay, I got to the cottages and no one was there, so I tried ringing Hugh's mobile, but he didn't answer."

"I was tied up at the accident and couldn't hear my phone," Hugh explained.

Doona nodded. "I wasn't sure what to do next. I couldn't decide if I should head for your cottage on my own or wait for Hugh or what. After a few minutes, I gave in and rang Inspector Rockwell. I thought that was in everyone's best interest."

Inspector Rockwell nodded. "She was right about that," he muttered under his breath. "My turn to pick up the story," he said. "Doona rang and told me about your, um, plan. I immediately headed up from Ramsey. I had told Doona to wait at the cottages for me, so I headed straight there. We were still assuming that the killer was going to drive over from Thie yn Traie after Bahey talked to everyone, so Doona was watching for anyone leaving. We weren't too worried about you because no one drove past the cottages while she was there."

"What about Bahey?" Bessie asked suddenly. "I thought she was going to come across to stay with me. What happened to her?"

"She was still trying to find someone to bring her over when I rang and told her not to bother after Donny was arrested. She was stunned when I told her what had happened. I'm sure she'll be in touch soon to hear all about it from you."

"Maybe," Bessie answered, "and maybe not. I'm pretty sure she saw or overheard something that made her suspect Donny, but she kept it to herself to protect the 'son she never had.' I suspect she's feeling very guilty about that right about now."

"I think I need to have another chat with Ms. Corlett," Inspector Rockwell said, making a quick note in his notebook.

"Sorry, I interrupted," Bessie said.

"It's fine," the inspector told her. "Anyway, as soon as I got to the cottages, Doona and I headed across the beach. We got here just in time to see Donny waving a knife around. At that point we just watched and waited. I didn't want to barge in and startle the man. I was afraid he would shove the knife into you without thinking. It was hard to watch him threaten you, but we couldn't work out what else to do. Doona tried ringing you, hoping to distract Donny, but your phone never rang."

Bessie frowned. "I think the ringer must have been turned off and forgotten," she said.

"I turned it off," Doona confessed. "I turned it off after we got you home from the hospital because I wanted you to get some sleep. And then I just forgot all about turning it back on."

"Anyway," Rockwell continued the story, "once we saw him put the knife down and grab the pillow, we came in through the back door. I rang for backup and an ambulance at the same time."

"Did Donny try to get away?" Bessie wondered.

"At first he just stared at us, like he couldn't believe that we were there. And all the while, he was holding the pillow over your face," Doona told her. "He didn't let go of it until Inspector Rockwell grabbed his arm."

"By that time I was coming in the front door," Hugh told her. "I got to see the ending."

Doona smiled. "Donny ran towards the front door and then tripped over his own feet and fell over. By the time he managed to get back up, Inspector Rockwell had handcuffs ready, and that was the end of that."

"He demanded his advocate right away, of course," Hugh told Bessie. "But once we searched his room and found the bloody coat,

Samantha's phone and enough illegal pharmaceuticals to keep Noble's going for a year, he decided to confess."

"Confess?" Bessie said.

"Yeah, I think he's going to claim insanity or something," Hugh shrugged.

"I suppose some high-priced solicitor will step in and he'll end up in a nice private mental hospital for a few years and then be out," Bessie sighed.

"I doubt it," Rockwell answered. "When I told Mr. Pierce that we'd arrested his son, he told me to ring the public defender's office. Apparently he's cutting Donny off without a penny."

"Can he do that?" Doona asked.

"According to his solicitor, absolutely. Donny's income was paid to him through a generous trust. There are numerous clauses within the trust that were meant, I suppose, to encourage good behaviour. Donny's drug abuse was already enough to get him cut off, but the trust specifically states that its funds cannot be used for legal representation in a criminal case. If Donny's found innocent, he might be able to fight his way back into some of the money, but since he's confessed, I think he's out of luck."

"Surely he has to realise that?" Bessie asked.

"I think Donny believed that his father would do everything in his power to help him, regardless of the specifications within the trust," the inspector replied. "He looked stunned when I told him that his father wasn't sending his solicitor to help."

"So he killed Danny so that his father wouldn't find out about his drug problem and cut him off, but now he's cut off anyway," Doona summarised the situation.

"Pretty much," Rockwell said. "I suspect his drug use had escalated to the point where he wasn't thinking very clearly, and poor Danny and Samantha died for nothing."

"I think I feel most sorry for Mrs. Pierce," Bessie said. "She's lost both of her sons now."

"She had to be sedated again after we told her that Donny had been arrested," Rockwell told Bessie. "But I think she was mostly surprised that he was caught and arrested, rather than anything else. I think she knew he was the killer, but expected our incompetence and her husband's money and influence to protect him."

Everyone was silent while they digested the thought.

"What about Jack White? What happens to him now?" Bessie questioned.

"We have plenty of evidence that he was supplying prescription drugs illegally back in the UK as well as here. He was dumb enough to keep very complete records of every transaction. We can even trace Donny's addictions back through Jack's records. I think it's safe to say that he's going to be behind bars for a very long time."

"Where does Vikky fit into all of that?" Bessie asked.

"There doesn't seem to be enough evidence to prosecute her for her part in the crimes," Rockwell told her. "It does seem clear that she knew what was going on. I suspect she might testify against her former lover in return for immunity from prosecution for the part she played. Anyway, White claims that the two of them were still a couple, in spite of her marriage to Danny."

"So she never really loved Danny?" Doona asked. "That's so sad."

"She still claims that she loved him," Rockwell told her, "but when she came across, supposedly on her honeymoon, she made arrangements to get together with Jack again."

"She did?" Bessie asked.

"Yep, the racy text that Danny got so angry about was actually a reply to a message Vikky had sent earlier in the day," Rockwell explained. "She'd suggested that they meet at midnight on the beach, and Jack was simply confirming the time and place."

"So Jack was on the beach that night, expecting to meet Vikky?" Doona asked.

"Apparently so," the inspector answered. "Instead he ran into Vikky's angry new husband. By that time, though, the drugs Donny had slipped him were taking effect. Jack claims that Danny shouted at him a bit and then staggered off, back towards Thie yn Traie."

"And right into Donny's arms," Bessie guessed.

"Exactly. Jack says he took off as soon as Danny turned his back, and I'm inclined to believe him. If he witnessed anything on the beach that night, I think he would be trying to use it as leverage for a reduced sentence on his own charges."

"So Vikky caused all the trouble and gets away with it all, including some share of Danny's money?" Doona asked.

"Apparently she'd already signed away her claims to Danny's estate. She's now arguing that she signed the documents under false pretenses." Inspector Rockwell shrugged. "It's a case for the solicitors and advocates now. I expect they'll do very well out if it anyway."

"So that's it then, I suppose," Bessie said. "Donny and Jack get locked up and the rest of us get on with our lives."

"I'm going to feel a little less safe here than I used to," Doona said sadly.

"You shouldn't," Rockwell told her firmly. "The island is a wonderful and very safe place and you shouldn't let bad behaviour by one or two people change how you feel about it."

Doona smiled at him. "I'll try to remember that," she said.

"I talked to the Chief Constable last night," the inspector told the others. "There are going to be a few changes at the station after everything that's happened."

"Oh no," Doona exclaimed. "You're not firing me, are you? I mean, I probably broke a dozen rules, but I love my job and...."

Inspector Rockwell held up his hand to stop Doona's outburst.

"No one is getting fired," he said.

Bessie grinned as both Doona and Hugh sat back with relieved expressions on their faces.

"However, Inspector Kelly is moving to the Ramsey headquarters building. He'll be taking over responsibility for the drugs and alcohol division for the north of the island."

"That should please him," Doona smiled.

"In the short term, I'll be taking over the day-to-day running of the Laxey station," Inspector Rockwell continued. "I'll still have CID responsibilities as well, but primarily for investigations here or in Lonan."

"Is that a promotion?" Bessie asked, blushing slightly at the nosiness of the question.

Rockwell smiled. "I'd call it more of a sideways move," he told her. "But not one I'm unhappy about. I've become quite fond of Laxey in the last week. I'm looking forward to spending more time here."

"You'll be doing lots of driving up and down the coast road," Doona remarked.

"Maybe," Rockwell shrugged and changed the subject. "One of the things I'm going to do, once I get settled in, is start some formal CID training up here for a few of the young constables."

Hugh raised his eyebrows.

Inspector Rockwell gave him a grin. "Are you interested in some more intensive training into criminal investigations?" he asked Hugh.

"Yes sir," Hugh said smartly. "Very interested."

Rockwell nodded. "I'll keep that in mind," he told him.

"Meanwhile," Doona said with a grin, "maybe one of you would like to take a beginner's Manx language class with Bessie and me? It starts right after Easter."

Both men laughed.

"I learned a little bit in primary school," Hugh said. I can just about remember 'moghrey mie' and that's it. It was hard work when I was eight and I'm sure it would be even harder now."

Doona looked at Inspector Rockwell.

"Oh, now, don't look at me," the man laughed. "I'm not even sure how much longer I'm going to be here. Scotland Yard might make me an offer I can't refuse."

"You'd refuse," Bessie said keenly. "You're hooked on the island now, I can tell. You'll be staying here for good. The island doesn't take everyone that way, but sometimes, for some people, it's just the only place that ever feels like home."

The foursome ate the rest of the pastries and drank another pot of tea. The conversation wandered aimlessly through topics of local interest. Just before nine Doona, Hugh and the inspector headed into the station to begin their working day.

Along the way Doona dropped Bessie off at her doctor's surgery where she was, once again, thoroughly checked over.

"You'll still have some aches and pains for a few days," the doctor told Bessie. "You'll want to take it easy, but otherwise, you should be fine."

Bessie walked out of the surgery and looked around at what qualified as the village centre of Laxey. She'd have a short wander around the shops and catch up on the latest skeet. Of course, everyone would probably rather hear what she had to say than tell her anything.

After that, she'd promised that she would pop into the police station and let Doona buy her lunch. Then she would go home and curl up with a good book. She smiled as she slowly walked down the pavement. She so loved her little island home.

# GLOSSARY OF TERMS

## MANX TO ENGLISH

- **fastyr mie** — good afternoon
- **kys t'ou** — How are you?
- **moghrey mie** — good morning
- **skeet** — gossip
- **ta mee braew** — I'm fine
- **traa-dy-liooar** — time enough (as in, no rush, we can get it done eventually)

## HOUSE NAMES – MANX TO ENGLISH

- **Thie yn Traie** — Beach House
- **Treoghe Bwaane** — Widow's Cottage

## ENGLISH TO AMERICAN TERMS

- **advocate** — Manx title for a lawyer (solicitor)

- **aye** — yes
- **biscuits** — cookies
- **car park** — parking lot
- **chemist** — pharmacist
- **crisps** — potato chips
- **cuddly toy** — stuffed animal
- **cuppa** — cup of tea (informally)
- **gaol** — jail
- **holiday** — vacation
- **midday** — noon
- **middlin** — tolerable
- **pavement** — sidewalk
- **pudding** — dessert
- **telly** — television

# OTHER NOTES

CID is the Criminal Investigation Department of the Isle of Man Constabulary (Police Force).

"Noble's" is Noble's Hospital, the main hospital on the Isle of Man. It is located in Douglas, the island's capital.

When talking about time, the English say, for example, "half seven" to mean "seven-thirty."

Bessie mentions "getting a telegram from the Queen" – British citizens used to receive telegrams from the ruling monarch on the occasion of their one-hundredth birthday. Cards replaced the telegrams in 1982, but the special greeting is still widely referred to as a telegram.

One character is referred to as living in a "4-bed semi", which is the short way of saying a four-bedroomed, semi-detached house. Semi-detached properties are two separate units that share a common wall down the centre. (In America they are often called "duplexes.") Each unit would be sold individually. Such properties are common in the United Kingdom where space is at a premium.

The "licence fee" referred to in the story is a television licence fee. This fee is required in the United Kingdom for anyone who owns and operates a television set. The money raised pays for public broadcasting, the British Broadcasting Corporation (or BBC) stations (both television and radio).

A charity shop is a store run by a non-profit organisation that sells second-hand items that have been donated to the store. All of the profits go to support the non-profit group running the store. They are a great source for second-hand books, furniture, toys, games, etc.

When island residents talk about someone being from "across," they mean that the person is from somewhere in the United Kingdom. (across the water)

In the United Kingdom (UK) a doctor's office is often referred to as a "surgery."

Bessie's adventures continue in:

Aunt Bessie Believes
An Isle of Man Cozy Mystery
Diana Xarissa

Aunt Bessie believes that Moirrey Teare is just about the most disagreeable woman she's ever had the misfortune to meet.

Elizabeth Cubbon, (Aunt Bessie to nearly everyone), is somewhere past sixty, and old enough to ignore the rude woman that does her best to ruin the first session of the beginning Manx language class they are both taking. Moirrey's sudden death is harder to ignore.

Aunt Bessie believes that Moirrey's death was the result of the heart condition that Moirrey always complained about.

The police investigation, however, suggests that someone switched some of the dead woman's essential medications for something far more deadly.

Aunt Bessie believes that she and her friends can find the killer.

But with Doona suspended from work and spending all of her time with the dead woman's long-lost brother, with Hugh caught up in a brand new romance and with Inspector Rockwell chasing after a man that might not even exist, Bessie finds herself believing that someone might just get away with murder.

# ALSO BY DIANA XARISSA

Boats and Bad Guys

Cars and Cold Cases

Dogs and Danger

Encounters and Enemies

Friends and Frauds

Guests and Guilt

Hop-tu-Naa and Homicide

Invitations and Investigations

Joy and Jealousy

Kittens and Killers

Letters and Lawsuits

The Markham Sisters Cozy Mystery Novellas

The Appleton Case

The Bennett Case

The Chalmers Case

The Donaldson Case

The Ellsworth Case

The Fenton Case

The Green Case

The Hampton Case

The Irwin Case

The Jackson Case

The Kingston Case

The Lawley Case

The Moody Case

The Norman Case

The Osborne Case

The Patrone Case

The Quinton Case

The Rhodes Case

The Isle of Man Romance Series

Island Escape

Island Inheritance

Island Heritage

Island Christmas

# ABOUT THE AUTHOR

Diana Xarissa was born and raised in Pennsylvania. She lived in Derbyshire and then on the Isle of Man for more than ten years before returning to the United States with her family. Now living near Buffalo, New York, she enjoys writing about the island and the UK.

Diana also writes mystery/thrillers set in the not-too-distant future under the pen name "Diana X. Dunn" and fantasy/adventure books for middle grade readers under the pen name "D.X. Dunn."

She would be delighted to know what you think of her work and can be contacted through the mail at:

Diana Xarissa Dunn
PO Box 72
Clarence, NY 14031.

*Or find Diana at:*
www.dianaxarissa.com
diana@dianaxarissa.com

Made in United States
North Haven, CT
06 November 2023

43689070R00124